The wall of compressed air painfully crushed his chest

For an unknown length of time, Bolan's universe was filled with deafening chaos, every hair on his body standing stiff, the fillings in his teeth growing uncomfortably hot.

That was when he realized that the magnetic field of lightning had to be creating eddying currents in anything made of metal.

Quickly Bolan tossed away his guns, throat mike, transceiver, spare ammo and knives. Yanking a grenade out of a pocket, he could feel how warm it was and whipped it as far away as possible. Then he tossed the remaining ones.

But the last grenade's detonation pounded the Executioner hard, ripping apart his clothing and peppering him with hot shrapnel....

Don Pendleton's Mack Bolan®

Fireburst

A GOLD EAGLE BOOK FROM
WORLDWIDE®

TORONTO • NEW YORK • LONDON
AMSTERDAM • PARIS • SYDNEY • HAMBURG
STOCKHOLM • ATHENS • TOKYO • MILAN
MADRID • WARSAW • BUDAPEST • AUCKLAND

Recycling programs
for this product may
not exist in your area.

First edition July 2012

ISBN-13: 978-0-373-61554-4

Special thanks and acknowledgment to
Nick Pollotta for his contribution to this work.

FIREBURST

Printed in U.S.A.

When I say that terrorism is war against civilization, I may be met by the objection that terrorists are often idealists pursuing worthy ultimate aims—national or regional independence, and so forth. I do not accept this argument. I cannot agree that a terrorist can ever be an idealist, or that the objects sought can ever justify terrorism. The impact of terrorism, not merely on individual nations, but on humanity as a whole, is intrinsically evil, necessarily evil and wholly evil.

—*Benjamin Netanyahu*
International Terrorism

Terrorists have no morals or ideals, no sense of what's right or what's wrong. Any end justifies the means. One thing has always been crystal clear—someone has to stop them. That's where I come in.

—*Mack Bolan*

PROLOGUE

New York City, New York

Following a rumble of thunder, lightning flashed across the night sky, illuminating the roiling storm clouds from within like misshapen Japanese lanterns.

"God, I hate the rain," a passenger on the jetliner growled under his breath, sliding shut the plastic cover to block his view out the window.

"Oh, sir, our aircraft is one of the safest planes in existence!" a pretty flight attendant said with a comforting smile. "We get hit by lightning two or three times every trip, and it doesn't even damage the paint! I can assure you that there is nothing to fear."

Completely unconcerned, the slim woman walked away to check on the other passengers.

Twenty miles ahead of the jetliner was John F. Kennedy International Airport, a glowing oasis of incandescent and halogen lights, mixing together into a whitish haze that dominated the night in open defiance of the rumbling storm.

"How's the traffic?" the pilot asked the navigator, keeping one hand on the yoke while reaching out to tap the glass front of a fuel gauge. The needle quivered, but didn't change position.

The curved banks of controls surrounded the three members of the cockpit crew in a rainbow of technology, while outside lightning flashed again, much closer, and then farther away.

"We're in the pipe," the navigator replied, infinitely adjusting the delicate controls on her radar screen. "There's nothing in the sky closer than a klick."

No other airplanes were visible because of the tumultuous summer storm, but the radar showed that the sky was full of flying metal, with an even dozen commercial jetliners steadily circling the busy airport, impatiently waiting for permission to land.

"This must be a slow day for Kennedy," the copilot said, keeping both hands on the yoke.

She shrugged. "Pretty much so, yeah."

"Bad for them, good for us," the pilot said, unclipping a hand mike and thumbing the transmit button. "Hello, Kennedy? This is flight one-nine-four out of Oslo. Do you copy? Over."

"This is Kennedy Tower, one-nine-four. We hear you five-by-five." The ceiling speaker crackled. "You're behind schedule. Should have been here an hour ago. Over."

"We hit a headwind over the Atlantic," the pilot replied. "Kennedy, could I please have an ETA?"

"Fifteen minutes until you can have a runway, one-nine-four. Stay on your heading and maintain—"

Suddenly, a blinding light filled the windows, and every instrument on the control boards flickered wildly.

"Say again, Kennedy. We got tickled," the pilot said with a laugh, as the instrument readings returned to normal once more.

"Any damage?" the navigator asked, glancing up from her screen.

"Nope," the copilot said, brushing back his thinning hair. "Just a—"

The terrible light filled the windows again, and the controls dimmed. But before they could reboot, another lightning bolt hit the aircraft, then another, and yet another, the force of the last one cracking a side window.

"What the fuck just happened?" the copilot demanded, looking around the flight deck. Nothing seemed to be damaged, but the overhead lights were dim, one of them flickering, and most of the control boards were dark and inert.

"Radar is down!" the navigator announced grimly. "The radio is dead, and ILM is off-line!"

"Maybe we blew a fuse," the pilot said, flipping switches with both hands. "Oh, Christ, we blew every fuse!"

"What about the backup circuits?"

"Dead! Everything is dead!"

Just then, the entire airplane shook as another bolt of lightning struck.

"Left engine is gone," the copilot announced in a strained voice. "Not dead. Gone. There's just a hole in the wing!"

"That's impossible!" the navigator stated furiously, twisting dials and pressing buttons. "This plane is designed to withstand any conceivable storm!"

The reply of the copilot was lost in the noise of a lightning bolt hitting them again. A spray of sparks erupted from a wall unit, and smoke trickled out from under the floor.

"Kennedy, this is one-nine-four!" the pilot said into the hand mike, but there was only silence from the overhead speaker. Tossing away the mike, he wrapped both arms around the yoke and braced his legs. "Fuck it, we're going straight in! Kennedy will just have to figure out what happened on their own!"

The copilot tightened his seat belt. "Okay, I'll tell the—"

This time the flash of the lightning came with the scream of ripping metal as a section of the roof broke off and sailed away in the storm. Instantly, the flight crew was hammered by a howling wind, and every loose item swirled around the compartment before vanishing into the rain.

With a wordless scream, the navigator was torn from her chair, the seat belt dangling loose. Flailing both arms, she was slammed against the ragged edge of the hole before tumbling away.

A split second later, lightning crashed in through the breech, killing both pilots, and drastically widening the hole. Lurching out of control, the aircraft flipped over sideways, the startled passengers screaming in terror. Then the lightning hit the plane several more times in rapid succession, and all of the fuel tanks simultaneously detonated.

The roiling fireball was briefly visible for several miles along the coastline of both New York and New Jersey before fading away.

Minutes passed in rainy silence. Then irregular chunks of burned metal and smoking corpses started to fall across the airport. An engine slammed into the main terminal, punching completely through to crash inside the concourse, killing people standing in line to check their bags. Next, bodies started to plummet from the sky, splattering across the tarmac, shattering windows and smashing into cars in the long-term parking lot.

As a strident siren began to howl from on top of the

control tower, a dozen other planes were trying to veer
away from the wreckage dropping onto the runways.
Not all of them were successful, several crashing into
one another in a seemingly endless chain reaction of
fire, death and destruction....

CHAPTER ONE

Colombia

Entering his tent, Mack Bolan, aka the Executioner, sat on a canvas cot, eased off his body armor and grabbed a medical kit. His latest strike against Colombia's leading cartel had resulted in minor injuries. None of his cuts were very bad, but things went septic very fast in the jungle, so even a tiny cut could soon become life threatening. When he was done, Bolan loaded a hypodermic syringe and injected himself with a double dose of strong antibiotics. Better safe than sorry. He had a long journey back to the airplane after he packed up his gear.

The soldier was just starting to make coffee when he heard a soft chime from inside his bedroll. Pulling out a laptop, he flipped up the lid, activated the decoder and established contact with a military satellite in orbit.

"Striker here," he said.

"Anchor," came the reply.

Tapping a button to activate the webcam, Bolan saw the screen clear into a view of a middle-aged man hunched over a desk covered with papers.

"Hi, Hal. Something wrong, or were you worried about me?"

"Not sure yet," Hal Brognola said, running a hand through his hair.

The big Fed was one of the top cops of the nation, a fixture at the Justice Department, and the head of the clandestine Sensitive Operations Group. Almost everything he did was covert, such as his alliance with Bolan, and he reported directly to the President.

"Okay, shoot," Bolan said, folding his bandaged hands.

Brognola frowned. "What do you know about lightning?"

"I know enough to get out of the rain when there's thunder."

"Then hold on to your ass, buddy. Within the past twenty-fours hours a commercial jetliner, a high-speed monorail train and fifteen individual people have been killed by lightning strikes."

"I'll assume the number is unusual?" Bolan asked.

"No, lots of people, places and things get zapped by lightning bolts every day. But ever since Ben Franklin invented the lightning rod, the death toll has been kept at a minimum," Brognola said, reaching past the monitor to get a manila folder. "However, according to the black box from the aircraft, the plane was hit fifty-seven times by lightning in a five-minute period."

Suddenly alert, Bolan sat up straight. "That's not possible, Hal."

"Bet your ass it's not," Brognola growled, opening the folder, to spread out some papers. "Yet it did happen. That's been confirmed. What's even worse, those fifteen people killed by lightning were all experts in advance electronics, specializing in—"

"Lightning?"

"Close. Tesla coils."

"Same thing."

"Near enough," Brognola admitted.

"All right, going with the idea that these weren't simply outrageous coincidences, what are we talking about, artificial lightning bolts from some sort of machine hidden inside the storm clouds?"

"Could be. Unless somebody has discovered a way to invoke a lightning strike, and then we're all in for a shitstorm of trouble."

"You got that right," Bolan replied, rubbing his unshaved chin. "What does a lightning bolt generate, a billion volts or so?"

"Right."

"Any of the people hit happen to survive?" Bolan asked.

"No way in hell. After the second strike, they were greasy smoke. The third lightning bolt made holes in the ground over a yard deep. Add the rain, and it'll take weeks to identify most of the remains. The FBI forensic lab was able to scrape some residue off nearby lampposts and store windows to try to run a match on the DNA, but no joy yet."

"Which means there must have been some eyewitnesses."

"Check. We managed to identify a few of the people killed. One was Professor Albert Goldman, the foremost expert in lightning storms in the world, another was Dr. David Thomas, an electrical engineer who had designed a radical new antilightning safeguard that would, he hoped, harness the power to channel into the power grid of a major city, and another was Dr. Kathleen Summer. She is...sorry, she *was* the woman who invented the Tesla antitank trap for the Pentagon ten years ago."

With each name, a picture scrolled across the bottom of the screen, along with a shot of the person's charred remains. Bolan snorted. Charred? They were damn near vaporized.

"Hal, how many people get killed by lightning in the U.S. in an average year?"

"About ninety."

"So fifteen are burned in a single day?" Bolan shook his head. "Good call, Hal. Clearly, somebody has found a way to control lightning strikes, and they've already removed most of the leading scientists in the field to forestall any attempts to analyze their equipment."

"Unfortunately, that was my guess, too." Brognola sighed, the picture distorted for a moment with a burst of static. "We won't know what these people want until they attack again."

"Were any of these scientists connected to one another? Went to the same school, had the same bookie, were they all heading toward a summit conference on weather—anything like that?"

"Nope, I checked, and then double-checked everything," Brognola stated, pushing the folder aside. "They had absolutely nothing in common aside from their field of expertise. Maybe when we identify the rest of the victims, some sort of pattern will emerge. But until then—"

"We're in the dark until these people start making demands," Bolan added. "And by then it may be too late to track them down."

"Agreed. All we can do is stay sharp, and be ready to move the instant something is learned."

"Okay, if I'm going to be chasing clouds, then I'll need some help on this," Bolan said. "Any chance of getting Able Team or Phoenix Force?" The two teams were the other field operatives of the Sensitive Operations Group, based at Stony Man Farm, Virginia.

"Sorry, they're both out of contact at the moment."

"Okay," Bolan stated. "If the Stony Man teams are unavailable, I have some people I can call in."

"Expect trouble?"

"Just prepared for it. You know me."

Brognola chuckled. "Yeah, I do. All right, stay in touch, and watch your ass."

Turning off the laptop, Bolan grabbed his gear and loaded it into the speedboat. He started the outboard motor and headed out. He had a long way to travel, and speed was of the essence.

In the distance, thunder softly rumbled.

He only hoped it wasn't already too late.

CHAPTER TWO

Bern, Switzerland

A thick blanket of glistening snow covered the jagged mountains surrounding the valley, puffy white clouds drifting lazily along the granite tors and snow-capped peaks.

Joyful singing could be heard coming from both the church and the synagogue. A frozen lake reflected the majestic Alps, the image slightly distorted by the laughing people skating arm in arm. Numerous people in snowmobiles scooted along the gentle hills, and a deadly serious snowball fight was raging out of control at the elementary school.

The town of Bern was a combination of the old and the very old. A stone tower attached to city hall boasted a gigantic clock with human-size figures that came out and performed a robotic dance every hour on the hour. There was an artesian well in the town square where people still drew water, even though they had modern plumbing, and there was the jingle of bells as teams of horses pulled colorful sleighs along the snowy streets.

Every wooden building was decorated with ornate carvings, every brick structure painted with highly stylized hex symbols of good luck and prosperity. The satellite dishes were concealed in the nearby woods, the cables laid under the ground so that they wouldn't mar the appearance of a classic Swiss village, and the fully functional Second World War antiaircraft cannons were well-hidden inside concrete bunkers designed to resemble stone cottages. As with just about everything else in the mountainous country, nothing was precisely what it seemed to be at first glance.

Just down the block from the town square was a crowd of people in heavy parkas and gloves. Standing politely behind the bright yellow "danger" tape, they talked in hushed whispers and took endless pictures with their cell phones.

On the other side of the barrier, gray smoke rose from the mounds of hot ashes and burned timbers that used to be a small bookstore. The firefighters had gone home hours earlier, and the chief constable of the village had trundled back to the station to write a report on the incident.

Suddenly, there was the roar of an engine, and a shiny Harley-Davidson motorcycle charged across the new bridge spanning the frozen lake. Revving the twin-V88 engine to maximum, the driver banked low around a corner, both wheels slipping in the ice under the snow in spite of the winter spikes. Cursing vehemently, the driver fought for control of the bike, and managed to right the Harley before jouncing over a frosty granite curb. For a split second, man and machine were airborne, then they came down hard, skittering along the slippery sidewalk until coming to a ragged halt at the danger tape.

Many people in the crowd frowned at the rude arrival of the outsider, but said nothing, merely moving aside to give the stranger a better view of the wreckage. Sitting on the purring motorcycle, the driver did nothing for several minutes but stare at the gaping black hole in the ground only a few yards away.

Turning off the Harley, the man kicked down the stand and walked to the edge of the pit, still trying to comprehend what he was seeing.

"Impossible," he muttered, lifting his visor. "This is impossible!"

Just then, cries of surprise rose from the skaters on the lake as a BMW snowmobile rocketed across the frozen expanse. Narrowly missing the scattering villagers, the big machine zoomed straight up the bank onto the snowy street and across the village green.

At breakneck speed, the driver dodged the well and several children and slammed through a snowman, reducing it back into its basic component. Blinded by the explosion of flakes, the driver zigzagged down the street, nearly clipping several parked cars and another snowman before crashing into the granite cornerstone of the local bank. Stone chips went flying, the fender crumpled, and the engine sputtered into silence. However, the driver managed to stay in the seat just long enough to ride out the recoil before hopping off and yanking open a rear compartment to haul out a bulky toolbox.

The driver was clearly a woman, and wearing the incongruous outfit of a ball gown and a thick puffy winter jacket. Satin slippers jutted from a pocket, and she was wearing heavy black snow boots.

"Damn it, Della, it took you long enough to get here," the driver of the motorcycle said, removing his helmet.

"Shut up, Zander. I live farther away than you do," Della Gotterstein countered, striding toward what remained of the bookstore. "How bad is the damage?"

"Total," Zander Meyers stated.

She scowled. "Bah, that is not possible."

"See for yourself!" Meyers said, making a sweeping gesture.

Pushing her way through the rapidly thinning crowd, Gotterstein halted at the danger tape to stare down into the charred hole.

"Good God," she whispered, setting down the toolbox to remove her own helmet. A wealth of golden hair cascaded to her trim waist.

"Told you," Meyers said, running a hand over his thick hair, the expensive toupee shifting ever so slightly.

"How in the… I mean…what could…" She glanced around at the surrounding building, then swallowed hard. "Is this an echo?"

Meyers frowned at that. *Echo* was code for a terrorist attack. "To be honest, I have no goddamn idea."

Displeased, Gotterstein pursed her lips at the blasphemy, but held her tongue. The man was an electronic genius, and that was all that mattered at the moment. His ridiculous belief in evolution was his own private affair.

As the last of the crowd politely departed, Meyers and Gotterstein ducked under the tape to walk carefully into the smoky crater. Only stacks of ash remained from the thousands of burned books, but there were also several puddles of congealed plastic, as well as a lot of melted wiring, and what might have been fried circuit boards. They were in such poor condition it was hard to tell.

"What do you think?" Meyers asked hopefully.

"Are you expecting a miracle?" Gotterstein retorted angrily, kicking over a bookcase. Underneath was a smashed keyboard. "Neither of us can repair this. There's nothing left of the bank's mainframe. It does not exist anymore!"

"Sadly, I concur." Meyers sighed as a light snow began to fall. The flakes vanished with a hiss as they landed on the broken timbers and smashed bricks.

"Billions of euros lost," Gotterstein said, glancing at the sky. "Are you sure this was not an echo?"

"According to the preliminary report from the fire department, this was caused by lightning," Meyers said, turning up his collar.

"Bah, impossible!" the woman scoffed. "The Swiss banking consortium had us install every safeguard known to modern science. No amount of lightning could have done this!"

"Are you sure?"

"Yes! It would take hundreds of bolts to smash through all of our shielding, antistatic defenses and Faraday cages!"

"So maybe there were hundreds of bolts."

"Are you insane?"

"Then how do you explain it?"

"I...I cannot."

"Let's check the garage," Meyers said, starting back toward the street.

The snowy town seemed deserted as the man and woman crossed the street to an old barn. The side door was painted to resemble wood, but up close it was clearly welded steel. Unlocking the door, they stepped inside and waited. After a few moments, the ceiling lights automatically flickered into life.

Proceeding along a bare concrete tunnel, they passed several massive cannon emplacements and ammunition bunkers. The air of the disguised fortress was stale, and the dust on the floor showed that no one had been inside the building for years.

At the end of the tunnel, they each inserted a special key into a pair of slots and turned them in unison. There was a low hum, and the wall broke apart to reveal a computer workstation.

Sitting alongside each other, Meyers and Gotterstein both ran a systems check, then started furiously typing for several minutes. Slowly, the room began to warm as the wall vents started sending out waves of heat.

Situated around them on the walls, a dozen plasma screens strobed into operation and began scrolling complex electrical schematics, data flow charts and endless lines of binary code.

"Dead?" Meyers asked without looking up from his work.

"Dead," Gotterstein muttered, brushing back a curl from her face. "But essentially undamaged."

"Excellent!"

"Agreed. The links are burned out. Those line fuses we installed last year apparently did the trick. The computer is off-line, but there has been no loss of memory, function or data. We can get this up and running in a couple of hours, and nobody will be the wiser that every bank in Switzerland temporarily lost all of their financial records."

"I concur," Meyers said, leaning back in his chair. Then he grinned widely. "Score one for the good guys, eh?"

"Praise Jesus!" She laughed.

Trying not to roll his eyes at the religious nonsense, Meyers said nothing. The woman was an expert at writing code and fixing hardware, a rare combination

these days. Her only flaw was a ridiculous belief in
supernatural mumbo-jumbo.

"I'll call my wife and let her know I'll be late for
dinner," Meyers said, rummaging in a pocket of his
heavy coat.

"Late for dinner tomorrow," Gotterstein countered,
extracting her own cell phone. "I'll call our contact at
FINMA and give him a preliminary report." She re-
ferred to the Swiss Financial Market Supervisory Authority, which oversaw Swiss banking.

"Be sure to tell him what a difficult job it is, but
we're more than capable of handling the repairs."

Glancing sideways, Gotterstein stroked a finger behind her ear, then displayed it to the man to show that
it was bone-dry.

Chuckling, Meyers hit speed dial. As the connec-
tion was made, the whole fortress shook as thunder
boomed directly overhead, the noise echoing among
the cannons and bunkers.

"Thunder snow." Gotterstein laughed, both thumbs
tapping on the miniature keyboard of her phone. "God,
that takes me back to my youth. Haven't heard it in
years."

"Me neither," he said with a worried expression as
the thunder sounded again. Louder, longer and much
closer.

"Della, let's get out here," Meyers said, quickly
standing. "If the primary computer across the street
actually was burned out of existence by lightning, then
perhaps—"

Just then, he was interrupted by a terrible crackling
noise as a lightning bolt crashed onto the barrel of an
antiaircraft cannon. The surge of power arced off the
melting breech to reach down the tunnel and hit the

control station. Still holding their cell phones, both Meyers and Gotterstein died instantly, without even knowing what had just happened.

Another bolt arrived, igniting the corpses, exploding the controls and flashing along the wiring. The power surge failed to reach the main CPU buried safely deep underground. But a third bolt hit, followed by a fourth, fifth, sixth.... The bombardment went on and on, arcing finally across the gap in the line fuses and burning out the main servers.

Instantly, every file was erased. But the attack continued, bolt after bolt, until the mainframe was on fire, the CPU a charred husk and all of the primary circuits melting.

Halogen gas hissed from the ceiling to try to extinguish the blaze, but the lightning flowed along the swirling fumes to spread along the fire-suppression system and reach into every room of the fortress. Almost immediately, a dozen of the bunkers full of high-explosive shells were reached, the combined reverberations echoing along the mountains and hills for a hundred miles.

Along the Amazon

MOTORING ALONG THE AMAZON River, Bolan landed at a trading post several miles downstream and caught a tramp steamer. A few hours later he reached Beln where a rental plane was waiting. Checking over the plane to make sure that it hadn't been tampered with in any way, Bolan took off and landed in Brasilia, the capital of Brazil, by early afternoon.

Changing his clothes in the plane, Bolan then proceeded to the security station. Customs inspectors in

Brazil were far less stringent than in America, especially since his diplomatic passport made Bolan legally untouchable, and his hunting permits were all in order. Over the years, he had found a dozen different ways to move military ordnance across borders. In third-world nations a simple bribe often did the trick. Brazil wasn't in that class anymore, and was rapidly on the way to becoming the first of the new superpowers. He would have to be more discreet. However, posing as a diplomatic aide for a politically neutral country like Finland, always facilitated Bolan's ease of entry, or a quick exit.

"I did not know that Finland had an embassy in our country," the inspector said in halting English.

"As a courtesy, I will refrain from mentioning that to the ambassador," Bolan said with a dignified sniff.

On the floor were several bags, an arsenal of ammunition and hunting rifles nestled inside soft gray foam.

"No, no! I only meant that I… Here is your passport, sir," the inspector said quickly to cover the gaff.

Slowly accepting the passport, Bolan tucked it away inside his white linen suit, then stared at the minor airport official in disdain, turned and walked away. So far, so good.

However, Bolan noted that the security cameras in the ceiling tracked his every step through the concourse, so he stayed rigidly in character until renting a car and driving away.

To throw off any possible tail, Bolan drove to an expensive hotel and switched to a different car from another rental agency. Then he did it again, exchanging the luxury car for an inconspicuous van.

Now far less noticeable, Bolan traveled to a storage-locker facility outside town, and paid for three adjoining units. As he unlocked the doors, he noticed a group of men playing a game of soccer in the grassy field across the street. They seemed a little old not to be working at this time of day, so Bolan watched them for a while. Located in remote locations, storage units were a favorite target for street gangs. However, the men played hard, and when they broke for beer, Bolan continued unloading the van.

In the first and third units, he installed a proximity sensor rigged to call his cell phone if the units were activated by an intruder. In the middle unit, he stashed the steamer bags, arming himself with a shoulder holster and Beretta. He left the body armor behind, but did don a thick undershirt of ballistic cloth. The resilient material would stop most shrapnel and small-caliber bullets. The impact would still break his bones, but he wouldn't die immediately. That wasn't much, but where he was going next it was all that he could risk wearing.

Driving back toward town, Bolan got a text message from Brognola about the lightning strikes in Bern. Temporarily, the ten largest banks in the world had no way to record a money transfer. The soldier knew that could have only a single purpose. The terrorists were preparing to sell the weapon. He scowled at that. First, they killed every expert in the field, then they made it impossible for the banks to reveal any details about a purchase.

Bolan noted sourly, maneuvering through heavy traffic, that these were Swiss banks, financial institutions world famous for never telling anybody anything at all.

Reaching the outskirts of the city, Bolan was immediately snared in rush-hour traffic. Exercising extreme patience, he spent the next two hours crawling along, dodging taxicabs, pedestrians, trucks and work crews, while listening to the radio for any news about recent attacks until he finally reached the Grand Imperial Casino and Resort.

Dominating the downtown area, the Grand Imperial rose from the surrounding office buildings and apartment blocks like a queen standing among hobos. The entire twenty stories glittered with neon lights in every possible color of the spectrum.

Music played from hidden speakers in the neatly trimmed hedges; a water fountain that looked suspiciously similar to the famous one in the Bellagio Casino in Las Vegas sprayed high columns of water in perfect time to the music. But then, William "The Gorgon" Kirkland wasn't known for being low-key, or overly concerned with the niceties of the law. His redeeming feature was a fanatical devotion to justice. Kirkland and Bolan went back a long way.

Stopping at the front portico, Bolan tossed the van's keys to a hesitant valet, whose demeanor changed instantly when the soldier flashed him a U.S. one-hundred bill for a tip, and strolled inside.

"Welcome to Grand Imperial, sir!" a showgirl said, flashing perfect teeth. She was dressed in nylons and sequins, feathers and a headdress, but her breasts were completely bare, aside from a light dusting of gold.

Smiling politely, Bolan shook her hand and went inside. The lobby was filled with slot machines, both the old-fashioned mechanical ones with an actual lever, the classic "one-armed bandit," plus the new computerized versions with a swipe for your credit card, and a cushioned seat where you could relax and comfortably lose every penny you had in the world.

The main room was enormous and overly decorated

with oil paintings, mirrors, ferns, chandeliers and velvet ropes. Just as in every other casino in existence, the crowd was excited but quiet, the general murmur of the patrons barely discernable over the chiming of the slot machines, ringing bells and the calls of the dealers. Most of it was in Portuguese, the language of Brazil. However, Bolan understood some of the more familiar phrases.

"Twenty-one, a winner!"

"Craps, sir, you lose."

"New player!"

"Fresh deck!"

"Next!"

An endless parade of feathered showgirls in outrageous outfits strolled along, offering free drinks to everybody. Lubricant for the opening of hesitant wallets. Along one wall were several small auditoriums with glass windows in front, soundproof, of course. Customers could see the show, but not hear what was being said, which lured them inside like sheep to the shearing. On one stage, a magician was sawing a topless woman in two, while in the next, fifty topless women were dancing in some bizarre version of the French cancan, and a third stage held a stand-up comic talking into a mike, the audience silently throwing back their heads with laughter.

Just then, a casino guard started to walk his way. The man held a radio in his hand to call for help in case of trouble, but his belt held a stun gun, pepper spray, handcuffs and a police baton. All of which weren't necessary, since he looked more than capable of benchpressing a fully loaded Cadillac Eldorado.

"I'm sorry, sir, but weapons are not permitted on the casino floor," the guard said in perfect English.

"Good to know," Bolan replied, impressed that the guard could tell he was armed. Most guards wouldn't have been able to do that. Clearly, he had been trained by an expert. "Now, please call the Gorgon, and tell him to haul ass down here, pronto."

The guard scowled. "Who was that again, sir?"

"Just ask Security, and tell them somebody has a message for the Gorgon."

"We have nobody here by that name, sir," the guard said, as four more guards come out of the crowd. Their faces were smiling, but their body language told an entirely different story.

"Just do it. Bill Kirkland and I are old friends," Bolan said calmly, keeping his hands by his side. A gunfight with unarmed men in the middle of a crowd was absolutely the very last thing he wanted here.

As the guards formed a tight wall around Bolan, the first one made the call. Almost instantly, there was a response.

"The Gorgon?" a voice crackled over the radio. "Nobody has ever had the balls to call me that except for... Mack, is that you?"

"None other, Bill," Bolan said toward the radio. "Nice to see you're doing so well."

"What was that?" William Kirkland crackled over the radio. "Sergeant Padestro! Please give Mr.... Smith the radio and return to your usual duties."

The cadre of guards visibly relaxed as the first passed over the radio. Then they departed without a backward glance.

"Your staff is well-trained," Bolan said, thumbing the transmit button, while turning toward the video camera in the ceiling.

"Damn well should be. Did it myself," Kirkland

told him. "Man, I never thought to see you again, old buddy. Head for the private elevator near that statue of Pegasus and come on up! I'll have the chef slap a couple of T-bones on the grill, and we'll start toasting the fact that we're not dead yet."

"Sounds good, but I'm here to collect on a debt."

There was a brief silence.

"Are you serious?"

"Absolutely."

"Be right down." Kirkland sighed, and the radio went dead.

Going over to the marble statue of the famous winged horse, Bolan gave the radio to a passing security guard. He had to wait only a few minutes before the gold-tinted doors to a private elevator opened and a large man walked out wearing an expensive three-piece suit.

Born and raised in the Scottish Highlands, former NATO Special Agent William "The Gorgon" Kirkland stood over six feet tall and appeared more than ready to repel Roman legionaries from his beloved homeland.

Painfully clean-shaven, with a dimple in his lantern jaw, Kirkland had a suit of military body armor slung over a shoulder and was carrying a black nylon equipment bag that clanked with every step.

"Bill," Bolan said in greeting.

"Prick," Kirkland muttered in reply, then broke into a broad smile. "Damn, it's good to you again. Even under these circumstances."

"Same here." Bolan chuckled. This close, he could catch glimpses of military tattoos under the other man's silk collar, and hidden up both sleeves. Having patched bulletholes in his friend, Bolan knew that Kirkland was covered with enough tattoos, some of them extremely unsuitable for public display, that he could have been an exhibit in one of his casino's sideshows.

"Okay, who do we kill?" Kirkland asked, shifting the body armor to a more comfortable position.

"As ever, the soul of tact." Bolan laughed, offering a hand.

"Why change perfection?" Kirkland grinned as they shook.

A passing waitress paused for a moment to smile openly at the two huge men, then sighed and walked away, but put a little more motion into her hind quarters than was normal.

"I think she likes you," Kirkland noted.

"I think she knows you own the place."

"Cynic."

"Dreamer."

"But hey, it came true!" Kirkland gestured grandly with his free arm. "I own a casino! Welcome to Wild Bill's Old West Palladium of Honest Cards, Easy Women and Cold Beer!"

"Now called the Grand Imperial."

"A minor name change, I assure you."

"Love to hear the story," Bolan said, checking his watch, "but we're short on time. Are you ready to travel?"

"Money, guns and passports, right here," Kirkland said, jiggling the equipment bag.

"Now why would a respectable citizen like yourself have need of more than one passport?" Bolan asked, suppressing a grin.

"Believe it or not, there are a couple of countries where William 'The Gorgon' Kirkland wouldn't be greeted with open arms."

"More like 'open fire'?"

"It has been known to happen," Kirkland said with a shrug. "Okay, where to first, Sarge?"

Bolan noted the change in address. "I have some supplies stored just outside of town, then I've arranged a very expensive off-the-grid flight to Miami," Bolan said as he began walking around the statue. "We need to pick up an expert in advanced electronics."

"Sure, not a problem. I know a guy… Wait, did you say Miami?" Kirkland asked, stopping in his tracks. "Oh, no, you wouldn't to do that to me."

Bolan said nothing.

"Damn it, Sarge, you *are* a prick," Kirkland growled, angrily starting forward once more. "Fine, okay, she can come! But if that crazy bitch ever mentions what happened in Hong Kong, I'll take her over my knee for a bare-bottom spanking that'll have her eating off a fireplace mantel for a week!"

"I'd love to see that," Bolan said. "Because immediately afterward, Heather would rip out your beating heart and shove it up your ass."

Kirkland grinned in memory. "Yeah, she's something special, all right."

"One of the best knife fighters I've ever seen."

"And I have the scars to prove it!"

"Me, too."

As the men exited the casino, Bolan saw that the staff had already brought around a Rolls-Royce, and a liveried chauffeur was holding open the rear door.

"Not today, James, I'll be slumming it with this hobo for a while," Kirkland said in passing. "Don't do anything on the Duesy until I get back."

"Whatever you say, sir," James said in heavily accented English. "Any idea when that might be?"

"None whatsoever."

"Very good, sir," James said, closing the door to the Rolls. "Then I shall continue the modifications on the Lamborghini until your return."

"Good man."

"You own a Duesenberg?" Bolan asked, giving the ticket for the van to a valet.

Casting a brief glance at Kirkland, the teenager bolted toward the parking garage as if his pants were on fire.

"I have a few," Kirkland boasted, then added, "Won the new one in a poker game. Okay, she's a total wreck, but Jimmy and I will get it running again. He's a wizard at remanufacturing antique parts."

"Nice to have a hobby," Bolan said cautiously, then felt compelled to add, "Bill, maybe you shouldn't come along on this. It could get rough."

"Rougher than Afghanistan, Beirut or the Congo?"

"Maybe," Bolan admitted, "and you've been pushing papers for a long time."

In a blur, Kirkland pulled a Webley .455 revolver from inside his jacket, only to see that Bolan had a Beretta out and ready.

"You were saying?" Kirkland asked coolly.

"Never mind," Bolan replied, holstering the weapon.

Just then, the van arrived. Bolan unlocked the rear doors and Kirkland stowed his equipment inside.

As Bolan got behind the wheel, Kirkland climbed in the passenger side and closed the door. "Okay, we're alone now," he said, pulling out the Webley to start loading the empty revolver. "Start talking."

"How much do you know about lightning?" Bolan asked, pulling away from the curb to merge into the busy stream of traffic.

CHAPTER THREE

Mumbai, India

A hard cold rain pelted the sprawling expanse of the eastern metropolis. Thunder constantly rumbled, and sheet lightning flashed from cloud to cloud, occasionally hitting the ground in a blazing display of nature unbridled.

Glistening skyscrapers of glass and steel dominated the vast landscape of gated homes, stores and tar-paper shacks. Freight trains moved slowly along the complex network of railroads, and the mighty Ganges River was high, threatening at any moment to overflow its banks and flood the city.

Washed clean by the unrelenting downpour, the downtown streets were nearly empty of merchants and tourists, unusual for the teeming city. The day's accumulation of trash was gone, flushed into the wide drains, and the traffic was reduced to taxicabs, trolley cars and the mandatory army of unstoppable bike messengers. Only the street people remained.

Music came from a hundred locations: tea shops, taverns, restaurants, discotheques, open apartment windows and electronics stores blaring their latest acquisitions to the world. In the hills, a wedding party continued full-force, undampened by the weather, a cadre of eunuchs dressed as women dancing in front of the house to wish the new couple good luck. Down by the busy docks, a Bollywood crew was frantically trying to film a sequel to an unexpectedly popular science fiction movie.

A gantry rose high above the crew, technicians, stunt men and government safety inspectors checking the rig attached to the hero. The maze of wires were all painted dark green so that a computer could easily remove them in the lab.

"Are we ready?" the director said into a hand mike, the words booming out of amplifiers safe inside canvas tents. "Okay then, we go on three...two...one!"

Backflipping through a store window, the dashingly handsome hero launched into the air using his high-tech battlesuit. Instantly, a woman screamed, a dozen prop cars exploded into wild flames, and a hundred bearded assassins opened fired on rooftops with Russian machine guns and Chinese assault weapons. Easily smashing his way through them, the hero scooped up the woman in his arms and launched into the sky, circling around a billboard promoting a local jeans company.

"Cut! Great job!" the director said. "Everybody to second marks, and we'll do the big fight scene!"

Standing on the sixteenth floor of the Chandra Building, the executive director of RAW scowled at the dimly heard commands. *"Everybody to the second marks."* If the hero didn't win the first time, then just do it again and again until he did. No problem. If only it was that simple in real life, the man thought.

In the room behind him, the top agents for RAW were sitting around a large conference desk reviewing Most Secret reports. If their conclusion matched his, then the entire world was in more danger than he could possibly imagine.

The agency was called RAW, the Research Analysis Wing, and was the external intelligence agency for India. Officially located in New Delhi, the covert agency actually operated out of Mumbai, posing as a legitimate business constructing desalination plants to make sea water drinkable. Which they did, but only as a sideline. Reporting only to the prime minister, the organization had stopped hundreds of terrorist attacks since its creation, and often joined forces with the Americans to eliminate terrorist training camps in Pakistan. RAW helped the Mossad capture Nazi war criminals, assisted Ukraine Intelligence to kill former KGB agents and joined forces with NATO in stopping human trafficking, as well as its usual duties of protecting the nation. But this new threat...

Watching the water trickle down the bulletproof window, the executive director briefly thought back to the warm summer rains of his childhood, playing in the mud puddles and sailing folded paperboats. Ah, youth. However, with the new information they had just obtained, it would seem as if those days were long gone, as antiquated as a coin-operated payphone.

"Sir, are you sure this HUMINT is hard?" the agent muttered, rifling through the sheath of documents.

"Yes, the human intelligence has been confirmed from two different sources," the executive director replied curtly, folding both hands behind his back.

"Then he's back," another agent stated, crumpling a sheet of paper in his fist.

With a scowl, the executive director turned away from the window. "So it would appear," he growled. "What's more—"

Suddenly, the unbreakable window vaporized into superheated plasma as it was hit by a lightning bolt, then a second came through the opening and the executive director exploded, his steaming internal organs blown across the conference table. The agents hastily dove for the floor, but a split second later it detonated into blackened splinters. Scrambling for the door, the agents got only halfway there before there was a flash of light, terrible pain and then an endless eternity of soothing darkness.

Again and again, lightning ravaged the office building, blowing out windows on every story and setting countless fires.

Meanwhile, the movie cameras continued rolling down on the dockyard. However, they were no longer pointed at the actors, but at the bizarre flurry of violent activity that was slowly destroying the entire Chandra Building.

Baghdad, Iraq

IT WAS A SURPRISINGLY COOL DAY in the desert, barely out of the nineties. There was no wind worth mentioning, and the sky was a deep azure-blue.

A trail of dust rose from behind a low swell in the hard-packed ground, and moments later a speeding Hummer came into view, jouncing and bouncing along the cracked pavement of the new road.

There had been a lot of new roads poured since the invasion and the subsequent fall of Saddam Hussein. Mostly because the loyalists, terrorists and others kept blowing them up with roadside bombs buried in the loose sand. The crazy Americans called them IEDs, improvised explosive devices. But everybody else in the world simply called them bombs.

For this day's mission, the three members of Project Ophiuchus were dressed in loose civilian clothing, black combat boots, sunglasses and kaffiyehs, the latter worn more to disguise their features from orbiting spy satellites than to keep the sand out of their mouths. The desert was merely a part of life, neither good or bad, just something to be endured or ignored.

"Almost there," Lieutenant Fahada Nasser said, shifting gears as the Hummer raced around a bomb crater. The sand was sprinkled with broken pieces of exploded machines, black ants feasting on any organic remains.

Although rather short, the lieutenant had a womanly figure that she did her best to hide under loose uniforms. But her eyes were a dark violet, described as "oddly mysterious" by Interpol in her wanted poster.

Her long black hair was tightly bound into a ponytail, and a jagged scar circled her neck where a Mossad agent had tried to slit her throat and failed. She was armed with a 9 mm Tariq pistol, which was partially hidden under an open jacket. But lying on the floor was an XM-25 grenade launcher, and her pockets bulged with extra shells.

"I used to live here, too," Major Zafar Armanjani replied, adjusting the red-and-black kaffiyeh covering the lower half of his face.

A tall man, Armanjani carried himself with a quiet sense of authority that gave other soldiers the urge to salute for no logical reason. Possessing the wide chest and thick arms of a professional weight lifter, Armanjani also had a strangely smooth face with tiny scars along the eyes and ears—the telltale marks of cheap plastic surgery. His only concession to vanity was a small silver scorpion hung around his neck as a good-luck charm. Tucked into a shoulder holster was a 13 mm Tariq Magnum pistol, and handcuffed to his wrist was an expensive leather briefcase.

In the rear seat, Sergeant Benjamin Hassan grunted, not because he had anything specific to say, but because he was grimly determined to be a part of every important conversation. The trouble was, Hassan couldn't really tell the important ones from the casual, so he chimed into every conversation just in case.

Abnormally wide, Hassan resembled a gorilla more than a man, the thick black hair covering his body only adding to the image. However, his face was closely shaved, a small nick on a lip showing his haste that morning. As befitting his role of a hired bodyguard, the sergeant was openly armed with two 9 mm Tariq pistols, one on each hip, and a machete. But resting on the seat nearby was an Atchisson autoshotgun, a big drum of 12-gauge cartridges inserted into the lower receiver.

Glancing sideways, Nasser and Armanjani exchanged a knowing look about the sergeant, then dismissed the matter. Ever since he had been kicked in the head by a camel as a child, Hassan wasn't able to understand many things that other people easily could. Normally, that would have been a serious detriment for a soldier. But his amazing marksmanship, brute strength and animal ferocity in battle more than made up for the minor inconvenience of his scrambled intelligence.

As the Hummer rumbled across a new wooden bridge, the major remembered how once it had been a beautiful concrete bridge decorated with a row of bronze statues of Saddam Hussein and equipped with steel hooks for hanging minor criminals. But that was all gone now.

Not so very long ago, the Republican Guard had

ruled this desert like the sultans of legend, obeying only the commands of their leader. Then the Americans came, endless waves of them, like a never-ending sandstorm.

Most of the army had broken rank and run away, stripping off their uniforms to try to hide among the civilians. But the clever Americans had established checkpoints along the roads, and simply arrested everybody not wearing shoes.

Realizing the futility of the trick, Armanjani had done the opposite, killed a lowly private and switched clothing. Then he attempted to attack a platoon of American soldiers with the safety still engaged on his rifle. He was arrested, searched and laughingly dismissed as a harmless conscript.

Armanjani grinned at that memory. The fools! A wise man fought like the scorpion, not the beetle. The beetle attacked dung, while the scorpion watched and waited in cool shadow as the hot sun made his enemies weak. Then he pounced and feasted.

Before the war, the Iraqi army had been equipped with the most modern of weapons that could be purchased either legally or on the black market—Russian AK-47 assault rifles, RPG-7 grenade launchers, T-72 battle tanks, Gazelle gunships and BM-25 multiple-rocket launchers. However, it had all proved useless against the laser-guided missiles, smart bombs and robot drones of the hated Americans. Within only a few hours, the armored might of the Iraqi army had been obliterated, most of the battle tanks and MRLs destroyed without firing a single shot.

But revenge was coming soon, the major thought smugly as the Hummer passed the burned-out shell of a Gazelle attack gunship. Everything of any value had been removed, leaving only the fire-blackened frame and twisted landing rails.

"I hate the sight of those," Nasser said in a husky voice. "They always remind me of a carcass the beetles have devoured."

"You're getting better at that," Armanjani said, looking out the window. "If I did not personally know better, I would swear that you were a man."

"Fuck you, too, sir," Nasser replied in a deep gravelly rumble.

"Much better," Armanjani stated. "Just remember to scratch your balls every now and then. Not under your damn breasts."

"My new bra itches."

"Too bad. The people we are dealing with do not like women, except as a vessel for their pleasure."

"Vessel. As in a toilet." Her voice was neutral, but her hands went white on the steering wheel. "Yes, I have met such men before."

"Just don't let them take you a prisoner and find out personally," he warned.

"I will have your back, cousin," Hassan growled, cradling the massive Atchisson autoshotgun.

Just then, the loose sand shifted on top of a nearby sand dune, and a lone figure in a tan ghillie suit stood, the loose material falling away.

As Nasser stopped the Hummer, the major made a complex gesture in the air.

With a nod, the armed figure went back into the hole, vanishing like a scorpion from the noon heat.

"Mark that spot," Armanjani commanded, as the Hummer started forward once more.

"He is already dead," Hassan replied, staring directly into the blazing sun.

"Not yet, my friend," Armanjani advised. "First we must talk with his masters."

Hassan only nodded in reply, his gloved hands tightening slightly on the deadly Atchisson.

"Do you really think that we can deal with al Qaeda?" Nasser asked in her real voice. It was soft and gentle, almost girlish, as if she were a child wearing the clothing of an adult. "They're animals! Not soldiers."

"We can deal with them," the major said. "And do not speak again until we are far away from here. These people have a very low opinion of women."

"They're fools."

"True. But rich fools who hate the same enemy that we do. Let us hope they will deal honestly, and we will drive away from here millionaires!"

"Billionaires," Hassan corrected hesitantly.

"Not after the split, no," the major said, checking the clip in the 13 mm Magnum pistol.

Settling back into the seat, Hassan grunted in grudging acceptance at that. Then he asked, "Why can we not simply sell our device directly to the Saudis? They are the real masters of the Middle East."

"Because their prince wishes to pretend that he is not a criminal, and thus keep the Americans from bombing his palace," Armanjani answered curtly. "As they did to Saddam and so many others."

"Bah, the Saudis are fools," Nasser snorted. "All men are fools!"

"Most women, too," Armanjani added with a chuckle.

Obscured by her kaffiyeh, Nasser's expression was unreadable, but the skin around her sunglasses crinkled as her cheeks rose in what might have been a smile.

A few miles later, they reached an intersection and

took a left turn. There were no street signs or mile markers. It resembled ten thousand other such intersections, ordinary and easily forgettable.

"Get hard," Armanjani commanded. "We are here to deal, but I trust these back-doors Muslims less than a UN negotiator."

As they crested a low hill, a shimmering expanse of blue appeared in the distance. Soon, they were driving along the shore of a small lake. In the middle was an artificial island with a white marble palace of domes, towers and spirals.

Once, this had been a minor palace owned by President Hussein, a paradise on earth. Now it was a burned-out hovel, barely able to stand against the evening breeze. Weeds filled the gardens, every window was broken and vile graffiti covered the outer walls in garish neon colors.

Parking the vehicle a safe distance away, Armanjani and the others exited the Hummer and did a quick recon around the palace before venturing through the sagging front doors. Their footfalls echoed off the bare walls as they walked into the shadowy mansion.

With their weapons at the ready, they eased across the spacious foyer, keeping apart from one another to prevent unseen snipers from getting a group shot. It was dark inside, the only light coming from a stained-glass skylight that had somehow escaped intact.

The palace had been stripped bare, everything of value removed, sometimes forcibly. Even marble columns and the electrical outlets had been yanked from the walls. The walls and ceiling were pockmarked with countless bullet holes, delicately carved doors had been reduced to jagged splinters, and there were dank piles in the corners that looked suspiciously like human waste.

Removing his sunglasses, Armanjani frowned in disapproval. This was sad. Saddam Hussein had been a father to his nation. A stern father, yes, but that was how you raised children—with the closed hand and the open heart. He simply couldn't understand the raw hatred his fellow countrymen harbored for their fallen leader. Our father is dead, can we not at least honor him in the grave? the major wondered.

Proceeding along the main corridor, the three people swept past a library, steam room, billiard room, armory and movie theater before reaching the living room.

Laid out in overlapping circular patterns, the cavernous room rose and fell in random patterns, giving it a rather unearthly feel. All of the furniture and artwork was gone, of course, and the waterfall had been turned off, leaving only the mosaic on the bottom of the basin. Some of the tiles had been removed, but it was still easily recognizable as President Hussein with several busty American movie stars clustered around him. He was in full military uniform, with a scimitar and a gold crown, while they were clothed in diaphanous veils.

Splintery wooden bridges crossed over empty swimming pools, and curved niches lined the walls where there had previously been antique suits of armor from around the world. What might have once been a throne occupied a central location, but it had been used for target practice so much that that was only a theory.

Moving to the pile of riddled lumber in the center of the room, Armanjani and his people looked up to see five men in nondescript military uniforms on the second-story balcony. A decorative banister of iron lace edged the platform, and there were rows of raised seats for spectators to look down into the living room as if it were a sports arena.

All of the men were heavily armed with assault rifles, pistols and knives. One man actually had a Russian RPG strapped across his back, while an elderly man with a bushy beard was carrying a battered leather briefcase.

"You're late," the man with the briefcase stated loudly.

Instantly, Armanjani and his people swung up their weapons and clicked off the safeties.

"That is not the correct greeting," the major stated, leveling the Tariq.

With a sneer, the old man waved that aside. "Bah, foolish games."

"Then we go," the major declared, backing away.

"Nicholas!" another man on the balcony said quickly.

There was a pause.

"Tesla," Armanjani replied in the countersign.

However, the members of al Qaeda and Ophiuchus didn't ease their stance or lower their weapons.

"Well?" Armanjani demanded impatiently, shaking the briefcase to make the handcuff chain jingle.

"We have seen the reports," the old man said, stroking his beard. "Each target was hit exactly as you said it would be."

"Most impressive," another of the men replied in a throaty growl.

"Then are you ready to do business?" Armanjani asked, lowering the pistol and tucking it into the holster.

"Yes and no," the old man replied.

"Meaning?"

"Your price is too high," a third man stated with a scowl. "Much, much too high!"

"The price is fair," the major replied, obviously annoyed. "Besides, this is not the marketplace, and we are not tourists!"

A fourth man laughed. "Everything is negotiable."

The major scowled. "Not this. The price is fair. Do you wish me to put it into an auction and have you bid against the Chinese and the Russians?"

At those words, the men on the balcony shifted their stances slightly, and Armanjani knew that he had just made a deadly mistake by admitting that he was in charge and not merely an emissary.

"I see a red dog," Nasser whispered.

"Agreed," Hassan muttered softly.

"So be it, *red dog*." Major Armanjani drew and fired the pistol in a single move.

The old man with the briefcase threw back his head as the 13 mm Magnum round smashed through his teeth, and then out the top of his head. A geyser of pink brains splattering across the bullet holes and graffiti.

"Kill them!" a second man bellowed, turning to run away.

"No, get the briefcase!" another countered, pulling an electronic device from a pocket and pressing the button on top.

When nothing happened, Hassan shouted a war cry and cut loose with the Atchisson. The autoshotgun discharged the entire magazine of double-O buckshot cartridges in a continuous roar, and sparks flew as a hundred pellets ricocheted off the iron railing. However, all of the remaining men vanished in the deafening maelstrom, their bloody bodies thrown backward to smack into the raised seats.

As Hassan reloaded the Atchisson, Armanjani quickly unlocked the handcuff from his wrist, and Nasser turned to aim the XM-25 at a suspiciously intact door.

A split second later, it slammed open and out rushed a dozen men brandishing AK-47 assault rifles. Instantly, she fired and the 25 mm shell exploded inside the chest of the lead man, his body parts smacking into his comrades and sending them tumbling in all directions. Then Nasser fired twice more, the 25 mm shells exploding on the floor, and blowing the scrambling men into screaming hamburger.

"Should we try for their briefcase, sir?" Hassan asked, sweeping the room for any further enemies.

"Ignore it, that's a trap," Armanjani answered, opening his briefcase to extract a bandolier of military canisters.

Draping it across his chest, the major yanked free a canister of white phosphorous, pulled the pin, flipped off the safety lever and threw the bomb down a dark hallway.

The canister bounced out of sight, then erupted into a writhing fireball that filled the hallway. Several human torches stumbled out of the flames screaming insanely and waving their arms.

Ignoring the walking corpses, Nasser fired shells down two other hallways. The HE charges detonated thunderously, shaking chunks of plaster off the walls, but invoking no additional death screams.

"Find the rest of them!" Armanjani snarled, moving to the cover of a bridge while firing random shots from the Tariq.

Nasser and Hassan followed his example, hammering the room with high-explosive death. Doors exploded off gilded frames, a chandelier crashed into a pool, a bridge collapsed, and then a false wall fell over, revealing a group of men loading a linked belt of ammunition into the breech of a .50-caliber machine gun.

Shooting as they moved, Armanjani and the others scattered. Half a heartbeat later, the machine gun sputtered into operation, the hammering stream of heavy-caliber combat rounds chewing a path of destruction across the room, across the pools, bridges and finishing the annihilation of the throne.

Ducking behind the waterfall, Hassan cried out as he caught some shrapnel.

Safe behind a concrete column supporting the balcony, Armanjani slapped a fresh clip into his handgun. "Green dog," he said.

Squatting under a bridge, Nasser nodded and shifted the XM-25 into a new position.

As the stream of .50-caliber rounds moved away from his position, Armanjani stepped into view and emptied the Tariq at the group of men. One of them fell clutching his throat, but the rest answered back with a volley from a variety of handguns, machine pistols and assault rifles. With a strangled cry, the major spun around and dropped.

"We got him!" a man cried, and the others stopped shooting to cheer in victory.

Fools, Nasser thought, swinging up the XM-25 to fire three shells at the domed skylight.

The bulletproof display of stained glass loudly shattered under the trip-hammer detonations of the 25 mm rounds, and a colorful rain of broken shards plummeted downward. The deluge hit the floor in front of the hidden machine gun, and noisily smashed into smaller pieces. The cheering stopped as the members of al Qaeda screamed and clawed at their bleeding faces.

Immediately, Armanjani started throwing more canisters of phosphorous while Nasser reloaded and Hassan cut loose with the Atchisson. In only seconds, the cries of pain ceased, and there was only the crackle of the chemical flames cooking the tattered corpses.

Moving fast, the major and the others charged down the main hallway just before the stacked belts of .50-caliber ammunition started cooking off, a stuttering barrage of wild bullets zinging everywhere.

Only seconds later, the personal ammunition carried by the terrorists did the same thing, exploding inside their guns and pockets. Bloody chunks of raw flesh were blown around in a ghastly abandonment.

"Black dog!" Armanjani yelled, scrambling up a steep flight of curved stairs.

Reloading as they ran, the three members of Ophiuchus ignored the second floor and continued to the third. Briefly, they ran across the exposed span of another bridge, and then directly into the private sleeping quarters of the former president of Iraq.

Easing their steps, the three of them slipped past the rows of barren guest quarters to reach the master bedroom and proceeded directly to the small linen closet.

While the others warily stood guard, Armanjani pushed open the door and fumbled along the top shelf. Unless his memory was wrong, it had to be here somewhere. It had to! In the distance, more ammunition detonated, and the machine gun briefly sputtered into action.

Finding the hidden switch, the major pressed it three

times, and a section of the wall moved aside to reveal a steel pole. Grabbing the pole, he slid down into the darkness.

The descent took a lot longer than he remembered, and it seemed impossibly long before Armanjani hit the floor of the sub-basement. Landing in a crouch, he instantly stepped aside. A moment later, Nasser arrived, closely followed by Hassan.

As the sergeant landed, they heard three fast clicks, and the entire length of the pole suddenly jutted razor-sharp blades. With a gasp, Hassan jerked his hands clear.

"I told you to move fast," Armanjani reminded him harshly.

"Yes, sir, you did," Sgt. Hassan panted, rubbing his undamaged palms, but unable to remove his eyes from the shimmering display of edged blades. There was a single drop of red blood on one, and he checked to find a finger nicked. That had been close.

Going to an open passageway, Nasser eased into the darkness, only to reappear a minute later.

"Clear," she announced.

Assuming the lead, Armanjani surged forward, making sure that he never removed his hand from the left wall. The antiradiation maze twisted and turned countless times through total darkness before there was a distant haze of light that grew steadily brighter.

Stepping into bright sunlight, the three people quickly scanned the ruins of a large greenhouse, but they seemed to be alone. The plastic windows, designed to withstand the worst possible sandstorm, were intact, but sandblasted dead-white, so that it was impossible to see what lay outside. Dust hung heavy in the air, and they stirred up small clouds shuffling past the rows of empty shelves and ornate pots. Dead plants lay underfoot, and their boots softly crunched on the desiccated foliage.

"Sir, why did we not simply go back out the front door?" Hassan asked in a terse whisper.

"Didn't you see the man on the balcony activate a remote control?" Nasser demanded impatiently. "What else could it have been but an antipersonnel device?"

"And where would you place such a thing?" Armanjani asked, peeking around an ornate column to check the next wing of the huge greenhouse.

"Front door, the exact way we got in," Hassan replied tightly. "Sorry, sir."

"Not to worry, old friend," Armanjani said, glancing at the hulking goliath. "That's why we're here."

Continuing on through the dusty buildings, the trio finally reached the last structure. Creeping along the sandy floor, they dimly heard voices discussing the battle.

"What do you think happened?"

"We'll find out soon enough."

"Give them another few minutes?"

"Let me finish this cigar first, eh?"

"Fair enough. Got one for me?"

"Of course!"

Rising in unison, the members of Ophiuchus aimed at the unseen enemy on the other side of the white plastic and fired in unison. The plastic windowpanes splintered under the furious assault, and several men screamed in pain, then went silent.

Kicking open the flimsy door, Armanjani moved out of the greenhouse with the others in flanking positions. A dozen bodies were sprawled on the sand, a few of the men still alive and choking on their own blood.

Parked nearby were a pair of Cadillac SUVs, the engines softly purring. The closest vehicle was missing all of the tinted windows along one side, and a corpse, missing most of his face, was slumped over the steering wheel. The second SUV was undamaged, the driver's door open, the man running for his life along the bank of the lake.

Taking careful aim, Armanjani stroked the trigger of his gun, and the fleeing man flipped over sideways to splash into the water.

With Nasser standing guard, Hassan used his 9 mm Tariq to shoot everybody on the ground twice in the face just to make sure they were dead.

Yanking open the door to the intact SUV, Armanjani wasn't surprised to find an old man huddled on the floor in the rear compartment.

"Please don't hurt me!" he begged, tears flowing down his cheeks.

Blowing the man away, Armanjani hauled out the body, then removed the corpse's white kaffiyeh to mop the fresh blood off the leather seats.

"Think there are any more hidden about?" Hassan asked, reloading the pistol.

"No, they were overconfident," Nasser said with a sneer as if that was the worst crime it was possible to commit.

Checking the trunk of the first Cadillac, the major found only the shipping case for the .50-caliber machine gun and some spare belts of ammunition. Useless. However, the other SUV contained extra fuel, military rations and a small arsenal of handguns, assault rifles and ammunition. But there was no money. The major stiffened in rage. Obviously, al Qaeda had never planned on paying for the weapon, even if a deal could have been reached. How could he have been so foolish as to trust them?

Slamming the hatch closed, Armanjani glanced across the lake to see that the abandoned palace was on fire, red flames licking out the shattered windows to slowly expand along the balconies.

"That secret exit was why you chose this palace for the meeting. Am I right, sir?" Nasser asked unexpectedly.

"Knowing where to fight is half the battle," Armanjani replied, holstering his weapon. "All right, let's go."

As Hassan got behind the wheel, Nasser took the passenger seat and Armanjani climbed into the rear, carefully avoiding the damp patch of sticky leather.

Taking a minute to familiarize himself with the controls of the new vehicle, Hassan then turned on the air conditioner and slowly drove away, following the double set of tire tracks in the sand.

"What now, sir?" he asked, turning onto the access road and accelerating. A wide dust cloud rose behind the speeding vehicle that soon obscured the view of the burning palace.

"We return to base and try to find more reasonable customers," Armanjani replied, removing his sunglasses and tucking them into a pocket.

Nasser scowled. "Sir, what if we can't find any reasonable customers, just more dogs like these fat fools?"

"Then we create some," the major said, pulling out a cell phone to start thumbing a text message.

CHAPTER FOUR

Washington, D.C.

Tugging his necktie loose, Hal Brognola used the heels of his palms to rub his eyes, and then poured himself yet another cup of strong black coffee from an insulated carafe. Only a few drops came out, so he rose from behind the desk and crossed the office to start making a fresh pot.

The office was orderly and neat, the walls decorated with pictures of his wife and children and law-enforcement certificates. His suit jacket was hung across the back of a chair, and an old police-issue .38 revolver was holstered at the small of his back. The grip was worn from decades of use in the field, and long hours at the shooting range every weekend. It had been a while since Brognola had drawn a weapon, but he knew that when the need arose there would be no advance warning.

The big Fed returned to his desk with a fresh cup of coffee. Tapping some keys on a keyboard, Brognola reviewed the fact sheet he had been assembling for Mack Bolan and the President on lightning. The voltage and wattage widely varied, but generally they were around a hundred-million volts, which was more than enough to kill a bull elephant, much less a human being. The earth was hit by roughly 50,000 lightning bolts a year, and an average 3,000 people died every year from being struck.

Single-strike, multistrike, forked, chain, sheet, sprite, elves, trolls, Brognola hadn't heard of half of the forms of lightning bolts he'd researched, and he had been startled to discover the old joke about a bolt from the blue was horrifyingly true. Blue lightning could arc in from five miles away. The sky would be perfectly clear, the wind calm, and a split second later you were a pile of ash in the grass.

"Good night, Chief!" his secretary, Kelly, called out from the other side of the office door. "See you tomorrow!"

"Drive safely!" Brognola answered back, casting a nervous glance out the window at the cloudy sky. It wasn't raining in D.C. yet, but it would soon, at which point all bets were off.

On top of everything else, the list of possible targets hit by these snake charmers, as they used to call people who claimed to be able to make it rain, was getting longer all the time, and the death toll was rising faster than Brognola could keep track of. At first, it was mostly meteorologists and weather scientists. Now, it was financial experts, bank computers and underworld informers. Obviously, the snake charmers were systematically clearing the way for when they came out of the shadows.

"That's when the blood will really hit the fan," Brognola said softly, starting to drink from his mug, only to find it empty once more.

Suddenly, an alarm began beeping. A new icon was spinning on the monitor. He double-clicked, and it expanded into a view of the President of the United States sitting at his desk in the Oval Office.

"Good evening, Hal," the President said, pulling his hand back from a keyboard. Then he frowned. "Although, to be honest, I don't think that it's going to be very good for either of us now."

"What has happened, sir?" Brognola asked.

"First, allow me to apologize," the President said, running both hands through his black hair. "I didn't believe in your theory of terrorists using lightning, but now..."

"What was hit?"

Tapping some keys, the President sighed. "See for yourself, my friend."

The view of the Oval Office reduced to a small rectangle in the corner, the rest of the screen shifting to an outside view of military base in the desert. Dark, jagged mountains filled the horizon.

"Five-Star, this is Fireball Forward!" a colonel shouted into a handmike while trying to hold his cap on top of his head against a stiff wind.

In the background were rows of Buffaloes and Hummers, a score of 4x6 trucks, a dozen Abrams tanks and two Black Hawk gunships. The Hummers were equipped with light machine guns, while the much bulkier Buffaloes were actually armed with .50-caliber machine guns. A burst from those would flip over a Hummer, but not even shake the road dust off an armored Buffalo.

"This is Five-Star," a voice stated. "Go ahead Fireball, we read you loud and clear!"

Brognola grunted at that. Five-Star was the code this month for the Pentagon.

"Five-Star, we've found the enemy camp," the colonel shouted, the wind kicking up dust clouds. Soldiers were running for cover as the buffeted trucks rocked slightly. "But we had to take cover—there is a major sandstorm coming this way!"

Just then, lightning flashed across the sky, painfully bright even on the laptop monitor, and the picture scrambled for a few seconds from the accompanying electromagnetic burst.

Leaning forward, Brognola held his breath. *Please guys, start running,* he silently urged.

"Say again, Fireball?" the Pentagon demanded.

"Sandstorm!" the colonel bellowed as, in the background, the horizon rose like a wave at sea.

Billowing and churning, the stormfront swept toward the army battalion. In only a matter of seconds it engulfed the makeshift base and visibility was reduced to only a few feet.

A deafening howl dominated the picture as dozens of soldiers were slammed to the ground, and every loose item was sent hurtling about into the turbulent brown air. Then lightning flashed, and a truck exploded, the concussion slamming other trucks aside and sending a dozen men flying away into the building storm.

"Say again, Fireball, where is your location?" the Pentagon operator demanded, the volume bar sliding all the way to maximum. "Do you need assistance?"

The colonel said something about northern mountains when the lightning appeared again, going straight into the open hatch of an Abrams tank. The armored machine seemed to bulge outward for a moment before erupting, the hellish corona of shrapnel, corpses and broken machinery spraying outward to decimate a group of soldiers and flip over both of the Black Hawks.

"Get in those caves," Brognola whispered, both hands clenched into fists.

Again and again, the lightning lanced out, destroying one tank after another, then the bolts began walking along the ground, leaving behind rivers of steaming lava. Screaming soldiers burst into flames, their weapons discharging, grenades mercifully ending their ghastly torment.

Feeling physically ill, Brognola wanted to look away, but forced himself to watch, filing away every detail of the savage attack. It lasted less than five minutes, then the lightning abruptly stopped, and there was only the howling wind. The dry sand quickly covering the tattered remains of what had once been a full battalion of men and women.

"Fireball, respond!" the Pentagon demanded. "Is there anybody still alive? Hello, is anybody there?" But the only response was the howling wind and the crackle of countless small fires.

The view froze and shrank, as the President returned.

"When did this happen?" Brognola asked, flexing his hands.

"Twenty minutes ago," the President stated grimly, sitting back in his chair. "Search and Rescue teams are already on the way, but there's little hope of finding anybody alive."

"After that? I would hardly think so," Brognola replied, fighting a rising wave of helplessness. An entire battalion destroyed in five minutes. Five minutes!

"Have you made any progress on finding these people? Or at least what they want?" the President asked. "These attacks are coming more and more often, and at bigger targets. Soon they'll start on cities, and then…"

His voice trailed off, his face a mask of repressed fury.
"We have got to do something!"

"Our best man is in the field, sir," Brognola said.
"But Striker hasn't reported anything so far."

"Nothing at all?"

"There's not much to go on yet, sir. It's all happening so damn fast! These snake charmers...I mean..."

The President held up a palm. "I understand the reference, Hal. It helps to give the enemy a name, that makes them less intimidating."

Brognola scowled. "Anyway, sir, these snake charmers have obviously planned out every detail far in advance, including all of our possible responses."

"Are there any preventive actions we can take?"

"Not at the moment. This isn't some fanatic with a truckload of dynamite," Brognola continued. "These are cool, calculating professionals. Right now, we're still just trying to catch up!"

"Accepted," the President said. "Granting the assumption that we fail to ascertain their ultimate goals, what happens then?"

Unexpectedly, thunder rumbled overhead.

"They win," Brognola stated in brutal honesty, as a soft rain began to patter against the window panes.

Miami, Florida

THE SUN WAS WARM ON THEIR faces as Bolan and Kirkland strolled along the boardwalk, the air full of the smell of saltwater mixing with delicious aromas wafting from nearby Cuban and French restaurants.

A steady stream of cars zoomed along the shorefront highway while crystal-blue waves crested on a smooth white shore. Colorful beach umbrellas dotted

the sand like psychedelic mushrooms, the small circles
of shadow mostly empty, aside from the very young or
the very old. The dichotomy of beachlife encapsulated.

There were numerous families playing in the shal-
lows, while small children built sand castles. Standing alert on a centrally located wooden tower, a burly
lifeguard dabbed zinc oxide on his nose to prevent
unsightly peeling.

Teams of armed police officers in T-shirts, shorts
and sneakers, pedaled their speed bikes along the
boardwalk, voices crackling from the compact radios
clipped to their gun belts. Safely out of the way, a
group of muscular young men lifted weights in the
glare of the noon sun, while countless dozens of young
women in bikinis lounged on oversized towels and
spread suntan lotion on their bare skin in a lazy, almost sensuous manner.

All along the length of the beach and boardwalk,
smiling vendors pushed along wheeled carts and sold
hot dogs, ice cream, cold beer, sandwiches, sunglasses,
cell phones and shark repellant.

Trying to blend into the crowd, Bolan and Kirkland
were wearing civilian clothing, loose white slacks, and
Hawaiian shirts of multicolored orchids. Bolan had the
Beretta holstered behind his back, a water bottle in a
nylon-mesh sling disguising the telltale lump. Kirkland had the same, a leather camera case masking the
presence of his big bore Webley.

Leaving the boardwalk, the two men turned inland
and crossed the street. Pausing for a traffic light, Bolan
suddenly took out his cell phone. "Cooper here," he
said, using a favored alias.

Watching the ebb and flow of humanity, Kirkland
waited patently until Bolan finished the call.

"What was hit?" Kirkland asked, waving off an approaching taxi.

"An army battalion in Afghanistan," Bolan replied. "Everybody was killed, and even the vehicles were destroyed—trucks, tanks and gunships."

"The sons of bitches are getting bold," Kirkland growled, glancing at the fleecy white clouds in the blue sky.

"There's no reason why they shouldn't be," Bolan replied, taking a sip from the water bottle.

"Think the strike was advertising?" Kirkland asked with a scowl. "Show the world what they could do to the mighty United States?"

"Unlikely. Afghanistan is too remote to receive proper TV coverage."

"Now, we could go there in person," Kirkland suggested, as a group of kids in tight formation zoomed by on roller skates. "But there are far too many terrorist groups in that part of the world for us to question. It would take years."

"I have something else in mind," Bolan said.

"Hey, there it is!" Kirkland said suddenly, pointing across a busy intersection.

Nestled among the rows of T-shirt emporiums, yogurt shops, hair salons and bars was a three-story building that occupied half of the block. A sign on top merely had the single word *Montenegro*.

"Let's go," Bolan said, starting across the street.

"Why did she paint the building pink?" Kirkland asked. "That doesn't really seem her style."

"Look around, brother. Most of the larger buildings are pink or blue," Bolan said, waving a hand. "I think the mayor wants the city to look the way it does in movies."

"Bloody tourists," Kirkland growled, as if expelling a piece of rotten fruit from his mouth.

Bolan laughed. "This from a man who runs a casino hotel?"

"Hey, my dice and wheels are honest! Tourists pay a lot for nothing. That just doesn't make any sense to me."

"Ever been to a museum?"

"Sure…okay, point taken. But I still don't like them and all their damn cameras!"

As they started toward the pink building, Bolan had a strong feeling that that was the real source of Kirkland's dislike. Undercover DEA agents, covert ops, spies and mercenaries had all taken a big hit the day the cell phone camera was invented. Jamming devices helped a lot, but nothing could stop all of them. There were just too many.

The row of windows along the top floor of the building were open, and as Bolan and Kirkland got closer they could hear the assorted cries, slaps and grunts of hard physical exercise in progress.

"We need her," Bolan said, pulling open the glass door. "So keep the safety locked on that smart-ass mouth."

"I'll do my best, Sarge," Kirkland said. "But no promises."

The lobby inside was cool and crisp, with potted ferns in every corner, and the walls covered with photographs of famous clients: professional athletes, politicians and a lot of movie stars.

"The woman is good," Kirkland said grudgingly.

"Few better," Bolan stated, going to the front desk.

"Hello, can I help you gentlemen?" the receptionist asked, switching her gaze back and forth between the two men.

A mature woman with mocha-colored skin and ebony hair, she was wearing a flower-print skirt, but above the waist a skin-tight leotard displayed her firm figure to its full advantage.

Any tighter and Bolan would have been able to see her religion. "We're here to meet Heather," he said. "We're old friends from out of town."

"How nice, Mr...." She waited.

"Dupree, Roger Dupree," Bolan said.

"A pleasure to meet you, Mr. Dupree."

"Roger, please."

She smiled, revealing unexpected dimples. "Hitesri Chandra... Sherry to my friends."

"A pleasure to meet you, Sherry."

She glanced at Kirkland.

He grinned. "Lamont Cranston."

She arched an eyebrow at that. "Is Ms. Montenegro expecting you?" Sherry asked hesitantly.

"No, this is a surprise visit," Bolan said.

"However, we did leave a message at her AA meeting," Kirkland suddenly added with a straight face.

Frowning at that, Sherry turned to look only at Bolan. "Well, I'm sorry, but Ms. Montenegro is conducting a private class at the moment. But if you'd care to wait..." She smiled invitingly and didn't finish the sentence.

"Mind if we just go straight up?" Kirkland asked, pulling open the stairwell door.

"Sir, that's not allowed!" Sherry shouted, reaching out a hand.

But Kirkland was already gone, taking the steps two at a time.

"Please excuse my friend," Bolan apologized, heading for the open doorway. "He was raised in a cave by bears."

"Pity they didn't eat him," Sherry muttered, sitting back down.

At the top of the stairs, a small landing led to a changing room lined with lockers. There were private showers, a steam room, and from down a short hallway came the familiar sounds of a fight in progress.

Heading that way, Bolan and Kirkland caught the smells of sweat, blood and some sort of stringent herbal compound.

"Ah, Tiger Balm, just the smell makes me ache," Kirkland said wistfully. "You know, I still carry some of the stuff in my bag?"

"Who doesn't?" Bolan replied, as they proceeded along the hallway.

"I just wish it didn't reek like the southern end of a northbound rhinosaurus."

As they'd expected, the room wasn't a gymnasium, but a dojo, a martial arts studio. Although it was large and well-lit by ceiling fixtures, there was no furniture of any kind, just thick mats covering the floor and punching bags hanging in every corner. On the walls were racks of blunt bamboo poles, cushioned wooden sticks, then uncushioned sticks, knives and swords, followed by a wide variety of more exotic weaponry. The only decorations were framed pictographs in Japanese, Chinese and Korean extolling the virtues of honor and courage.

There were a dozen people of various ages sitting on the mats. Everybody was barefoot and wearing a loose cotton judo uniform, the twill jackets held shut with twisted cloth belts. Most of the students wore the red belts of advanced pupils, but there were also a few beginners in white belts and one high-ranking brown belt.

Standing at the front of the class was a tall woman with flaming red hair tied off her face with a strip of rawhide. She was completely without cosmetics and strikingly beautiful, with a full mouth and slightly slanting eyes of emerald-green that spoke of a mixed ancestry. Her white uniform was edged with black piping, and she wore the black belt of a teacher tied around a trim waist.

"So that's the deal. The first person to physically touch me gets a full refund on all of their fees," Heather Montenegro said, tightening her belt.

"That's all?" a burly black man asked suspiciously. "Just touch you? Not put you down or draw blood?"

Tolerantly, Montenegro smiled. "If you manage either of those, Mr. Cortland, you can have the building. Now, everybody stand!"

In unison, the students rose smoothly to their feet, many of them going immediately into an attack stance.

"Any volunteers for today's demonstration?" Montenegro asked, adjusting the rawhide around her forehead.

Three men and two women stepped forward, everybody else stayed in place.

"All right, begin," Montenegro said calmly, both hands at her side.

Instantly, the group of five charged forward, three of the students assuming the cat stance, the last two dropping into the horse position. Separating fast, they all converged on Montenegro from different directions.

"Pitiful," Kirkland muttered. "Five will get you six she drops them all in under a minute."

"No bet," Bolan said, shaking his head.

As the first student got close, she collapsed into a dragon crouch and did a leg sweep. Swaying out of the way, Montenegro caught the foot by the ankle, and twisted, sending the woman tumbling away.

Extending both arms, a man dove forward, obviously intent on trying merely to touch the teacher. Montenegro ducked under the arms, then spun around the man and slammed him in the back, adding her force to his own rush. Out of control, he slammed into the cushioned wall and rebounded, bleeding profusely from a broken nose.

The third student flipped over backward like an acrobat to land in the drunken monkey position, both arms raised for a double strike. A split second later, Montenegro buried her heel into the stomach of the man. Turning bright red, he doubled over, gasping and choking.

The last two students immediately retreated slightly, circling the motionless Montenegro. Then they both moved with blinding speed, the man chopping for her neck, while the woman kicked for a knee. A classic hi-lo formation.

Swatting aside the punch, Montenegro lashed out a foot to block the kick, then threw the man over her shoulder to crash into the woman. They went down in a tangle of limbs.

"Enough!" Montenegro called, straightening her stance. "Now, class, what was wrong with—" Spinning, she blocked a punch from the man with the bloody nose, then effortlessly flipped him sideways.

"While I applaud your tenacity, Steven," Montenegro said, walking closer to stand over the panting man. "The next time you attack after I called a stop, I'll break both of your arms."

"Yes, *sensei*," he muttered, his face pressed into the mat.

"Only try something fancy when you're desperate," Montenegro continued, kneeling to massage his spine with her knuckles. Almost instantly, the bleeding stopped and he began to breath more easily.

"Better?" Montenegro asked, ceasing the administrations.

"Better," he muttered, stiffly getting to his feet. "You're fast, sensei."

"True. So never underestimate an opponent," Montenegro said sternly, then turned about. "All right, class, as I was saying…" Her voice faded away at the sight of Bolan and Kirkland across the room.

"What the hell are you two doing…aw, crap," Montenegro said, yanking off the rawhide strip.

Politely, Bolan gave a short bow of respect, while Kirkland waved in greeting. "Hiya, toots! How's tricks?"

Scowling in annoyance, Montenegro deeply inhaled, then sighed. "Barbara!"

"Yes, ma'am?" replied the short blonde wearing the brown belt.

"Please take over for me. Work on disarming an opponent armed with a knife without breaking their bones. I'll be back in a few minutes."

"Days," Bolan corrected.

"After that, who knows?" Kirkland added with a grin.

Frowning for a moment, Montenegro then shrugged

in acceptance. "Barbara, the class is yours until further notice."

Barbara seemed flustered. "But, ma'am—"

"Hey now, wait just a damn minute!" said a burly man wearing a white belt. "I came here for Montenegro, not some teenager barely out of diapers!"

Without comment, Barbara stepped sideways to grab him by the wrist, then twisted hard, sending him to the mat. Then she buried a thumbnail into his throat. Twitching with unbelievable pain, the man broke into a sweat, his mouth opening and closing, but nothing coming out.

"What were you saying again?" Barbara asked, easing her grip.

"Yes, *sensei,*" he wheezed softly.

"Senpai," Barbara corrected. "I'm only a teacher, not a master."

Seeing that everything was in order, Montenegro bowed to the class, then crossed the mats to kiss Bolan warmly on the cheek. "Nice to see you again, Blackie."

"Same here, Heather." Bolan smiled. "You look great."

"You, too!" Montenegro chuckled.

"I see you've updated the curriculum," Kirkland said diplomatically.

"Shut up! Never speak to me again," Montenegro growled. "And just who the hell do you think you are?"

Confused by that, Kirkland struggled to formulate a response as Montenegro strode down the hallway to the locker room.

After a moment, the men followed.

"So, where are we going, jungle or desert?" Montenegro asked, taking off the black belt before going into a private changing stall.

"We'll discuss that somewhere less public," Bolan said, leaning against the wall. "But pack light."

There came the sound of a running shower. "Guns, guts and garters?"

"That sounds about right."

"If you need any help with the garters, just let me know," Kirkland said teasingly.

"Why, are yours slipping?" Montenegro asked as the shower stopped. "Colonel, are you sure that we need the shaved ape?"

"Wouldn't have brought Bill along if he wasn't necessary," Bolan said, trying not to grin. "And call me Matt during this gig."

"Matt it is," Montenegro replied. "I suppose that somebody has to carry the luggage."

"Heather, don't say things like that!" Kirkland exclaimed in a shocked voice. "We don't think of you as the luggage! More like…deadweight."

Just then, the door swung open and Montenegro stepped out of a steamy cloud. She was still barefoot, but was now wearing a loose khaki shirt tucked into cargo shorts that showed a lot of leg. Her tousled hair was damp, but Montenegro was wearing full makeup, with jade earrings and a silver necklace.

"What happened to your legs?" Bolan asked in surprise.

"Laser surgery," she replied, stepping into sneakers. "Scars make a man look tough, but aren't very attractive on a woman."

Just then, his cell phone vibrated and he took the call.

"Heads up! The main NASA launch facility at Cape Canaveral has just been attacked," Bolan announced.

"Over a hundred dead, including the head of NASA. The assembly building is gone, along with the prototype for the new Falcon rocket. Most of the base is on fire…"

He scowled. "Okay, Base. Striker out." He put away the cell phone.

Instantly, the atmosphere in the locker room changed.

"Okay, I brought a full kit, and Matt has an arsenal," Kirkland said quickly. "Anything special you need at home?"

"Yes, some new Glocks that I've been training with, and my body armor," Montenegro replied, tucking away the knife.

"Don't worry about it. We've got enough level four body armor to sink Manhattan."

"General issue level four, or some specifically tailored for female soldiers?"

"General issue." He gestured at the door. "Okay, you're right. Lead the way."

As Montenegro started down the stairs, she asked over a shoulder, "What's our first move, Matt?"

"I have our ride waiting at the airport," Bolan said. "From Miami we fly directly to Andrews Air Force Base where we pick up some heavy ordnance and switch to a C-130 Hercules."

"And then?" Montenegro asked, pushing open the ground-floor door and rushing across the lobby.

Both men said nothing until they were outside and on the street.

"Sri Lanka," Kirkland replied. "We're going after the White Tigers."

She paused. "They're behind the attack on NASA?"

"Not a chance in hell," Bolan said honestly.

Furrowing her brow, Montenegro started to ask a question, then comprehension flared.

"You clever bastards," she said, slowly smiling. "Come on, my Hummer is this way. Let's go!"

CHAPTER FIVE

Eyl Bay, Somalia

The morning sun was bright and hot enough to melt the flesh off a person's back.

The sluggish water in the bay moved thick and gray, foamy with toxic chemicals, and raw sewage floated about on the surface. Seagulls screamed in annoyance overhead, and dead fish lay rotting on the pebble shore. Not even the local insect population was interested.

Clustered protectively along a torpid river were hundreds of ramshackle buildings. Most of them were squat and ugly, the ancient engineering adage of "form follows function" played out here as the impoverished inhabitants were forced to make do with whatever they could get their hands on. However, there were a handful of large buildings, made of tan brick instead of crude adobe bricks. The roofs were beautiful blue domes that reflected the bright sunlight, and more than a few had television antennas or shiny satellite dishes. The cracked streets were strewn with garbage, dotted with potholes and puddles of human waste.

There were no cars or any other form of motorized conveyance in sight. No music could be heard playing anywhere. There were no factory whistles, fire alarms, church bells, school bells or police sirens, only a deafening silence to go with the oppressive heat. The starving people shuffled along like an army of the damned heading back into Hell.

The town boasted a crude dockyard, the concrete pilings pitting under the salty spray. The workers were lean, but seemed almost fat in comparison to the people in town. Their clothing was a mixture of old and new, all of it clean, and they were heavily armed with multiple pistols, knives, machetes and well-oiled AK-47 assault rifles.

Using a plastic funnel, a tall man was carefully pouring gasoline into an engine bolted to a speedboat. "Is that enough, cousin?" he asked, stopping to straighten a kink in his sore back.

"More than enough," the captain replied, screwing down the cap to the fuel tank. "With luck we should make a fine haul today. Our scouts along the coastline report that there is a yacht only fifty miles away."

"A rich yacht full of fat men and their pale wives with big breasts?"

"There almost always is." He grinned. "But more importantly they are secretly carrying the payroll for the French Foreign Legion."

The tall man squinted. "How do you know such things?"

"That is why I am the captain and you pour the gas."

"Fair enough." The tall man laughed, displaying gold-capped teeth.

Sitting along the tattered edge of a street, a small crowd of people watched the pirates performing their chores in a mixture of wonder and raw envy.

Out in the harbor several container ships moved slowly along, their decks lined with armed men as protection from the local pirates. Off to the side was a shiny new warship from Saudi Arabia, located just on the other side of the harbor.

Much farther out a couple of European cruise ships skirted along the horizon, trying to keep the dismal villages lining the shore out of the sight of their vacationing passengers.

Only one ship was anchored in the bay, and there were no sailors in sight on the deck, nor any obvious defenses, such as barbed wire or Claymore mines attached to the hull.

"A fine ship, eh, cousin?" the tall man said, stroking his small beard.

"No, it is not," the captain replied in a growl. "That is a ship of death."

"Ah, the crew are good shots."

"Worse."

The tall man gasped. "They're American?"

"Even worse than that," the captain muttered, rubbing a fresh bandage hidden under his loose shirt. "Just keep moving, cousin, and keep breathing. There is no ship in our harbor. Understand?"

The tall man scowled at the bizarre statement, then slowly nodded in comprehension and went to check the manacles belowdecks. As the old saying went, a wise man knew when to be blind. There were just some things in the world that were too dangerous even to talk about, and, apparently, that ship was one of them. Then again...

"Would it really hurt if we did swing past the ship?" the tall man asked, the greed obvious in his voice. "A simple look, that's all. What could that harm?"

"Hmm, I suppose so," the captain replied, turning to glance at the vessel.

There was a distant boom, and a split second later

the face of the captain erupted, teeth and eyes spraying out across the water.

The tall man had no time to cry out before his chest exploded. For a very brief instant, he felt himself falling backward, but never seemed to reach the water....

A THOUSAND YARDS OFFSHORE, the guard on the stern deck of the ULCV *Red Rose* worked the arming bolt on his .50-caliber Barrett sniper rifle to chamber a fresh round. The empty six-inch brass shell hit the steel deck with a *ring-a-ling* noise, and rolled out a wash port in the gunwale to splash into the bay.

Normally, a sniper rifle would be a poor choice for a defensive weapon on a ship. But the *Red Rose* was no ordinary vessel, no matter how much it looked like one. The massive container ship was so broad and heavy that there was never any real sensation of being on the waves. Even when it was in motion, the ship felt oddly stationery.

"Alpha to Command. The danger is neutralized," the guard whispered into his throat mike. "Area four secure."

"COMMAND TO ALPHA, CONFIRM," Lieutenant Naser replied into a gooseneck mike attached to a control board. "Continue your sweep, Alpha. Neutralize any possible threats at your discretion, over."

The nearby walls were covered with monitors showing the real-time weather over every major city in the world, along with matching clocks and a glowing vector graphic of every telecommunication satellite in orbit.

"Alpha to Command. Roger. Over and out."

"Trouble, Lieutenant?" Major Armanjani said, leaning over a table covered with maps. He had a ruler in one hand and a compass, in the other. A cold cup of coffee sat nearby, along with a plate of untouched sandwiches.

Prepared for a meeting later that day, the major was wearing an expensive business suit that cost more than he'd made in a month as a major in the Republican Guard. His necktie was raw silk, the stickpin solid platinum. A gold Rolex gleamed on a wrist, and an aluminum tube bearing the logo of a Montecristo cigar jutted from his breast pocket. Armanjani didn't smoke, but the cigar was just the sort of tiny detail that made his public persona of wealthy man absolutely believable.

"Nothing of importance, sir," Nasser replied, swiveling in the chair. "Some of the locals joked about taking this ship, so our rear sniper convinced them it was a bad idea."

"Good riddance," the major said, checking the wind patterns over Australia. "The village elders should have tried harder to teach them restraint."

Raising an eyebrow at that, Nasser said nothing. What village elders? There was nobody in the entire city more than thirty years old!

In a desperate attempt to make money to buy food, the Somalian government had leased the rights for foreign powers to dump garbage offshore. Now, this area of the ocean was so heavily polluted the men didn't even dare to go swimming out of fear of catching a deadly disease. The Somalians had fouled their own nest. It made the major angry to think that any Arab had acted so foolishly. The government tried to feed the poor, and end up killing more of them than starvation ever could have done. It was pitiful.

Then again, to be brutally honest, she noted, this

huge ship lying anchored so close off the coastline
must seem like an irresistible target.

Registered out of Edinburgh, Scotland, the *Red Rose*
was a typical container ship, deliberately designed to
not be noticeable in any way. The ship was a thousand
feet long and capable of hauling 20,000 of the standard twenty-foot-wide, ten-foot-high, forty-foot-long
shipping containers. To maximize their speed, the *Red
Rose* was only carrying only half that amount, most of
it legitimate cargo just in case they were ever stopped
for an inspection. It was mostly home appliances, rice
and farming equipment. Nobody sane would ever try
to check 10,000 containers. That would take weeks!

However, past that outer layer were reinforced
containers stuffed with BM-25 Hail multiple-rocket
launchers. Designed to destroy land fortifications, the
122 mm rockets were more than capable of destroying any attacking enemy vessel, whether it was a jet
fighter, battleship or submarine.

Next came a buffer zone of containers filled with
ordinary sand, a bulwark able to withstand any bombardment for a short while. Past those, safely located
deep inside the main hold, was the prefabricated command module made of six cargo containers welded together, which made it just barely large enough to hold
all of the equipment necessary to operate the Scimitar
of God, as the new weapon was called. There was a
mainframe computer sealed behind a Plexiglas wall, a
bank of control boards, a compact emergency genera-
tor, pressurized containers of oxygen and a few chairs.

In an emergency, the command module could be
sealed airtight to sink to the bottom of the sea, far
away from any battle raging on the surface, giving the

people inside plenty of time to assemble a small submersible pod and quietly leave unnoticed.

Their trip to Somalia from the construction shacks in southern Peru had been harrowing, almost nerve-racking. Zigzagging across two oceans, the major had closely followed every storm possible, endlessly fine-tuning the Scimitar to new and even more deadly accuracy. They had destroyed islands, icebergs and a dozen assorted small craft along the way.

Just then, a polite knock sounded and a slim man appeared at the open hatchway. Professor Kazim Khandis was dark and handsome, with hair so black that it appeared to have blue highlights, and a small European-style mustache, meaning that he used no oils or wax.

"Yes, what is it?" Armanjani asked without looking up from his work.

"We should have Tokyo online in a few minutes," Khandis announced in cultured tones.

"Excellent!" Armanjani said, putting aside a ruler. "Was there any trouble with the relay?"

"None whatsoever," Khandis said, flashing a wide grin, then disappearing around the bulkhead once more.

Leaving the command module, Armanjani awkwardly stepped over to the next container. A scarred hand reached out of the shadows, and Hassan pulled the major across.

"Thank you, Benjamin. Is everything ready?" Armanjani asked, straightening his lapels.

"Seems to be, sir," Hassan replied, turning a wheel to seal the entrance airtight. "But I'm no tech."

"Not a problem, old friend, the professor is," Armanjani replied. "Just remember not to speak after the red light goes on. Understand? No matter what happens, you must remain silent."

The sergeant nodded.

Chuckling, the major patted the other man on the shoulder and turned to start down a short passageway lined with heavy curtains.

The interior walls of the container were covered with rubber sheets studded with foam cones to render it soundproof. The floor was a thick shag carpet, and the ceiling was covered with acoustic tiles.

Going to a corner of the room, Armanjani sat behind a wooden desk bolted to the floor. There were potted ferns on one side, and a small fishbowl containing a stuffed goldfish that had been carefully glued into place. The wall behind the major was draped with a soundproof curtain, devoid of any possible details that might reveal his mode of transportation, or location.

"Ready," Armanjani said, booting up a desktop computer, the monitor topped with a webcam.

While the machine cycled into operation, the muted sounds of New York City traffic began playing softly from speakers hidden under the desk.

"Lower, please, Professor," the major said, smoothing down his hair. "We don't want them to think it's a trick."

Obediently, the recorded sound-effects fell away to a distant murmur barely discernable.

"Perfect. Now add the train."

Almost imperceptibly, the click-clack of iron wheels started to play. Major Armanjani nodded in satisfaction. Now, if there were any odd motions in the room from the ship it would be discounted as merely the motion of a rolling train.

"How many satellites are we relaying this through?"

Armanjani asked, adjusting the empty picture frames on the desk.

"One hundred and six," Khandis said through a speaker in the ceiling.

"Camel dung," Hassan snorted. "There aren't that many satellites in existence."

Ignoring that, Armanjani switched on a microphone and tapped it with a finger for a sound check. "Ready?" he asked.

On the other side of the room, behind a thick sheet of clear plastic, the professor looked up from a soundboard. Raising his hand, he splayed five fingers, then four, three, two, then pointed at the major.

Major Armanjani pulled in a deep breath, then let it out slowly. *Showtime.*

Gradually, the monitor cleared into a view of a small garden with a splashing fountain, and caged hummingbirds hanging from the branches of the trees. Three Asian men and a middle-aged Asian woman were sitting in wicker chairs.

They were dressed in Western business suits, except for the woman who was in some sort of a business dress, the hem halfway down her trim calves, but a hint of nylon still visible. The top button on her blouse was undone, and the stylized horns of some mythological creature were just barely visible on the swell of her breasts.

As if in counterpoint, every inch of exposed skin on the men was heavily covered with tattoos, almost garish, as if they were freaks in a circus. Their yellowish skin looked like ancient parchment, old and brittle, as if they would fall apart at the slightest touch.

All of them were wearing shoulder holsters without weapons. Armanjani could only assume this was

some sort of Japanese protocol. But whether they were
being polite or announcing that they didn't fear him
was completely unknown. Ordinary Japanese were difficult enough to understand, while these elite members
of the ruling council of the secret criminal organization known as the Yakuza were absolutely inscrutable.

"Asalamu alaikum," one of the men said in ritual
Muslim greeting.

"Koniciwa," Armanjani replied in smooth Japanese.
"Genki desu ka?"

That clearly caught the council members off guard.
Only the woman had the grace to give a small bow of
respect.

That was when Armanjani noticed that the tip of a
finger was missing from her left hand. That meant she
had once made a very serious mistake, yet now was
on the High Council of the Yakuza. It was very unusual for a woman to have such a position. Suddenly,
he had the feeling that she was actually in charge, and
the old men were there purely as window dressing. The
Yakuza had to know that Arabs preferred to deal with
men. *Smart. Very smart.*

"Ah, you see with more than your eyes," she said,
straightening both cuffs. "Good. I dislike dealing with
fools. Shall we switch to a neutral language? It would
be much easier than waiting for a translation."

"That is fine. Which would you prefer, German,
French or English?"

"English will be fine," she replied. "Especially since
I do not speak Arabic, Major."

That caught him by surprise, and Armanjani fought
hard not to let the shock show. Who was this wiz-
ened old crone, and how much more about him did
she know?

Suddenly, Khandis held up a clipboard with a name hastily written across the back in magic marker.

"My thanks, while I appreciate your honesty…Lady Hoto," the major said coolly.

Smiling faintly, Lady Rashomora Hoto gave no outward reaction to the identification, but her eyes darkened.

Major Armanjani recognized the name. Rashomora Hoto had previously been the top assassin for the Yakuza, and had personally killed more people with her bare hands than he had done with an entire army. She was old now, but not weak by any means. Even through the monitor the major could feel the power of her presence. He would have to be extremely careful from this point onward. One wrong move, and he would start a war with these bloodthirsty infidels.

"No, not a fool at all," Hoto muttered, then shrugged. "Fine, let us begin."

"Are you satisfied that the Scimitar is everything we promised?" Armanjani asked, leaning forward on his elbows.

"Yes, I am convinced," Hoto said, folding her hands. "Every target that we requested has been completely destroyed after a storm passed over. Clearly, the weapon can do exactly what you claim."

"Good. The price is five hundred million U.S. dollars."

There was a short pause while the old men glanced at one another, then at Hoto.

"The price is acceptable," she announced. "When and where can you make the delivery?"

"Right now if you wish. Our codes are unbreakable."

"No codes are unbreakable," Hoto snorted. "It is

all that we can do to keep Interpol from recording this brief conversation!"

"All right, I know the perfect location where we can make the exchange in person," Armanjani said, tapping a few buttons on the keyboard. A small map of the world appeared on his screen, rotating and turning, while it shrank to an aerial view of an atoll off the coast of Fiji.

Squinting at something off-camera, Hoto scowled, then nodded. "A good choice. Shall we say tomorrow at noon?"

"Noon."

"Agreed. See you then."

As the screen went dark, Armanjani disconnected the microphone before exhaling. "Victory, my friends! In twenty-four hours we will retire immensely rich!"

"And what will the Yakuza do with the Scimitar?" Khandis asked, turning off the sound effects.

With a dismissive wave, Armanjani stood. "That is not our concern," he declared, walking slowly from the steel room.

CHAPTER SIX

Haifa, Israel

Strolling along the brick-lined tunnel, Deborah Stone whistled a classic Broadway show tune and thought about a hot bubble bath. It had been a very long day in the archives, and she deserved a small treat. After all, today was her birthday!

When first recruited into the Mossad, she had foolishly thought her job would involve danger, excitement, travel to foreign lands and being seduced by handsome counterspies.

Hefting the sheaf of reports, Stone sighed. In truth, most of her work involved sorting HUMINT reports and filing requisition requests. It was boring but vital work in the defense of her homeland.

Unfortunately, she was forbidden to talk about the work to family or friends. Which meant that she couldn't even have the therapeutic release of ordinary bitching and moaning. Stone knew that dentists had the highest percentage of suicides, and hadn't been surprised to learn that the next highest was intelligence operatives.

Passing a security checkpoint, Stone was surprised to find the guard missing from his post. That was a very big deal in the agency. However, the steel gate sealing off the side tunnel was still firmly locked, so she naturally assumed that the man was simply in a stairwell catching a smoke.

Debating the matter, Stone decided to let the minor breach of security slide. Everybody deserved a second chance. If it ever happened again she would have to report him to the chief.

Shifting the stack of reports tucked under her arm, Stone continued on to the board room. The chief and the executive council were waiting for these reports.

Pushing open the ornate wooden door, Stone recoiled as a searing blast of heat washed out of the room, carrying the reek of ozone, burning carpet and roasted flesh.

Still carrying the reports, Stone rushed over to a fire alarm, broke the glass and flipped the switch. Instantly halogen gas issued from vents in the ceiling, and a strident alarm began to clang steadily.

As the gas extinguished the blaze, she anxiously waited for somebody to arrive. When that didn't happen, Stone suddenly noticed exactly how quiet the base was—no chatter from any of the offices, no clacking of keyboards, no laughter. There was only a deep stillness permeating the air, broken only by the crackle of the fire.

Pulling in a deep lungful of air, Stone cut loose with a blood-curdling scream. The noise echoed along the hallways and empty offices invoking no response. Where was everybody?

Hurrying down the smoky tunnel, Stone burst into the private office of the unit's director.

"Sir, please excuse…" Which was as far as Stone got. The room was full of what resembled mummies sitting around the big desk. Both male and female, the mummies were wearing the charred clothing of her coworkers, right down to the melted remains of Solomon Goldman's truly awful toupee.

In the middle of the singed table was a melted puddle of goo on a platter that might have been an ice cream cake, and there were several wrapped gifts scattered about on the floor, as if the mummies had tossed them aside for some bizarre reason.

Even stranger, the desktop computers were flashing random bits of nonsense on their flickering screens, the coffeemaker was loudly gurgling even though the reservoir was empty, and the clock on the wall was running backward. Transfixed, Stone couldn't believe what she was seeing. What had happened here? It was almost as if the base had been hit by a tactical nuclear weapon!

Just then, the emergency light in the corner came on, the beams much brighter than she ever remembered. They continued to increase in power, reaching nearly blinding levels when the bulbs shattered, and the battery pack burst into flames. Unexpectedly, the carpeting began to smolder, thick dark fumes rising from the melting plastic to curl about in the air like living things.

Exhaling completely, Stone slapped a hand over her mouth to keep from breathing in the toxic fumes, and turned to sprint away for the emergency exit.

Slamming aside the door, Stone dropped the stack of reports as she bolted up the stairs to the top level.

Bursting out the double doors, she stopped at the sight of death and destruction. There were several large burn marks on the wooden floor and along the brick walls. The big aquarium was softly boiling, the fish inside floating on the surface. Fried human bodies were strewed about the floor, some of them holding weapons, while others were crouched behind furniture as if trying to hide from an invader. Was that it? Had Hezbollah found the agency? To be honest, she would have expected far worse destruction than this.

Just in case, Stone clawed for the 9 mm Jerico pistol holstered behind her back. Clumsily, she clicked off the safety and worked the slide.

Just then, a stark white light filled the room from outside, and one of the heavy plastic windows exploded, sending out a shotgun blast of jagged pieces of the resilient bulletproof material.

As she retreated backward, an aluminum ladder melted before her startled eyes, and the stacks of nearby paint cans popped like chestnuts in a microwave, splattering the room in multicolor splendor.

Suddenly, every alarm the agency possessed cut loose, warning of fire, floor, radiation, poison gas and a dozen other impossible hazards. The noise was deafening, and Stone cringed, covering her ears until the racket stopped.

Outside, thunder rumbled again.

Pulling out her cell phone, she felt that the casing was warm and Stone instinctively threw it out the shattered window. As the phone hit the sidewalk, a crackling bolt of lightning lashed down to vaporize the device.

With a feeling in her guts as if the cable had just been cut in an elevator, Stone holstered the pistol and glanced at the front door only a few yards away. A cool rain was falling outside, reducing visibility to only a few yards. She couldn't even see the parking lot, much less the highway and farms beyond.

The decision made, Stone spun and dashed pellmell down a side corridor. Going outside would be suicide; her only hope was to go deeper into the base, as far underground as possible, which meant the vault.

For ease of access during the day for the people putting away files, the half-ton door wasn't locked. If she could just make it inside, she stood a fighting chance against whatever had hit the agency! Some new kind of energy weapon? she wondered.

Thunder rumbled ominously outside, shaking the framed photographs on the cracked walls. That added speed to her flight, and she dove forward to land sprawling inside the vault.

"Emergency shut-down alpha, kappa, alpha!" Stone shouted desperately.

For a long second it seemed as if nothing would happen. Then Stone heard a low thumping of working hydraulics, and the massive door rolled shut with a deafening boom. Seconds later a crackling explosion sounded and the vault door visibly shook, the locking wheel turned a bright cherry-red in color. Scrambling to the farthest corner, Stone crawled onto a wooden pallet filled with cardboard boxes of plain paper. If this was lightning, then she had to get off the metal floor fast or get electrocuted!

"Contact Tel Aviv!" Stone shouted at the ceiling, hoping the emergency circuits were still working. "Request immediate extraction, and—"

Without any warning, lightning exploded from the locking wheel to slam into the file cabinet. The self-destruct charges attached to the sealed folders promptly detonated, spewing out a snowstorm of disintegrated documents, and making every hair on her body stand painfully stiff.

Realizing that she was also carrying explosives,

Stone quickly drew her service automatic and flipped it away from her.

The entire vault trembled slightly as a glowing red spot appeared on the opposite wall, then another bolt crackled from the locking wheel to slam into the floor only inches away.

Braced for death, Stone was startled when the light faded away. However, the aftereffects of the strike were amazingly painful. Every muscle was sore, her teeth ached, the titanium pin in her shoulder from an old bullet wound was uncomfortably warm, and the wooden pallet felt warm under her bare buttocks. Holy Moses, I'm freaking naked! she thought.

Quickly, Stone checked for any burns or cuts, but she was undamaged. Except for the fact that all of her clothing was strewn about the vault in tattered pieces.

Fighting off a wave of panic, Stone laughed nervously. She had heard that lightning could blow the clothes off whatever poor bastard it hit, but nine times out of ten the target was reduced to a charcoal briquette. Only the thick metal walls had to have made the difference.

Just then, the vault shook again, much harder than before, and a glowing red spot appeared in the middle of the floor. She watched in horror as it slowly changed into orange on the way to a blazing-white, nearly hot enough to melt through. Then she cheered in victory as it began to cool back into orange.

"Is that all you got?" Stone screamed defiantly at the unseen storm.

As if in reply, a fast series of lightning bolts slammed into the building again and again, the terrible noise steadily increasing in fury and power until it sounded like the end of the world....

Kandy, Sri Lanka

RATTLING AND CLANKING OVER every pothole, bump and rock, the U.S. Army M-1114 O'Garra-Hess armored vehicle charged along the jungle road, leaving a wide trail of churned earth in its wake. The up-armored Humvee was usually equipped with a 7.62 mm machine gun, this rented civilian model only came with air-conditioning and a rather surprisingly good stereo system. But that was turned off at the moment. This far into the northern jungle of the island nation, Bolan and the others were staying alert for anything suspicious in the lush foliage. As with so many other Third World nations, the rule of law usually ended where the paved streets did. Space was a little tight inside the vehicle because of the three BMW motorcycles stacked in the back, but nobody was eating elbow.

Prepared for combat, Bolan and his companions were wearing camouflaged fatigues, their chests oddly angled from the level four body armor underneath. Designed with overlapping ceramic plates, the NATO body armor was proof to anything short of a .50-caliber round, and cushioned trauma pads underneath offered serious protection from impact damage.

Bolan and the others were also wearing throat mikes with compact transceivers clipped to their belts. But those were turned off at the moment. Radio silence was vital for this mission. The target this morning was the White Tigers, a radical splinter group of the infamous Tamil Tigers. Officially, the White Tigers had been disbanded a few years ago under a United Nations peace treaty. In reality, the leaders had simply gone underground, and were still waging their war against the Sri Lankan government for reasons lost in an ocean of blood.

Following a curve in the road, Bolan just managed to squeeze past a troop of Sri Lankan soldiers marching through the steaming jungle. A mixture of men and women, the soldiers were carrying a wide assortment of weaponry: AK-47 assault rifles, M-16 assault rifles, Uzi machine guns, Browning Automatic Rifles and MP-5 submachine guns. Basically, anything that the government could get in bulk.

"How big is the Sri Lankan military?" Montenegro asked, thumbing 12-gauge cartridges into a Neostead shotgun.

"About half a million," Bolan answered, keeping a tight grip on the wheel as he downshifted to take a steep hill.

Tilting back his cap, Kirkland gave a low whistle. "That is a lot of ground-pounders for an island about the size of Brooklyn."

"Not when you consider how many terrorist groups they have," Bolan countered, shifting again to accelerate along a smooth patch of dirt road.

"True enough," Montenegro grunted. Aside from several terrorist organizations that operated out of the jungle, there were also roving bands of criminals that assaulted and robbed anybody foolish enough to leave the safety of the city.

"Sure would be nice if we had a machine gun," Kirkland stated, watching the bushes, ferns and tall grass blur past the armored windows.

"You have a machine gun," Montenegro retorted, cradling the Neostead shotgun in her arms.

"I meant mounted on the roof," Kirkland replied,

adjusting a chest harness. "The two-fourteen here is for getting up close and personal, not rattling the trees."

Affectionately, he patted the XM-214 electric machine gun resting on his lap. The six-barrel weapon was mounted on a chest harness to help distribute its considerable weight. There was a belt of battery packs, and a backpack of ammunition that used an enclosed Niagara belt to feed the special 5.56 mm rounds into the breech of the rotating man-killer. The XM-214 had to be fired in very short bursts, or else it would run out of ammunition in only a few minutes.

Lying on the floor was a bolt-action rifle, the barrel tipped with an oversize sound suppressor. The Zastava Black Arrow was one of the best sniper rifles in the world. Chambered for a .50-caliber round, it was a man-stopper of the first order, with an accurate range of roughly a mile, and fully capable of blowing holes in most armored limousines and bank trucks.

"I prefer flexibility," Montenegro retorted, hefting the Neostead.

Invented in South Africa for crowd control, the bizarre weapon had a pair of ammunition tubes mounted on top, each holding six 12-gauge cartridges. What made the shotgun unique was a switch that let the operator alternately feed from one tube or the other. Thus, one tube could be packed with deadly fléchettes, while the other contained harmless stun bags, allowing the operator to choose between kill or capture. However, for this mission, Montenegro had packed the tubes with a scenario load designed to get the dirty job done as fast as possible.

Passing the crumbling ruins of a temple, the up-armored Humvee jounced along as the land rose and fell into steep ravines, waterfalls and rivers appearing in no discernable pattern.

"Pretty landscape," Kirkland noted.

"And dangerous," Montenegro added.

He grinned. "Okay, pretty dangerous."

"Oh, shut up."

Chuckling, Bolan suddenly slowed to touch his earbud. "This is Striker, go ahead, Base." He said nothing for a few minutes, then grunted. "Confirm, Base, I'll inform Casino and Amazon."

"God, I hate that code name," Montenegro muttered under her breath.

"Where did they hit now?" Kirkland asked.

"A fertilizer warehouse in Israel."

"A fertilizer warehouse?" Montenegro said thoughtfully. "Any chance it was just outside of Haifa?"

"Mossad?" Kirkland asked. "Damn, these guys got guts. The Mossad never forgives and never forgets. How much damage was done?"

"In Israel the warehouse was flattened. There was only one survivor," Bolan said.

"The terrorists are upping the ante. We have to pull this mission off double-time," Kirkland grimly added. "Time is not on our side."

"If it ever was," Bolan said, then snarled a curse and wildly veered into the jungle.

Crashing through bushes, he plowed the armored vehicle over a small tree before swinging back onto the dirt road.

"Spot a landmine or something?" Kirkland asked, releasing his grip on a ceiling strap.

"Just a dead elephant blocking the road," Bolan replied accelerating once more.

"Think it was a trap?" Montenegro asked, squint-

ing at the sideview mirror. Covered with feasting birds
and rats, the huge corpse lay like a grisly mountain of
mottled flesh amid the lush greenery.

"I didn't before," Bolan stated braking to a fast stop.
"Get hard, people!"

Straight ahead of them was a pair of old Saracen
ACPs parked at right angles to the road. Each of the
vehicles had a Browning .30-caliber machine gun
mounted into a cupola, and a Bren .303 light machine
gun.

Equipped with six wheels, the British-made armored personnel carriers were backed by a steep cliff
on the left and a deep ravine on the right. There was
no way past, or around the obstruction, or the armed
men standing partially hidden amid the tall bushes.

"Think they're legit?" Montenegro asked softly,
keeping her expression neutral.

Kirkland snorted. "Not a chance."

"Agreed. Sri Lanka hasn't used a Saracen in decades," Bolan noted. "And the government insignia
is missing from the doors. That's a capital offense in
their army."

"Okay, I only count ten men," Montenegro whispered, unlocking her door.

"But each Saracen could hold ten, maybe twelve,"
Kirkland added, as the six barrels whirred into operation once more. "Which means there are more hiding."

"The elephant?" Montenegro asked out of the corner of her mouth.

"More than likely," Bolan replied. His instincts said
that these men were hijackers, street criminals just
out to rob tourists. But until they made a move, there
was nothing he could do. Low on manpower, the Sri

Lankan government often had the military do police
work. Bolan had no desire to kill cops.

"Okay, you want this soft or hard?" Kirkland asked,
thumbing a switch. With a low whir, the six barrels of
the XM-214 began to spin rapidly.

"That's for them to decide," Bolan replied, loosening the Desert Eagle in his holster. Unfortunately,
the Black Arrow was too powerful to use inside the
confines of their vehicle. The blowback would have
permanently deafened everybody inside the vehicle.

Tense minutes passed with nobody talking, then
a fat sergeant lurched away from the other men and
started along the dirt road.

"Stop right there!" Bolan ordered through the open
window. "Who are you, and what do you want?"

Stopping halfway between the Saracens and the
Humvee, the sergeant scowled at the foreign language.
"Government checkpoint!" he proclaimed in heavily
accented English, resting a hand on the Beretta at his
side. "Everybody out vehicle! We search for contra-
band!"

The group of soldiers chuckled among themselves
over that statement, a couple of them openly leering
at Montenegro. Coolly, she looked back at them with
no more interest than a concrete abutment.

Keeping the engine running, Bolan leaned out the
window. "We're neutral observers from Switzerland,"
he stated, displaying a forged document bearing all of
the correct seals. "We have full diplomatic immunity
from any and all searches."

"Everybody searched!" the sergeant reiterated with
a snarl. "No exceptions!"

"That is not legal," Bolan said, keeping the words

simple. "Perhaps you should check with your superiors in Colombo."

"Colombo? I am the law here!" the sergeant declared, drawing the Beretta. "Now get out of truck, or die!"

In response, Bolan fired the .50-caliber Desert Eagle through the gunport in the door, and the sergeant staggered backward minus his face.

"Incoming!" Montenegro bellowed, as the trees and bushes around the vehicle came to life with machine-gun fire. Bullets musically ricocheted off the armored side of the vehicle and slapped deep into the thick Plexiglas windows.

Throwing open the rear canvas flap, Kirkland stepped into view with the XM-214 at waist level. "Showtime!" he shouted, clenching a fist on the firing bar.

Already spinning at operational speed, the six barrels erupted into a stuttering stream of high-velocity lead that swept through the jungle plants. Birds filled the sky as a hurricane of leaves and torn pieces of bark exploded into the air and several men cried out in shock, then went silent forever.

Swinging open the door, Bolan fired the Desert Eagle four times at the group of hijackers, the big-bore rounds removing their lives in bloody sprays. The rest of the hijackers dove for cover, rolling underneath the Saracens before sporadically returning fire. Bolan was nearly hit twice before he got behind their armored vehicle.

As the cupola on top of a Saracen started to rotate, Montenegro jumped onto the road and cut loose with a double blast from the Neostead. The barrage of stainless-steel fléchettes peppered the top of the enemy vehicle, a lot of them going through the tiny view slot and gunport. A man inside the APC shrieked in pain and the Bren discharged randomly, blowing up a bush alongside the dirt road. Howling monkeys scattered into the trees, a few of them boldly scampering past the armed men and over the military vehicles.

Now the Browning machine gun on the other Saracen chattered into life, the stream of bullets chewing a path along the road and across the angular front of the Humvee. The headlights shattered and a tire blew, but the barrage of .30-caliber rounds failed to penetrate the windshield, merely leaving behind a crazy quilt of radiating cracks.

Using the flat tire as cover, Bolan crawled under the vehicle and unleashed the Beretta 93-R. The machine gun yammered a stream of 9 mm rounds that riddled two more hijackers. One of them fell to the ground, but the other began howling as he clutched the ruin of his left arm. Hastily slapping a fresh magazine into the Beretta, Bolan tracked after the mortally wounded criminal to finally end his pain with a single shot into the left temple.

Sweeping a path of destruction through the opposite side of the jungle, Kirkland got two more death screams, then hosed both of the Saracens with the XM-214, the hundreds of 5.56 mm bullets zinging off the armored hulls to ricochet back and forth, tearing the rest of the hijackers into crimson shreds.

Emptying the Neostead at the second Saracen, Montenegro killed the man in the cupola, blood gushing out the view port. That was when the APC suddenly revved its engine and jerked forward, charging directly for the M-1114 armored vehicle.

Unleashing both of their weapons, Kirkland and Montenegro hammered the APC, trying for the driver.

Meanwhile, Bolan rolled onto the road and came up in a kneeling position, the Desert Eagle held steady in a two-handed grip. As the Saracen zoomed toward him, the Executioner paused for a full second, then stroked the trigger. The .50 Desert Eagle boomed, the driver inside the Saracen cried out, and the APC lurched to the side. Scraping past the Humvee, it went into the jungle, careened off a tree and disappeared from sight.

"I think it's headed for the cliff," Montenegro said, thumbing fresh cartridges into the Neostead.

"Good riddance," Kirkland snorted, turning off the power to the microgun.

As the barrels slowed to a halt, there came a distant crash, and a few seconds later a black plume of smoke rose above the trees.

Holding up a fist, Bolan signaled for silence, and everybody listened intently for the sound of movement in the jungle or whimpers of pain. But there was only the low murmur of the Humvee's V8 engine and the gentle murmur of the multiple waterfalls.

"Okay, Heather stands guard!" Bolan said, turning away from the array of corpses. "Bill and I will swap out the flat. We need to get moving. That army platoon we passed must have heard the fight, and they will be on the way here double-time."

"Or we could take the remaining Saracen," Kirkland suggested. "That way, if we get spotted by the White Tigers, they'll think it's only these morons."

"Plus, we get a little extra firepower," Montenegro added, resting the Neostead on a shoulder.

"Sounds good," Bolan said, holstering his weapons.

"Okay, people. You know the drill. Let's move those motorcycles inside the APC and get rolling!"

In only a few minutes, the bodies inside the APC were removed and the supplies transferred.

"We better leave the road and travel through the jungle," Bolan announced, strapping into the driver seat. "That'll slow down the army if they decide to follow."

"We should wreck the Humvee first," Kirkland said, clumsily feeding a fresh belt of ammunition to the Bren.

"Not a problem," Montenegro said, triggering the Bren. In yammering fury, the gun strafed the armored vehicle, the reaming tires blowing off the rims as the windows shattered, the doors buckled, the hood was ripped aside, and the engine burst into flames.

"That'll do it," Bolan said, starting the engine.

Driving off the road, the six big tires of the APC rolled over the former owners, audibly cracking the bones, and spraying out a grisly residue of tattered clothing, fecal matter and internal organs.

"Damn, I thought it smelled bad in here before," Montenegro muttered wrinkling her nose.

"Better us inside smelling them, than them smelling us outside," Kirkland stated with conviction.

"I couldn't agree with you more," she said, starting to reload the Bren.

As Bolan drove the vehicle into the lush greenery, thick shadows reduced his visibility to only a few yards. He was forced to turn on the headlights. Then flowering vines, fat insects and green leaves began slapping against the Saracen's armored prow. Soon, a juice spray covered the headlights until they were useless.

"I better get the GPS operating before we drive off a cliff," Kirkland said, rummaging in an equipment bag.

"Give me a five-mile warning before we reach the target valley," Bolan directed him, slowing their advance. "We'll stop a mile away and finish the rest on foot."

"Any estimation on how many of them will be there?" Montenegro asked, closing the breech on the Bren.

"Fifty or sixty," Bolan said, struggling to shift gears. "But there could be more, so stay sharp."

"If the numbers are bad, what's the backup plan?" Kirkland asked, sliding into the gunner seat and attaching the GPS to the control board.

"There isn't one," Bolan stated, veering away from the mossy ruins of another crumbling temple. "This is our best chance to find the people behind the lightning strikes, so no matter what, we're going in and blitzing the place."

"Just don't shoot any of the buildings," Montenegro reminded him, taking a jumpseat.

"Agreed," Bolan stated gruffly. "This mission is a total failure unless we capture the White Tigers' computer intact and undamaged!"

CHAPTER SEVEN

Indian Ocean

Dark exhaust pouring from its main stack, the *Red Rose* steadily built speed as it headed toward Japan.

Evening was starting to fall across the calm ocean, the running lights of the colossal ship like imprisoned stars. Armed sailors walked along the deck surrounded by the mountain of cargo containers, and soft music could be dimly heard playing from the bridge set on top of the aft cabins.

Relieving himself over the edge of the ship, Major Armanjani could see the captain standing at the wheel, smoking a pipe and looking every inch a sailor. Born and raised in the desert, the major simply couldn't understand the unnatural love that sailors felt for the sea. How could he? It was cold, unforgiving and tried to kill you in every way possible.

Zipping his trousers closed, Armanjani was forced to admit that many people couldn't comprehend an Arab's love for the desert. The deep spiritual silence, and the endless peace. Sand was delightfully warm during the day, wonderfully cool at night, and filled with just as much hidden life as any ridiculous ocean.

Walking along the edge of the great ship, Armanjani was lost in dark thoughts of distant home when a young soldier approached and threw a salute.

"Sir, if I may interrupt?" he asked.

For a brief moment, the major fumbled for a name. "Yes, what is it, Corporal Akhmed?" he asked tolerantly.

At the use of his name, the youth preened. "The name of this ship, *Red Rose,* does that have some meaning to us, sir? I have thought about this for some time, but cannot see how it reflects our goals, or needs or…" His voice trailed away uncertainly.

"That is a good question, Corporal," Armanjani said. "The answer is no. The name has nothing to do with Ophiuchus, and that is the whole point."

"Sir?"

"The name comes from a Scottish poem. That is where the ship is registered—Edinburgh, Scotland."

"That is in England?"

"The United Kingdom, but very close."

The youth shifted uncomfortably. "If the name means nothing, then why do we use it, sir?"

"Perhaps you think the vessel should be called the *Secret Warriors Against America,* or *Saddam's Revenge?*" the major asked with a chuckle.

"Yes, it should!" Akhmed answered defiantly, then lowered his voice. "But obviously that would not be very wise."

The major nodded. "No, it would not. When walking into a den of thieves, a policeman wears the robes of a criminal, not his uniform."

"Yes, sir. Of course, you are correct," the corporal muttered, then saluted. "Praise God!"

"Praise God," Armanjani repeated, then scowled. "Akhmed, is that a cell phone I see in your pocket?"

His smile vanishing, the youth said, "Sir?"

"I specifically ordered everybody to divest themselves of anything that could reveal our true identify," Armanjani growled. "That included money, passports, letters from home and cell phones. Nothing! We are to carry nothing from our homeland until the great task is done!"

"It is just a cell phone, sir," the youth whispered, sweat appearing on his brow. "I never use it! Never!"

"Akhmed, Akhmed," Armanjani said, shaking his head. "If I tell you not to step on any unusual lumps alongside a road, is that for my glory or to keep you from being blown up by a landmine?"

"Sir? I... That is..."

"Damn it, Corporal, have you made any calls to your family? Yes or no?" Armanjani demanded. "Calm down, son. You wouldn't be in any trouble, if you tell me the truth. Have you made any calls?"

"No, sir! Never! That is...just one," the corporal replied in a small voice, pulling out a very expensive cell phone. His name was blazoned across the lid in diamonds. "It had been so long since I heard from my father, and I—"

In a single motion, Armanjani pulled out the Tariq and fired at point-blank range. The range was so short that the muzzle-flash actually engulfed the hand of the youth. The 9 mm rounds exploded the cell phone into a million pieces, then continued onward to punch through the chest of the teenager, spraying the gunwale with hot blood.

As the dying corporal staggered, his arms flailing, Armanjani turned sideways to lash out a boot and send the teenager tumbling over the gunwale. It seemed to take a very long time for the body to splash into the dark sea below.

Only moments later, Hassan appeared with six more people behind him, their arms full of weapons.

"White dog!" the sergeant snapped, his hands tight on an Atchisson auto-shotgun.

"Brown dog," Armanjani replied, lighting a cigarette.

Everybody relaxed at the countersign, then scowled at the fresh blood pooled on the deck.

"What happened, sir?" Hassan asked, quickly glancing around at the darkness for anything suspicious.

"Sadly, Corporal Akhmed had a weapon malfunction and died," the major said, drawing in the pungent smoke. "His family is still to receive his full share of the profits, and from now on list him as Sergeant Eljar Akhmed."

"Yes, sir," Hassan replied, barely moving his lips. "Should we attempt to recover the body?"

"Any sharks in the area?"

"No, but the crabs are abundant on the ocean floor. They will consume everything within a few minutes."

"Astonishing. Crabs live in this bay?"

"Inedible, of course, sir. Their flesh stinks of chemicals and waste."

"Then let him be. Poor Akhmed with be a feast to them. Truly, manna from heaven."

"Such a shame," a private muttered. "The corporal was a good man and a good friend."

"Just not a very good soldier," Hassan added bluntly. "This is just another mistake in a long line of them."

"We all make mistakes," the private added hesitantly, looking back and forth between the other men. Wisely, the other soldiers said nothing.

"That is true," Armanjani said, exhaling a long

stream of dark smoke at the stars. "Just be sure to remember that while God forgives, I do not."

Northern Sri Lanka

FOLLOWING THE GPS COORDINATES, Bolan drove the Saracen north. The road snaked through the sloping jungle, meandering past boulders, the crumbling ruins of ancient temples, thick groves of clattering bamboo, the charred remains of a Volkswagen Beetle and along white-water rivers.

"Heads up!" Bolan announced. "I see the waterfall!"

"Thank God," Kirkland growled with obvious relief.

Fording a shallow creek, Bolan drove the APC up a hill and stopped on the crest. Spread out before them was a lush river valley thick with trees. On the opposite side were triple waterfalls, the low rumble of the diverging columns sounding oddly similar to distant thunder. A white mist rose from the catch basin.

"That must be them," Montenegro said, looking through a monocular. "I can't find any animal life nearby. Birds or monkeys."

"The White Tigers probably chase the animals away so that they can hear an approaching APC or gunboat," Bolan guessed, starting down the slope.

"Idiots," Kirkland said with a sneer. "Only people and monkeys sweat ammonia. Keeping some around would have been a great way to confuse any chemical sniffers."

Reaching the bottom of the hill, Bolan maneuvered the APC into a thick grove of bamboo. As he turned off the engine, the others opened the rear hatch to cool down the interior, then everybody took turns applying camouflage paint to each other's face.

Adding more rosin to their hands, they checked over their weapons, then proceeded on foot toward the campsite. The terrain was rough, and snakes were constantly underfoot. But the air was cool from the mist of the waterfalls and lightly scented with a sweet perfume coming from the thousands of flowering vines.

Leading the way, Bolan zigzagged down a gentle incline, and suddenly raised a clenched fist.

Everybody froze.

Slinging the Black Arrow over a shoulder, Bolan eased forward carefully. He had almost missed the thin black wire stretched across the open field. Following it to the bushes, he found the wire connected to a French-made landmine. Anybody touching the tripwire would have set off an explosion that would have leveled a wide patch of the jungle.

Pulling out a pair of insulated pliers, Bolan started to cut the wire, then decided to check underneath the landmine first. Sure enough, as expected, there was a second pressure switch hidden in the dirt below that was connected to a U.S. Army Claymore mine hidden under a thick pile of leaves.

"Just the two mines?" Kirkland said with a scowl. "Pretty basic defense."

"Officially, nobody is after them," Bolan reminded him. "The UN peace treaty is still in effect."

"And unofficially?"

"Both the Sri Lankan government and the Tamil Tigers want these people dead and buried."

"That's a lot of dead. Any chance of a reward?"

"Not on these guys," Bolan said.

"Pity."

"Now, I thought you were richer than Croesus?" Montenegro asked Kirkwood, slowly raising an eyebrow.

"True, but there is no such thing as too much money, too much firepower or too many friends."

"My God, we actually agree on something?"

He shrugged. "It had to happen eventually," Kirkland said.

"Heather, better check for cameras and proximity sensors," Bolan ordered, starting to disarm the Claymore.

"Already did," Montenegro said, displaying a compact EM scanner. "There's nothing in the area but more land mines."

"Double-check," Bolan directed her, glancing around the area.

"Got a feeling, Matt?" Montenegro asked.

"Something's not right," Bolan replied.

That was good enough for her. Montenegro put no stock in the notion of extra sensory perception. However, any good soldier knew when there was something wrong with a combat situation. There was nothing supernatural about it. In fact, it was about as natural as anything could be—merely a million years of evolution hardwired into a functional survival instinct, the subconscious mind processing information faster than the conscious mind could register.

Wordlessly, she melted back into the foliage and circled the area. In only a few seconds, she found the real deathtrap, a ring of Claymore mines equipped with proximity sensors. You merely had to get close to them, and your world ended in a strident blast of C-4 high-explosive mixed with steel ball bearings.

However, an EM scanner neutralized the sensors long enough for Montenegro to disarm the Claymores, one at a time. It was delicate work, and nobody complained about how long it took. When working with landmines there were only two settings: careful and dead.

"No cameras," she reported afterward. "But there are signs that these are replacement mines."

Kirkland grunted. "Meaning they've been attacked before."

"My guess would be not successfully."

"Good," Bolan stated. "With luck, they'll be overconfident."

Sweeping past the landmines, they soon located the campsite hidden in a shallow ravine. There were a dozen low structures made of logs and concrete, pillboxes for lack of a better word. They were laid out in an irregular pattern to fool any surveillance planes or spy satellites. The two streams splashed over jumbled rocks, cooling the air to a comfortable level, and, more importantly, helping to mask the heat-signatures of the terrorists.

The fuel dump was located under a different camouflage net, at the delta of the two rivers. Stacks of fifty-five-gallon drums were stored on plastic pallets, and nearby was a hand-cranked pump.

A fishing boat was tied at a crude wooden dock, which was merely a few planks extending over the gentle waters. There was nothing that resembled a barracks, just the pillboxes and a series of low tents set alongside the sloping hillside under the huge trees. More protection from aerial surveillance.

There were a couple of machine-gun nests made from logs and sandbags, along with an old antiaircraft gun.

It was obvious that the White Tigers couldn't possibly use the weapon with this much greenery as cover, and Bolan realized it was here for ground troops or enemy boats. At such a close range, almost point-blank, the antiquated antiaircraft weapon would be death incarnate to any boat foolhardy enough to approach.

Camouflage netting was stretched over the entire camp, and there were several wooden platforms built into the leafy tops of the tall trees. Armed men sat inside the dense foliage, smoking cigarettes.

"Overconfident," Bolan whispered in frank disapproval.

"Apparently with good reason," Kirkland muttered.

Off to the side of the clearing, a dead man hung from a wooden post. He was stark naked, the body covered with burn marks and deep cuts, the eyes and genitals removed. The ground underneath him was alive with scurrying ants.

"Tortured, but not by an expert," Bolan noted emotionlessly. "Just a sadist who loved his work."

"How do you know that?" Montenegro asked curiously.

Bolan grunted. "A professional would never have cut off his testicles. Keeping them intact gives the prisoner false hope, which makes them weak. Cut them off, and the poor bastard has nothing more to lose, then he'll die before talking. His last great act of defiance."

"The things you know worry me sometimes, Matt," Kirkland said, checking the feed to the XM-214. "Okay, how do you want this done, a blitzkrieg or ghosts in the night?"

"Clean sweep," Bolan replied, leveling the Black Arrow. "There can't be one of these people alive afterward."

"Check," Montenegro said, sliding off a bulky backpack. Folding back the top, she removed four short plastic tubes. The light antitank weapon—LAW—was a 66 mm single-shot, disposable weapon.

"I'll take one of those," Kirkland said, holding out a hand.

"Be careful of the backwash," Montenegro warned, passing over a tube. "It can easily set the bushes on fire, and you'll get backlit. A perfect target."

"Rock and roll," he replied, tucking the tube under an arm before easing off into the jungle.

"Give us ninety," Montenegro said, heading in the opposite direction.

Grunting assent, Bolan swung up the Black Arrow and took careful aim, gauging the force of the wind from the fluttering of the flowers on some nearby vines. Looking through the telescopic sights, he marked each target carefully, then did it again until ninety seconds had passed. Taking a deep breath, he moved back to the first target and stroked the trigger.

The massive Black Arrow sniper rifle boomed like unchained thunder, and a guard smoking a cigarette on top of the radio shack was thrown backward from the arrival of the 700-grain bone-shredding round. He hit a tree with a sickening crunch of smashing bones and slid down to the ground, leaving behind a red smear of life.

No alarms sounded. There were no bells or sirens. But armed men boiled out of the tents and pillboxes and started firing blindly into the jungle. The patter of the hot lead tearing through the green leaves sounded strangely like rain.

Riding out the recoil, Bolan moved to the next target and took out two more guards, then punched holes in the speedboat until it began to sink into the river.

Suddenly, there was a flash of fiery smoke, and a LAW rocket streaked out of the jungle to lance straight into one of the pillboxes. Instantly, the structure erupted in a stentorian column of fire, smoke, logs and dead bodies. There was a microsecond pause, and then the stores of ammunition ignited, the blast sending out a corona of shrapnel that flattened the jungle for a dozen yards in every direction. A guard standing on the dock screamed as a log slammed into his chest, sending him flying across the water and out of sight into the dappled shadows.

Firing as fast as he could work the arming lever, Bolan maintained the sniper fire while Kirkland and Montenegro put two more LAW rockets into the base, taking out the treetop fortifications, the firebase on the island and the main structure. Only the radio shack wasn't hit, the equipment inside far too precious to risk damaging in any way.

Scrambling behind a stockade, a White Tiger managed to get a heavy machine gun into action. Tracers were visible in the air as the terrorist racked the hillside, the big .50-caliber rounds clipping off vines and leaves to create a whirlwind of flying greenery.

Pouring streams of hot lead into the pillboxes, Kirkland and Montenegro kept the terrorists busy as Bolan levered a fresh round into the Black Arrow, aimed and fired.

There was a small puff of dust from the outside of a log as the big round hit, then the man inside shouted in pain and the machine gun went silent.

Now rising into view, Kirkland unleashed the XM-214, sweeping a visible stream of high-velocity lead across the campsite. A dozen men were literally cut in two from the stream of 5.56 mm bullets, their torsos flailing backward as their legs continued on for a few steps before the men toppled over.

As the hopper became empty, Kirkland ducked behind the rock, and Montenegro appeared on the bluff, the Neostead vomiting hot-lead death. Two men climbing into a military-style jeep seemed to fall apart from the incoming barrage of stainless-steel buckshot, the vehicle flipping over to burst into flames as it rolled away.

Bolan cursed as he realized that the vehicle was heading straight for the radio shack. Changing targets, he poured .50-caliber rounds into the burning jeep, blowing away pieces to slightly change its course. Tumbling directly past the radio shack, the vehicle rolled into the river and vanished below the waves.

Just then, three men appeared from a pillbox wearing old-fashioned body armor, each of them cradling an M-60 machine gun, a long belt of linked ammunition dangling from the side. In orchestrated attack pattern, they began to advance, spraying the treetops and the bushes at the same time, while the third man fired short bursts into random stands of vegetation.

Dozens of birds and monkeys died in the maelstrom, and Bolan grunted as a .308 hardball round ricocheted off a rock and slammed him in the side. His NATO body armor held, but glancing down he saw a nick in the ceramic plates right along the edge. A quarter-inch more and he would have died, drowning as his lungs filled with blood.

As one of the belts of an M-60 got short, the other men would bracket that shooter in protective fire while he shoved in a fresh belt from the lumpy canvas bag hanging at a side.

Struggling to clear a jam from the breech of the

XM-214, Kirkland slapped the release on the harness
and the bulky weapon dropped to the ground. Drawing both a Glock 18 and the Webley, he started forward at a full sprint, jumping over bodies and rocks to
dive behind a smoldering chunk of a destroyed pillbox.

Instinctively, Kirkland started to report the loss of
the weapon over a throat mike, then stopped. This
blitz had to be done silently. There couldn't be any
broadcasts of an outside invasion. That could ruin everything.

As a White Tiger rushed by firing a Kalashnikov,
Kirkland waited until he passed, then stood and triggered a single round from the Webley. The huge revolver boomed, and the terrorist ceased to exist from
the neck upward.

Inserting a fresh drum of 12-gauge cartridges into
the Neostead, Montenegro saw a subtle motion in the
corner of her eyes, and just barely swung the weapon
around in time to stop the knife from slashing open her
throat. Steel clanged on steel as the machete rebounded
from the barrel, then the White Tiger hacked for her
belly. Montenegro rammed the unloaded autoshotgun
down on his wrist, and the machete went flying as his
bones shattered. Muttering curses, he staggered backward, holding the crushed wrist, then turned sideways
to kick a boot at her chest.

Moving fast, Montenegro tried to dodge out of the
way, but the boot hit, and the air exploded from her
lungs. The body armor took the brunt of the attack, but
her left breast still felt as though it had been stomped
flat. But then, hitting a woman in the breast was like
kicking a man in the balls. The pain temporarily ren-
dered the victim unable to do much of anything but
gasp in pain.

As her vision blurred, Montenegro swung around the Neostead and blindly fired. The range was only a few feet, and the terrorist was lifted off the ground by the hammering arrival of the double-O buckshot, his chest spreading wide into raw meaty wings as his organs burst across the bushes in a ghastly crimson spray.

Skirting along the edge of the trail, Bolan was attacked by two more White Tigers, one of them hiding in a muddy pond, and the other pretending to be dead, a blood-soaked shirt draped over his undamaged shoulders. The first got a .50-caliber round in the face, and his head exploded like a dropped watermelon. The second White Tiger managed to get off two rounds from a 9 mm Beretta before Bolan finished him with a boot to the throat, and then a bullet to the chest.

Levering a fresh round into the Black Arrow, Bolan swept the campsite and found a White Tiger scrambling for the radio shack. Starting to fire, Bolan realized the 700-grain rounds would go through the man and endanger the equipment inside the pillbox.

Instantly changing tactics, Bolan stroked the trigger, and a thick branch was blasted off a tall tree. It came straight down onto the terrorist just as he reached the entrance. His head caved in from the blow, the eyes popping from his face. Screaming obscenities, the terrorist clawed at his dangling eyes just as the Executioner drew his Beretta and squeezed off a fast shot, sending the disfigured man into the bushes to die.

A half-second later, the man and bushes erupted as Montenegro unleashed a burst of buckshot from the Neostead.

On the other side of the camp, Kirkland came striding out of the trees, the XM-214 whining a song of death. Hiding behind a water barrel, a White Tiger died kneeling in the mud, his AK-47 assault rifle firing into the ground, kicking up leaves and rocks.

Ducking low, Kirkland got hit anyway as a rock slammed into his chest, ripping a hole in his shirt to reveal the molded body armor underneath. Then another hit the spinning barrels of the XM-214. The rock shattered into pieces, and Kirkland staggered backward with blood covering his face.

Just then, a grenade fell from the trees to explode near the dock. The eruption threw out large clouds of dirt and leaves, closely followed by two grenades that created a larger cloud of swirling debris.

"Shoot the explosion!" Montenegro yelled, just as a White Tiger appeared from the bushes to charge straight for the radio shack. Obviously, somebody had realized that was the one location not being attacked.

Changing targets, Bolan fired fast, but the White Tiger was only grazed, and made it inside the radio shack alive. But there was a red smear of blood on the entrance.

Springing across the open ground, Montenegro raced into the shack and almost fired. But the terrorist was standing behind the precious radio, slapping a fresh clip into his assault rifle. Damn!

Throwing herself to the concrete floor, Montenegro unleashed a burst of buckshot at the man's boots, his legs below the knees disappearing in a bloody explosion. Shrieking in agony, the crippled terrorist fell into view, and his brief time on earth swiftly ended as she fired one more time.

Shadowy figures filled the entrance, and Montenegro stopped herself from shooting just in time as she recognized Bolan and Kirkland.

"You okay?" Bolan demanded, the barrel of the Black Arrow sweeping the pillbox for targets.

"Undamaged," she growled, slowly standing. "What happened to your fancy popgun there, William?"

"Ran out of pop," Kirkland replied, holstering the Webley. "Radio intact?"

She started toward it. "Let's see."

Converging on the radio, Bolan checked the controls while Kirkland looked over the transceiver and Montenegro inspected the car batteries it used.

"Everything looks good," Bolan said hesitantly. "Bill and I will give you some cover in case there are any more Tigers around."

"Stay close. It won't take me a minute to broadcast our message," Montenegro said, pulling out a small code book that was tucked inside her body armor.

"Should we prep the bikes?"

"Running is not my style. But it sure as hell can't hurt."

Going outside, Bolan and Kirkland took defensive positions alongside the entrance. One of them reloaded while the other stood guard, then they switched. There was nothing moving in the camp aside from loose leaves and a few scattered fires. The only sounds were the gentle murmur of the river and a soft shushing caused by the breeze blowing through the trees. Then a tiger roared in the distance, closely followed by the high-pitched scream of a monkey.

"Lunchtime," Kirkland muttered, wiping the blood off his face with a handkerchief. "Tell me the truth, Matt, how do I look?"

"Like you've been dead for a week."

"So it's an improvement? Cool."

Just then, Montenegro appeared. "Done and done,"

she crisply reported. "I podcast the message so that it
goes out over the air and across the internet. Any decent hacker should be able to figure out it came from
the White Tigers, and where they're located."

"Then the ball is in the air," Kirkland said, turning
off the XM-214 to save battery power. "How soon do
you think it'll be before they hit?"

"Immediately, if not sooner," Bolan said, removing
the magazine from the Black Arrow to start thumbing in fresh rounds. "So we better get ready. A hard
rain is coming."

"It's not the rain that worries me," Montenegro said,
looking upward.

Past the lacy canopy of tree branches, the blue sky
was clear of any clouds. But in the distance, thunder
softly rumbled, and everybody redoubled their efforts
to get ready for the coming maelstrom.

MAJOR ARMANJANI STOOD AT THE railing staring at the
Sea of Japan. He felt a presence at his side.

"What is it?" the major demanded.

"The White Tigers have claimed responsibility for
our attack on Mossad," Lieutenant Nasser replied.

"Who did you say?" he demanded in confusion.

"The White Tigers, sir. A small terrorist unit that
operates in Sri Lanka."

"And for this you bother me?" the major snarled in
annoyance. "Broadcast a denial, then kill them."

"Sir...I... That is... Sir, the Yakuza believe them
and have canceled the deal," Nasser replied quickly.
"They warn us never to contact them again, or else."

"They dare to warn me?" Inhaling sharply, Armanjani did nothing for a long moment.

"Meet me in Control in five minutes!" he snarled.

"Bring me everything we have on these people, and get the satellites ready!"

"Which ones, sir?"

"All of them!" Armanjani bellowed, starting up the metal stairs. "Every fucking one we have!"

CHAPTER EIGHT

White Tiger Base, Sri Lanka

Going back to the Saracen APC, Bolan and the others drove a safe distance from the terrorist campsite then parked on the sloping side of a grassy hill.

"We should have a grand view of the lightning strikes," Montenegro said, turning off the engine. "After which all we have to do is… Shit!"

"Now, I'd do that first, if I was you," Kirkland quipped, then the smile left his face as he caught a distant movement. "Aw, fuck me running, Matt! Friendlies, seven o-clock!"

Grabbing a set of binoculars, Bolan stepped to a gunport and looked in that direction. Following the path of crushed plants left behind by the Saracen was the platoon of Sri Lankan soldiers, closely followed by a big 4x6 BMW truck. Obviously, they had heard the gunfight and were coming to investigate. They were heading straight for the terrorist camp and right into oblivion. It was pure bad luck, and there was nothing they could really do about that. Except…maybe…

"Okay, we have no choice," Bolan growled, turning on his transceiver. "We have to lure them away from the terrorist camp!"

"That BMW can move a lot faster than this Saracen," Montenegro stated, tucking an earbud into place. "We're going to have to use the bikes!"

"They're trained in jungle warfare," Kirkland said, stuffing grenades into his pockets. "No way we're going to outfox them without speed!"

"Okay, use the bikes!" Bolan declared. "We have to get them far away from here, or they're all going into the ground."

"Three against fifty," Kirkland muttered, sliding on a throat mike and transceiver. "Time to see just how good we are!"

"See you in hell, handsome!" Montenegro said, awkwardly rolling a BMW motorcycle out of the APC.

"You, too, babe," Kirkland answered in unaccustomed frankness. He started to add something more, but the woman was already disappearing into the bushes.

"Now, what makes you think she was talking to you?" Bolan asked, leaving by the side door.

"Bite me, Matt." Kirkland chuckled under his breath. Pushing a BMW out of the APC, he kicked the machine alive. The engine started with a soft purr barely discernable above the murmur of the nearby river. He drove across the hillside before switching on the microgun.

As the six barrels spun into operational speed, Kirkland braced himself on the bike to help steady his aim, then squeezed the firing handle and unleashed a whining stream of high-velocity rounds.

Barely visible in the mixture of shadows and sunlight, the fusillade of 5.56 bullets chewed a path of destruction across the jungle to eat a deep hole in a thick teak tree, bark and wood chips flying everywhere.

Even before the soldiers had a chance to respond,

the colossal tree began to tilt and groan. Creaking loudly, it toppled over and crashed directly down on the hood of the BMW truck. The windshield and headlights shattered as both front tires blew. Nosing into the dirt, the truck rammed to a halt, the driver slamming into the steering wheel and rebounding, her lips bloody and several teeth missing.

"Better than dying," Bolan muttered, marking his targets through the powerful scope on the sniper rifle. This next part was going to be tricky....

The vehicle was still rocking when a dozen men and women armed with American-made M-16 assault rifles poured out of the back. They hit the ground running, and separated, preventing their unseen enemy the opportunity to fire on a group target.

"Damn, they're good," Montenegro said over the earbuds.

"Be better," Bolan commanded sternly, then added, "Best of luck."

"You, too, Matt!" Montenegro muttered, lurching into motion even as she fired several bursts from the Neostead straight up into the air.

Moving low and fast, the soldiers assumed a combat formation and quickly secured anchor points behind a pair of trees, while the rest surged forward. But nobody fired a weapon.

Kneeling behind a giant fern, Bolan grunted. They weren't frightened or firing blind. These were combat veterans, and that just made the situation ten times more difficult.

With no choice, Bolan set the crosshairs on the biggest person he could find in the platoon, a burly woman wearing the chevrons of a sergeant. Aiming carefully, he squeezed off a round and saw blood spray from her shoulder. The soldier staggered and fell, then rose again, a Beretta firing in her undamaged hand.

It was only a flesh wound, but that should be enough to make the others nervous. Moving slowly and cautiously, the soldiers were a serious threat. Angry and charging, they were more dangerous, but could be directed where to go. Hopefully.

"Good shooting there, Tex," Kirkland said, into his throat mike. "Don't think I could have made that shot."

"Not unless you were aiming for her head," Montenegro retorted, stopping the purring bike in a stand of ferns before thumbing fresh cartridges into the Neostead. She then aimed and fired in a single motion. The 12-gauge shell slammed into a tree and violently exploded, sending out a halo of sizzling flames. Rapidly, she added five more rounds, creating a crude firewall off to the side.

Instantly, the Sri Lankan soldiers swept around the barrier and charged into the jungle in the wrong direction.

"Heather, you're a genius!" Kirkland laughed.

"She told you that years ago," Bolan whispered, stroking the trigger of the Black Arrow.

The first 700-grain round slammed through a burning tree, but the next hit the hood of the BMW truck. The metal crumpled like a used tissue. He fired again at an angle, and the side of the truck dented deep as thick oil pumped onto the ground like greasy blood.

"That's not going anywhere soon," Kirkland stated, as the Sri Lankan soldiers cut loose with their assault rifles in the wrong direction.

Dividing into teams of three, the men and women swarmed through the thick plant life, using every possible bit of cover as they raced deeper into the jungle and soon vanished from sight.

However, the soldiers continued to fire their weapons as if carrying an unlimited supply of ammunition. Birds and monkeys voiced their strong disapproval of the actions.

"Anybody in the truck?" Bolan asked, moving to a new position.

"Can't tell for sure," Montenegro said, then she cursed and the Neostead fired.

"Report!" Kirkland barked.

"There…was a…'gator…in the river," Montenegro panted breathlessly.

"Was?"

"Deader than disco, brother."

"Groovy."

"Unfortunately, our new friends heard your handiwork," Bolan said, watching some of the soldiers heading that way. "Okay, both of you join up near the river, then separate again. Lead them as far away from here as possible! Keep them moving at all costs! If you get captured, go peacefully and I'll bust you out of jail at midnight!"

"Sounds like fun." Kirkland sighed. "Okay, sweet pea, let's dance for the man!"

"Never call me that again!" Montenegro snarled, the bike lurching into action as the Neostead ripped off a fast series of shots into the air.

As tattered leaves rained down from a tree, the Sri Lankan soldiers charged in that direction, then Bolan heard the XM-214 whine into operation, and a tree was cut in two to come crashing down directly in their path. Scrambling out of the way, the soldiers took cover and responded with a flurry of gunfire.

Moving away from the camp of the White Tigers, Montenegro and Kirkland zigzagged through the jungle, driving like madmen, only pausing to maintain the sham battle. Carefully aimed grenades rained down to decimate whole sections of the jungle. The Sri Lankan soldiers arched around the explosions, and accelerated their running advance.

As the sounds of combat faded into the distance, Bolan hid his BMW inside a copse of trees and took refuge in the bushes. He knew that the tree offered no protection from a lightning strike, but he felt sure that Kirkland and Montenegro would continue the mission if he didn't make it. The bikes had been a last-minute addition, but without them it would be impossible to get the job done.

Thunder rumbled in the clear sky, and Bolan snapped up his head just in time to see a bright flash as a lightning bolt arched down from the clear sky to hit the terrorist camp. The radio shack exploded into splinters, flaming debris flying away hundreds of yards.

Using his cell phone, Bolan took some pictures, then a solid bar of lightning slammed into the camp. The bolt of crackling electricity moved through the camp, annihilating everything in its path. The ground melted into bubbling lava, trees exploding as the sap inside boiled, and mounds of green vegetation burst into smoky flames.

Still taking pictures, Bolan had to admit that he had never seen anything like it, and suddenly knew just how powerful a weapon their unknown enemy possessed. Was there anything, any fortress, military base, or warship in existence that could survive such an attack? He tried not to imagine what it could do to a civilian target, such as New York, London or Paris.

The death toll would be staggering. Even worse, there was no limit to their supply. These people could burn down major cities across the planet until civilization fell into savagery. Then they could come out of hiding and claim the world as their own, still armed with their doomsday weapon.

As the lightning zigzagged along the camp, dozens of hidden land mines detonated, then a tarpaulin was blown aside to reveal a buried cache of fuel drums. They ignited simultaneously, the fireball expanding across the campsite to reach into the jungle and across the river.

Instantly dropping the cell phone, Bolan opened his mouth and slapped both hands over his vulnerable ears to try to ride out the concussion. Half a heartbeat later, the shock wave arrived. The wall of compressed air painfully crushed his chest and threw Bolan backward into a tangle of vines. He became disoriented for a brief span, then jerked awake to the sound of land mines and other munitions cooking off like holiday firecrackers. The hammering series of violent explosions only serving to weakly counterpoint the triphammer strike of the lightning bolts.

For an unknown length of time, Bolan's universe was filled with deafening chaos, every hair on his body standing stiff, the fillings in his teeth growing uncomfortably hot. That was when he realized that the magnetic field of lightning had to be creating eddy currents in anything made of metal.

Quickly, Bolan tossed away his guns, throat mike, transceiver, computerized monocular, spare ammunition and knives. Yanking a grenade out of a pocket, he could feel how warm it was, and desperately whipped the sphere as far away as possible. Then he tossed the rest, but the last one detonated before reaching the ground. The blast pounded the man hard, ripping apart his clothing, hot shrapnel peppering his ceramic body armor....

CHAPTER NINE

Indian Ocean

Deliberately leaving the bathroom door open, Lieutenant Fahada Nasser stood washing her face in the sink. Her khaki shirt and sports bra were hung from the inside doorknob. When she finished, the woman started washing her stomach, breasts and underarms. The soap was plain and unscented and lathered nicely in the spring water from the reserve tanks. The massive ship had a desalination plant that made sea water drinkable, but soap still wouldn't lather properly in the stuff. As always, the difference between potable and drinkable was small, but significant.

A canvas gun belt circled her trim waist, and a 9 mm Tariq pistol was holstered at her hip. Her skin was marked with numerous scars, the classic "railroad" pattern of a poorly stitched knife slash, the irregular glassy patches of old bullet holes, and the long slashes of a military caning.

"How is it going, Kazim?" Nasser asked, drying her face on a terry cloth towel.

"Almost there, Fahada," Dr. Khandis replied, hunched over the control board and typing steadily on a keyboard. An unlit cigarette dangled from his mouth, and nearby was a plate of crumbs that only minutes ago had been a stack of sandwiches.

Mounted in an arc around him, a series of submonitors scrolled binary commands while another showed his slow but steady progress. Creating a virtual-reality room was easy enough, and there had to be a backdoor for the customers to enter. It was the satellites that were tricky. He needed to switch the combined signals halfway across the globe, leaving behind false trails, doppelgänger signals and ghost echoes to outfox some of the smartest hackers alive. Now that was a challenge!

Slinging the bra over a shoulder, Nasser strolled into the view, allowing her breasts to move freely. When the man didn't seem to notice, she leaned over his shoulder, brushing one across his cheek. She was pleased when his ardent typing paused, and he had to backspace to clear a mistake.

"My dear, please," Khandis muttered glancing sideways.

"Sorry." Nasser chuckled, tousling his hair.

"Apology accepted," he said.

"Do we have enough time…?" she asked, not finishing the question.

"Let's find out," he growled eagerly.

Just then, the intercom crackled. "Any responses yet, Doctor?" Major Armanjani asked brusquely.

For a long moment, there was no reply.

"Doctor, do you copy? Have there been any responses yet about the auction?" Armanjani demanded.

"Getting in the first results," Khandis replied, pulling away from his lover. "The Red Star said no, but the Sicilian Mafia says yes."

"Excellent! Never did trust the damn Chinese anyway," Armanjani snarled. "What about the Fifteen Families?"

With a sigh Nasser went back to the bathroom to finish drying and get dressed.

"The Fifteen Families say yes," Khandis reported. "As do the Russian mob, a Colombian cartel and Hezbollah."

"Hezbollah?" Armanjani laughed. "Those poor bastards barely have enough funds to buy bullets. How could they possibly afford the Scimitar?"

"They say there is enough."

"They lie! Ignore them. The leaders of Hezbollah are so accustomed to lying they do not know when to stop."

"As you wish, sir."

"Is Lieutenant Nasser there by any chance?"

"Here, sir!" she reported crisply.

"Have you found a location for the auction yet?"

"Yes, sir, I have," Nasser reported, buttoning closed her shirt. "But I must again state in the strongest possible terms my objection to a physical auction. The danger is too great to risk. This should be done safely over the internet."

"I see," the major said. "And what do you think, Doctor?"

"No matter how heavily coded and hidden, any internet auction can be traced," Khandis said, spreading his hands in an apology to the frowning woman. "It must be done in person, using the Scimitar itself to guard us from enemy action."

"Sir, I disagree," Nasser declared, walking out of the bathroom. "It is much too dangerous. Remember what al Qaeda tried, and that was on our homeland!"

"A freak occurrence of bravery," Khandis scoffed. "After the loss of their leader, they've been running amuck like dogs in the gutter!"

"Your concern touches me deeply," Armanjani said over the speaker. "However, I agree with the good doctor. The auction will be done in person at a suitable location chosen by the lieutenant. I want the two of you working closely on the matter of security. This is your only concern. All other duties have been suspended until there is a successful climax."

"But sir," Nasser stated, "that could take all night!"

"Then take all night!" Armanjani bellowed, rattling the intercom. "Take however long is necessary! But I want results by dawn. Am I understood?"

"Absolutely, sir," Khandis said. "We shall give it our all!"

"Good. Are the White Tigers taken care of?"

"Burned off the face of the Earth, sir," Nasser said.

"Excellent!" Armanjani chuckled. "Lieutenant, hire some local people to make sure there were no survivors, then help the doctor find a suitable target for the demonstration."

"Already done," Khandis said. "There are heavy clouds over Léon, France."

"The city of Léon! Is…is such a thing possible?" Armanjani asked hesitantly.

"Yes, sir," the doctor boasted proudly. "The target will be leveled immediately after the announcement of the auction."

"Very well. Then I will leave everything in your capable hands."

"Yes, sir!" the doctor replied.

"Let me know when the details are confirmed," Armanjani stated gruffly.

White Tiger Base, Sri Lanka

THE JUNGLE WAS STILL, all of the animal life chased away by the lightning strikes. Not even a breeze was stirring among the trees, as if the very air itself had been frightened into submission by the display of nature unchained. The only sounds were the crackling of the numerous small fires and the gentle murmur of the river.

Crawling over to the BMW, Bolan found the bike lying on its side, the chassis dimpled from the rain of shrapnel. However, the motorcycle was undamaged, just dirty and badly scratched.

Settling in for a long wait, Bolan open a canteen and poured some water into a palm to wet his hair back down. The secondary effects of that many lightning bolts were pronounced. His compass was dead, the needle spinning randomly. The GPS was dead, as was the Starlite scope on the Black Arrow. The glass lenses still worked, of course, but the electronics were frazzled. Only the transceiver was still operational. It was shielded from electromagnetic fields to prevent the device from triggering proximity detectors.

Bolan heard the mechanical thunder of a powerful engine, and an old Russian M-3 half-track appeared on the dirt road along the crest. Starting down the slope, the M-3 crushed a path through the tall grass and the bamboo and stopped on a low hill overlooking the former campsite of the White Tigers.

The driver and commander stayed inside the enclosed cupola, while six men climbed out of the back. Each was dressed in loose camouflage uniforms, the kind that could be purchased at most shopping malls, and each was armed with a wide assortment of pistols and submachine guns.

"Spread out," a bald man commanded, working the arming bolt on his weapon. "I want a fifty-meter sweep of the whole area! Check under every bush."

Staying motionless in the stand of trees, Bolan noted that the men showed some skill at what they were doing, but not much order. They could be mercenaries, perhaps hired by the people behind the lightning strikes to make sure this had been a clean sweep and all of the White Tigers were dead.

Listening to the men converse, Bolan was intrigued by their thick accents. They were clearly not from Sri Lanka, but from the India mainland just across Adam's Bridge, a string of sand bars and shoals that loosely connected the island nation to the mainland. Local legend said that was where Adam and Eve crossed over from the Garden of Eden after they got kicked out. Nice story, but theology was not his main concern at the moment. Staying alive was.

Many years ago, there had been a ferry service connecting the two nations, but a cyclone destroyed the Sri Lankan port, and it was never rebuilt for a combination of reasons. Bolan could only assume that the mercenaries had some private way across the watery border. Some kind of old LARC cargo vessel would be the logical answer. These guys didn't look wealthy enough to own a hovercraft that could support the massive weight of a Soviet M3.

With a finger on the trigger of the Black Arrow, Bolan kept as still as possible as the mercenaries walked around the fused landscape, warily turning over bodies, checking inside hollow logs, and even probing the shallow depths of a muddy creek. Then two of them dived into the river to check for bodies. They seemed surprised by all the damage, and avoided the fused craters in the ground as if they were radioactive.

Just then, a man growled something in a foreign language. There was a long jagged scar across his throat where it looked like somebody had tried to remove his head with an ax and failed.

"Speak English!" the bald man snarled. "These scum don't speak of a word of it."

"Very well," the man rumbled. "The area is clear, sir. If there were any survivors, I'll eat my own gun."

"They're all dead!" the bald man shouted at the M3 half-track.

"Find a head!" an amplified voice ordered from the cupola.

As there were so many of them scattered about, the grisly object was easily located. A mercenary tried to lift up the head by the hair, but the cooked scalp slipped right off the bone, and another had to be found. This time it was cradled in both hands, the unhappy man twitching his nose in an effort to not inhale the fumes coming off the cooked flesh.

"Damn, it does smell like pork," another man noted, covering his mouth with a hand.

"Shut up, fool. Ramel! Get me their website," the bald man snapped, holding out a hand.

A barrel-chested man passed over a satellite phone, and the bald man looked at something on the tiny screen, then back at the head. Frowning slightly, he did this several times before grinning.

"Yeah, this is one of them," he stated with a chuckle. "The idiots actually posted pictures of themselves in dramatic poses."

"Were they insane?" a tall man asked, the accent so

thick that it took Bolan a few moments to understand what had been said.

"No, not insane," the bald man said, dropping the head then kicking it toward the river. "Just total amateurs." Splashing into the water, the head sank from sight.

"Easy money." A burly man laughed, resting his MP-5 on a broad shoulder. "Every assignment should be like this!"

"Where would be the fun in that?" a thin man asked, his head moving like a pendulum as he steadily glanced back and forth at the wreckage. "They certainly have a lot of expensive weaponry."

"There is some nice stuff around here," a hairy man said, rubbing a hand across his mouth. "Sir, mind if we check the bodies for anything valuable?"

"Why not?" the bald man said with a laugh.

Scowling darkly, Bolan moved away from the BMW. If anybody started to walk his way, he would lead them away from the motorcycle, then circle back and ride for his life.

"None of that! Everybody back in the truck!" the unseen commander ordered. "Pival, leave the repeater, and set the timer for ten minutes! I want to be far away from here before radioing back what we found!"

"You don't trust them?" the bald man asked, looking up at the clear sky.

A panel slid back in the cupola, and an old man glared out. "Do you?"

"People who claim that they can control lightning?" The bald man sneered. "Not under any circumstances!"

Using his monocular, Bolan watched from the shadows as the mercs set up a repeater radio in the middle of the decimated campsite.

"And…it's live!" the bald man shouted, as he set a timer and stepped away quickly. "We have five minutes and counting. Move it."

Hustling a lot faster than they had before, the mercs scrambled back into the half-track, and it roared up the road heading north.

Waiting a minute to give them some distance, Bolan then climbed onto the BMW and kicked the big engine alive. It sputtered at first, then surged with power, and Bolan streaked away from the campsite, plowing straight through the leaves, vines and bushes to climb the hill and jounce onto the road.

Maintaining a low speed, Bolan had only gone a few miles when lightning flashed from behind. Looking in the rearview mirror, he saw the campsite erupt into fire as another lightning bolt arched down from the clear sky, the boom of its arrival sounding like artillery. Glancing at his watch, Bolan saw that a little over five minutes had passed. Right on schedule. If nothing else, their unknown enemy was punctual, and that could be used against them.

Catching the rumble of the Soviet half-track, Bolan lowered his speed even more. There really was no problem following the vehicle as a half-track left highly distinctive marks on the ground. Several times the mercs stopped to make sure they weren't being followed, but there was no way he could have lost them if this had been the middle of the night during a monsoon.

As with most jungle roads, this one had been built along the lines of least resistance, curving around natural formations and always trying to stay level. That facilitated Bolan's progress enormously, and he was easily able to stay just out of sight across several bridges, and through a bird sanctuary, until finally reaching the northern coast of Mannar Island.

The road abruptly stopped in the middle of what might be called a town, but was barely more than a settlement. The existing buildings were few and far between, a ramshackle collection of plywood huts, tar-paper shacks and a couple of rusty prefab huts.

Just past the end of the road, the remnant of the destroyed dockyard was now only a ragged outline of broken masonry near the beach. But clustered on either side were crude homemade docks, little more than splintery planks chained to boulders. Dozens of fishing nets hung off tall bamboo poles to dry in the sun, and the ocean was dotted with a wide assortment of boats, ships and rafts trawling the shallow waters for whatever came their way.

Parked alongside the main road was a Bradley Fighting Vehicle flying the Sri Lankan flag. Several uniformed soldiers were lounging against the APC, assault rifles slung across their chests.

Angling off the road, the mercenaries in the M-3 did not even pause as they rolled toward the APC. The Sri Lankan soldiers casually nodded in greeting as the half-track passed, and one of the mercenaries in the rear tossed out a small package. Sauntering over, a lieutenant recovered the package and tucked it out of sight inside his shirt.

Parking behind some bushes, Bolan watched as the mercenaries continued to the shoreline. Sure enough a battered old U.S. Navy LARC was resting on the beach, the rear ramp down and waiting for them. Resembling a flat-bottom boat with wheels, the LARC had a tiny pilothouse full of armed men, and a Finnish 20 mm cannon mounted on the port gunwale. Although

it looked about as seaworthy as a toilet seat, Bolan
knew that the tough little LARC had more than enough
brute horsepower to speedily haul the Soviet half-track
across the strait to India. The U.S. Navy crest had been
scraped off long ago, and nothing new had replaced it.
The LARC also didn't have a name painted across the
bow, or even running lights.

The vehicles trundled up the ramp, the mercs parking it in the middle of the LARC, and the armed crew
started chaining it into place for the brief sea voyage
home.

Realizing that this was the end of directly following them, Bolan swung off the road and drove his bike
around the tiny fishing village, desperately searching for some alternate method of pursuit. If necessary,
he would steal a boat, but the local people looked as
though they were living on the ragged edge, and his
theft might mean disaster for an entire family. Come
on, he thought, there had to be some other way...yes!

Floating just off the beach was a small fishing boat
with three men clustered around a torn net hanging
from the broken rig. No catch meant no pay. Perfect.

Driving directly over, Bolan parked the bike and
sharply whistled. Curious, the fishermen approached,
then paused at the sight of the huge Black Arrow
strapped across his back.

"English?" Bolan asked, killing the engine.

"Little. Captain," a man gruffly replied, stabbing
himself in the chest with a thumb. "Who you?"

Without bothering to answer, Bolan hauled out his
emergency cash and fanned the collection of bills. The
eyes of the crew went wide, and one man actually
wiped the drool off his unshaven face with a sleeve.

"Me, my bike, follow them," Bolan said, pointing with his free hand.

"No. Many guns," the captain said, waving a hand in dismissal.

"No fight, only follow," Bolan said, pulling out the last of his cash. "Nothing more. Just follow."

Turning around, the captain held a fast conversation with his crew. Glancing down the beach, Bolan saw the LARC preparing to leave.

"All?" the captain asked, rubbing two fingers together.

Bolan nodded agreement.

"Deal." The captain sighed, clearly unhappy about the matter. "But follow. No fight!"

"No fight," Bolan agreed, dividing the stack and passing over half of the money. "All money after land."

It took all four of the men to hoist the BMW onto the trawler. But the crew seemed to have done this sort of job before, and the Sri Lankan boat stayed far away from the Indian LARC, constantly dipping below the horizon in an effort to stay of sight. The 20 mm cannon wasn't much, but it could easily have blown the trawler into flotsam with a single shell.

The strait was only thirty-odd miles, and soon Bolan was back on dry land again, absolutely broke, but now on Panban Island, India, and still in hot pursuit.

Driving into the grassy hills, Bolan studied the Soviet half-track through his monocular. Several miles down the road was a large Indian military outpost, a fortified base surrounded by real pillboxes, heliports full of armed helicopters, and landing strips holding neat rows of strike fighters.

The roadway went right past the huge base, concrete

K-rails funneling the four lanes into one, and that was
blocked with a brick guard kiosk, a thick wooden rail
and a squat monolith of steel that rose from the middle
of the pavement.

Bolan was impressed. He had seen those before
many times. Any car, truck or even armored personnel carrier that tried to ram past that low lump of steel
would stop dead in its tracks as if slamming into the
side of a mountain. That squat monolith was actually fifty feet long, and reinforced by countless yards
of ferro-concrete. It was very similar to the monolith
used to block the front driveway of the White House.
Only an army tank would have a chance to get by,
and there were enough concrete tank traps lining the
berms to slow down even an Abrams M-1 battle tank.
The Indian military really knew its business. Nobody
was getting past this point without being inspected.

So exactly how did the mercs do it on a regular
basis? Bolan wondered.

As expected, the answer was simple. As if they
had done this a thousand times before, the mercs sent
the half-track off the side of the road, and down into
a muddy creek that flowed along a culvert. Without
slowing, the half-track disappeared inside a huge storm
drain.

Muttering a curse, Bolan kicked the BMW into life
and raced after them. This was unexpected! If Kirkland and Montenegro got away from the Sri Lankan
military and came after him, Bolan hoped that they
noticed the culvert. If not, they would never find one
another again without using the radios. And after what
Bolan had seen happen to the merc radio, he would be
extremely hesitant to broadcast his location to anybody,
even with a heavily coded signal.

Knowing that even the purr of the BMW would be clearly heard inside the confines of a tunnel, Bolan was forced to let the half-track get almost completely out of sight before he dared to drive into the drain.

Unable to use his headlight, Bolan had to lower his speed again, and squinted into the darkness ahead, trying to stay alert for any sudden turns. Expectedly, he slammed into an open drain, and almost cracked a rib when the motorcycle toppled over, the sideview mirror exploding into shards of plastic and glass.

As the BMW skidded along the tunnel, Bolan saw the concrete wall flowing past his unprotected head only an inch away. With a deafening screech, the handlebar sent out a bright spray of sparks, and only the body armor saved his right arm from being ground into mincemeat.

When the bike finally stopped moving, Bolan stiffly crawled out from under it and used the Black Arrow to lever the machine back onto its wheels. Then he waited for an attack. But the half-track didn't return. He could only assume they hadn't heard his accident over their own engine.

Or else they're laying a trap for me at the exit, Bolan thought grimly, checking over the Black Arrow for any damage done by using it as a prybar. However, the resilient weapon was unscathed.

Unfortunately, the same couldn't be said for the Desert Eagle. The holster on his hip had been ripped open, and the safety on the big-bore pistol was badly bent. Bolan tried several times, but he couldn't get it to move. With no choice, he tucked it into his belt. The pistol was dead until he could gain access to a machine shop. What was worse, the transceiver had busted open along his sideways journey. Half the cir-

cuits were missing, and the rest looked like a rainbow
of spaghetti. With no way to repair the radio, Bolan
placed it prominently in sight on a small mound of debris for Kirkland and Montenegro to find if they came
this way. Hope for the best, but always plan for failure.
That was the key to staying alive in combat.

Finally getting back into motion, Bolan rode along
in the featureless dark, straining to hear the half-track
again.

Slowly, the long miles passed with Bolan pausing
at every side tunnel to check to see if the mercs had
gone that way. Several times he was forced to use his
cell phone as a light source to hunt for tire tracks in
the reeking mud. However, all he ever found were big
fat rats. Or at least something very ratlike, but much
bigger. The animals hissed at his approach, and Bolan
backed away quickly. A gunshot would echo for miles
along the tunnels and give away everything.

Only one of the rats was ever bold enough to attack. Moving fast, Bolan kicked it away, and the animal crunched against the side of the tunnel, leaving
a gory trail of bloody intestines as it slid back down.
Instantly, all of the other animals converged on their
fallen brother, and that started a fight that steadily
grew in volume and savagery.

With the Beretta in his hand, Bolan retreated from
the horrid feast and started the bike to quickly leave
the area.

Luckily, the mercs seemed always to be driving fast
and straight. Which meant either that they were speeding past a known enemy, or else Bolan was dangerously close to their base of operations. Possibly both.

Suddenly, Bolan saw a patch of sunlight ahead, and
immediately braked to a full stop. Parking the bike,

he eased forward with the Beretta and Black Arrow at the ready. Dimly, he heard the sound of splashing water, and came out of the tunnel into another culvert, a feeder pipe sticking out of the wall, and a stream of water arcing down to flow into a grated drain.

Checking his watch, Bolan was surprised to find that it was now late afternoon. The sun was low on the horizon, and thick shadows covered the landscape.

Using that to his advantage, Bolan crept along the muddy ground, zigzagging among the clumps of weeds and oddly perfumed bushes. He couldn't identify the plant, but the smell was wonderful. A tiny bit of heaven hidden amid the cruddy weeds and muddy rats.

The sloping side of the culvert was an easy climb, and Bolan reached dry ground without breaking a sweat. A paved road cut through a wide field, heading east and west. But Bolan spotted the tracks of the half-track and proceeded due north, past crumbling old buildings of unknown purpose, wrecked cars and tall shining towers of steel, their high-voltage power cables softly humming.

Reaching the edge of a low cliff, Bolan looked down upon a huge automobile junkyard. Mounds of rusting vehicles stretched across the dark landscape in crude rows. A crane stood behind the ramshackle building, and parked in front of a garage was the half-track. Bingo.

Unfortunately, the outer perimeter was tight, an outer fence of barbed wire that was topped with coils of concertina wire. The endless razor blades gleamed in the dying light. Then Bolan frowned. Correction, there were two wire fences, each twenty feet tall, and the space between them was clearly a dog run. He could spot the occasional pile of excrement and a broken leather collar.

There had to be another way. If necessary, Bolan would blast a path into the place, but then he might accidentally kill somebody with useful information. No, same as before, this had to be a soft recon. Slip in, slip out. A ghost in the darkness.

Scouting along the crumbling cliff, Bolan found an access road branching off to what appeared to be a major highway. Continuing onward, Bolan unexpectedly found an abandoned drive-in movie theater. He'd honestly had no idea that those were used anywhere other than North America.

The huge sign out front was lacking any letters, and all of the light bulbs were either missing or smashed. However, a city sticker identified this as Devakottai. He had never heard of the place. The parking lot was laid out in neat rows of raised gravel so that each car could see over the one in front. There were rusty steel posts jutting from the gravel, some of them still containing speakers to hang from the car windows. But there was also a lot of windblown trash and huge potholes, a few of them growing trees large enough to bear fruit.

Located in the exact middle of the drive-in was the two-story projection building. The walls were covered with graffiti in Hindi, and the missing doors revealed that the entire building had been stripped clean. The 35 mm cameras, winding plates, everything was gone.

Oddly, the concession stand seemed intact, although the windows were so dirty they might as well have been sandblasted white. Bolan headed straight for the movie screen. That would be his way into the junkyard.

The screen's protective coating was badly ripped in

the corner, and stained in numerous places from the
weather, thrown sodas and decades of bird droppings.

Vaulting over a wooden gate, Bolan circled past
a rusty set of kids' swings to reach the base of the
screen. There was a ladder built into the frame. The
inset handholds were covered with big flakes of corrosion. He tested one, and it seemed strong enough to
take his weight. But there was only one way to know
for sure.

Listening to the wind for a few minutes to try to
hear anything, or anybody coming this way, Bolan
then started to climb. Several times, his hands slipped,
coming away with a fistful of corrosion.

Finally reaching the top of the screen, the soldier
moved carefully forward through a thick morass of
leaves, desiccated pigeon corpses, beer cans and hundreds of crumpled newspapers. Some of them were so
old that they were printed in English, from back when
the United Kingdom used to rule the former colony.

From this angle, Bolan could see everything inside
the junkyard: the mountains of spare parts, old refrig-
erators, farm tractors, electric ovens and hundreds of
car bodies creating a desolate lunar landscape of enam-
eled wreckage.

Pulling out the monocular, Bolan could see the garage and the half-track. There was nobody in sight at
the moment, but he knew that wouldn't last for long.
The Executioner had only a few minutes to get inside
and back out again before being discovered. Time was
very much against him.

Going to the far edge of the platform, Bolan found
that the towering movie screen cast him into shadow
darkness, streamers of dying sunlight dappling the
landscape like a kitchen colander. That would hide

him from anybody on the highway. He grunted. This
was probably why the mercs had taken the location.
The screen of a drive-in theater had to be isolated from
the headlights of passing cars or else the movie would
be ruined. Out of sight, out of mind.

At the end of the screen, Bolan discovered that he
was only a few yards away from the double fence.
However, the drop was a good twenty feet. He couldn't
risk injury. An old Reliance Gasoline sign hung from
a streaked pole squeaking steadily as it blew back and
forth.

Retreating as far he could, Bolan took off in a full
run and launched himself into the air. He hit the pole
hard and almost rebounded free, but his fingers clawed
along the metal, and he managed to find purchase.
Wrapping both his arms and legs around the pole, the
soldier slid down the entire length, disturbing a great
cloud of rust before landing on the hood of an old
Verma sedan.

Trying to maneuver off the roof, Bolan slipped and
went sailing to land on the vented hood of an ICML
Rhino. The impact knocked the breath out of him, and
Bolan lay there for a few moments, waiting for the
world to stop spinning. Slowly, the Earth got back on
its axis once more.

Sliding off the Rhino, Bolan crawled across a Chev-
rolet sedan to reach the ground. Crumpled cars and
trucks of all sorts surrounded him on every side, tire-
less wheels jutting randomly and the ground sparkling
with thousands of tiny squares of busted safety glass.
Pausing for a moment in the growing shadows, he listened for any approaching sounds. But apparently nobody had heard his arrival.

Checking the Beretta, he proceeded around a collection of rusty sawblades and headed toward the garage. The building was silent, and the door was locked. However, that wasn't a problem. Removing a set of lockpicks from his pocket, Bolan went to work and gained entry in only a few moments.

Using his cell phone again as a makeshift flashlight, he quickly moved through the building in search of a computer. The mercenaries had to have gotten their orders over the internet. Anything else was much too risky. They had sat phones, but their base had to have a computer. If he could find that email, and extract an ISP address, he would have the first solid lead to the people behind these attacks.

If his EM scanner were still working, Bolan would have simply done a sweep for anything with a strong magnetic field. But now he was reduced to physically checking every room in the garage.

Unfortunately, there was no personal computer that he could locate. However, he did find a cache of stun grenades and tucked a couple of the flash-bangs into a pocket for later. Getting into the junkyard was going to prove much easier than getting out again. But first, he needed that computer! Or the man in charge. Either would do.

Starting along a hallway, Bolan opened a door and found himself looking directly into the face of a titanic guard dog, the colossal animal looked to be three feet tall at the shoulder, and possessed a head even larger than his own.

Uncharacteristically baring its fangs, the monster-size dog snarled, and Bolan was forced to pistol-whip it across the forehead. The stunned animal dropped heavily to the floor.

From behind another door, a man asked a question

in Hindi, and another man answered with a guttural laugh. Deciding to take a gamble, Bolan softly whimpered like a dog in pain. The voices talked to each other, then the door unlocked.

Instantly, Bolan lashed out a boot, driving the door into the person on the other side. There was an explosion of words, followed by a clatter of wooden chairs falling over. As the door swung closed once more, the Executioner kicked it again, and this time a man shouted in pain.

Charging into the next room, Bolan saw a man on the floor nursing a bloody nose, while another man was stumbling away, cradling a hand to his chest. Before either of them could react, the big American clubbed them both down with the Beretta. One man fell to the floor with a low moan, while the other dropped lifeless in the corner, blood pouring from his open mouth.

Quickly checking them both, Bolan recovered a pair of cell phones, both with internet capability. Tucking both of the phones safely away inside his body armor, the soldier decided that he had pushed his luck hard enough and headed for the exit.

He was almost at the door when a powerful engine surged into life somewhere close, and Bolan recognized it as belonging to a Russian half-track.

Arming a stun grenade, Bolan tossed it out the exit and waited until he heard the blast and saw the flash before charging outside. Night had fallen, but he could still see a dozen men clawing at their faces, while six more lay sprawled unconscious on the littered ground.

Triggering the Beretta machine pistol, Bolan mowed down the disorientated men with a hail of 9 mm Parabellum rounds. They tumbled backward into forever just as a pair of older men appeared from around a mountain of crushed cars. They blinked in surprise at the sight of Bolan, then clawed for weapons under their windbreakers.

Emptying the Beretta's magazine, Bolan removed them from this plane of existence, then quickly reloaded only seconds before a bald man came out of the garage with a Jackhammer shotgun blasting death in every direction.

A score of buckshot hit Bolan in the chest and he was slammed backward into the mountain of cars. Spinning away, he took cover behind a pile of tires as the bald man fired again, this time the spray of double-O pellets riddling the tires and shattering a sideview mirror.

A used tire slammed into the Executioner's head, almost knocking Bolan out. The world went blurry for a second, and he blindly fired at the bald man, trusting his combat instincts. As the Beretta coughed twice, the man screamed, and the shotgun clattered to the ground.

Just then, the garage door began to rise. Quickly arming another stun grenade, Bolan bounced it off the ground to land inside the garage. But just as it thunderously flashed, the door exploded into pieces as the half-track crashed through.

As Bolan reloaded the Beretta, the half-track ran over several of the unconscious men, the tires and treads reducing them to unrecognizable gore. Then the headlights turned on, twin yellow beams lancing across the junkyard to banish the night.

Diving to the side, Bolan raked the cupola with a full magazine from the Beretta, but the flurry of 9 mm rounds merely glanced off the old Soviet Union armor to musically ricochet away.

Somebody inside the cupola thrust the barrel of an

assault rifle out a gunport and started shooting back. The 7.62 mm rounds raked across the rusty piles of metal, punching holes in the bodywork of the cars and slapping hard into old tires.

Bolan armed his last stun grenade and charged the half-track, scrambling into the open rear compartment.

Angry voices came from inside the cupola at the front, and as a gunport opened, Bolan rammed the grenade inside. It hit the metal floor with a clatter. The men inside snarled in rage, then the cupola exploded with blinding light and deafening noise.

Instantly, the voices stopped, and the half-track began to sharply veer to the left, heading straight for a pile of old iron sinks.

Scrambling over the side, Bolan hit the ground running. More voices were coming toward the garage, and a second dog had joined the hunt. He recognized the breed as a Presa Canario, a widely feared animal.

As Bolan raced around the piles of wrecks and refuse, the Soviet half-track plowed into the pile of sinks, smashing them aside in a ringing cacophony that was louder than the grenades. Suddenly, lights appeared all across the yard, and men rushed to join the fray, AK-47s up and ready.

Heading for the entrance to the junkyard, Bolan shot out a cluster of halogen bulbs just as a big man stepped out of a wooden hut carrying a flashlight.

Seeing that the fellow was unarmed, Bolan switched targets from the man's chest to a leg, and shot him in the knee. Howling in agony, the man fell and reached behind his back to produce a 9 mm Tokarev pistol. Now, Bolan fired again just as the mercenary squeezed off a shot.

He missed; Bolan did not.

Reaching the front gate, the Executioner saw that
it was made of heavy wooden timbers covered with
barbed wire, and closed with an enormous padlock
that would have seemed right at home on a bank vault.

With more men appearing, Bolan shot off the padlock with a burst from the Beretta. As the gate swung
open, he charged down the access road, then angled
across a marshy field. His combat boots sank into the
soft mire, slowing him to a jerky walk.

Suddenly, a siren began to wail, and Bolan redoubled his efforts for speed. Assault rifles began chattering, the bullets zinging through the dense weeds.
More dogs started barking. Then a shotgun boomed,
and a round slammed Bolan in the middle of the back,
driving him into the mud.

Rolling aside, he got back on his feet and was sprinting forward when he was stabbed in the unprotected
part of his arm with something sharp. Darts! Instinctively, he twisted away just as a terrible racking pain
filled his body and the whole world went black.

CHAPTER TEN

Aboard the Red Rose, *Atlantic Ocean*

As the huge cargo ship steamed steadily toward the southwest, a tense hush filled the control room while Major Armanjani carefully studied a large, three-dimensional map of North America that completely filled the main monitor.

"Is this real-time?" he demanded with a darkening scowl.

He was still seething over the foolishness of the White Tigers that had cost them the sale to the rich Yakuza. He felt almost drunk with the overpowering need to spill blood. A half-billion dollars gone! Somebody had to pay for the crime.

"Yes, sir, absolutely real-time," Dr. Khandis replied, tapping the screen with a laser pen. "Check the timestamp for yourself."

"Bah, are there no storms in America?"

"None, sir."

"Anywhere?"

"All right, there are a few," Khandis relented grudgingly, touching the screen in several places to magnify that part of the image. "But none of them are near anything significant."

"Very well, Doctor," Armanjani stated, folding his

arms. "What other targets *do* have a storm nearby? Any U.S. Navy ships at sea will do for now."

"Choose for yourself," Khandis replied, typing on a keyboard. A list of possible targets scrolled on the screen.

"Hold right there!" Armanjani commanded as a smile grew. "Yes, that will do nicely. Can you show me any details?"

"Of course, sir," he said, adjusting some controls.

The satellite image on the monitor shifted into an aerial view of heavy cloud banks.

"How can I see anything with the storm in the way?" Armanjani snarled in annoyance.

"Switching to thermal," Khandis said, and the image changed to a black-and-white view of a large city.

"Is that the best you can do?" the major asked, rubbing his cheek with the back of a hand.

"Not at all," Khandis replied smoothly, and the image swirled to clarify into a full-color view of the inside of a shopping mall.

"Amazing," Nasser whispered, feeling a rush of pride. She cast a brief glance at the man, then quickly looked away before anybody noticed.

"Indeed, this is much better," Armanjani said. "Where are these cameras located?"

"Security feeds, traffic lights and the long-distance views are from the closed-circuit television system at a local college. Their firewall was laughable, and it is just far enough away that there will be minimum distortion from the second effects of the strike."

"Excellent! Well done, Kazim," Armanjani said, pulling an aluminum tube from a pocket.

Unscrewing the cap, he extracted a slim cigar, and using a pocketknife, he trimmed the end, careful not to bruise the tobacco. Then he lit a match and let the sulfur burn off before applying the flame to the tip. When it was glowing red, he inhaled deeply, and exhaled through his nose, twin streams of dark smoke issuing as from a dragon.

"Proceed when you are ready," Armanjani commanded, settling the cigar into the corner of his mouth.

Grunting in reply, the doctor fine-tuned the controls for a few moments, then activated a series of macro files. Binary commands flowed across the bottom of the screen and a few seconds later a lightning bolt lanced down from the sky to strike the Léon, France, airport fuel dump.

A writhing fireball expanded across the airport, engulfing airplanes, buildings and dozens of people. The picture was silent, but the grotesque death throes of the burning civilians were painfully obvious.

"Hit them again," the major commanded, smiling around his cigar.

Lightning flashed once more. "The local power grid is down," Khandis reported crisply as another bright flash appeared. "And there go the telephone lines."

"Good. Now take out the main target," Major Armanjani growled, leaning into the glowing screen. "I want Interpol to die screaming. Do you understand? Die screaming!"

Standing at the back of the room, Hassan and Nasser said nothing, but Dr. Khandis openly scowled in disapproval of the command. But he still adjusted the delicate controls, his hands flowing across the keyboard like a concert pianist performing on stage.

Again and again, the terrible white light filled the monitor as lighting bolts slammed down on a large unmarked building. The windows shattered as portions of the structure exploded, bodies flying away in tattered pieces. A prolonged bolt crawled through the parking lot, detonating hundreds of cars, leaving only bubbling lava and melted wrecks in its wake. An armored truck violently exploded, the blast sending the wreck hurtling through the rainy sky, a snowstorm of documents fluttering out of the swinging doors. Lifting off a helipad, an unmarked Black Hawk helicopter raced for the mountains, but lightning hit it in the air, and it vanished, only tiny bits of charred machinery sprinkling down across the dark suburbs.

"Enough foreplay. Take out their mainframe," Armanjani ordered.

With a blank expression, the doctor obeyed.

The screen flickered and rolled as bolt after bolt slammed into the building, hammering away at the crumpling masonry until its middle section was revealed, a massive supercomputer enshrouded in a swirling white mist. As the next bolt hit, the mist vanished, and a thousand servers visibly crackled with the static discharge before exploding and catching fire.

As a cloud of dark smoke rose from the decimated supercomputer, dozens of men and women grabbed backup disks and raced for the emergency exits. The technicians died before reaching the doors, lightning blowing off their arms and legs, the disks vaporized.

Now a prolonged bolt hit, the searing rod of condensed electricity moving through the ruin of the building like the wrath of God. What wasn't immediately destroyed soon exploded into flames as sheets of static electricity crackled over everything in a horrid display of wanton destruction.

In the offices, wooden desks simply exploded, metal desks melted, their contents annihilated. Armored file cabinets turned bright orange then white and melted into glowing puddles of steel, the top-secret reports gone forever. Gunracks on the walls jerked about as the stores of ammunition cooked off, sending out a deadly flurry of wild ricochets. Wounded, bleeding, choking on the polluted air, their clothing on fire, screaming people limped toward the gaping holes in the thick walls, only to be met with fresh lightning, bolt after bolt, an endless barrage of hammering fury.

"Enough! That settles many old debts." Major Armanjani grinned, blowing a long stream of dark smoke at the monitor.

"That is only a crippling blow to Interpol," Hassan stated. "They are far from destroyed."

"True, but it is enough for now." Armanjani chuckled, dismissing the matter with a wave of his hand. "Now, tell me how the auction is progressing."

"We're ready to go, sir," Nasser reported crisply. "A suitable venue has been chosen, security is arranged and a decoy auction has been established to confuse anybody trying to find us."

"Which of our enemies is still alive even to try?" Dr. Khandis laughed contemptuously.

"There are always new enemies," Armanjani growled, rolling the cigar thoughtfully between his fingers. "Lieutenant, create several more fake auctions. Sergeant, double whatever security you already have for the real one. Doctor, prepare a disaster scenario."

"Sir?" Khandis asked, confused.

The major sighed. "Pretend that the American CIA,

Russian Special Forces, the Mossad and the British MI-6 have joined forces to attack us in unison," he explained tolerantly for the scientist. "Then detail a plan to kill them, and for us to escape anyway."

"Sir…is such a thing possible?" Khandis asked with a nervous laugh.

"All of them joining together?" Armanjani stated, shifting the cigar to a more comfortable position in his mouth. "Possible? Of course. Not highly unlikely." He snorted smoke. "However, the way to stay alive in combat is to plan for disaster."

"Yes, I see," the doctor muttered. "That…makes good sense."

"Glad you agree. Now get to work, and make no mistakes," Armanjani growled, standing to look menacingly down at the scientist. "Because you're coming with us to the auction."

"Me?" Khandis gasped. "Why bring me along?"

Removing the cigar, the major inspected the glowing red tip. "Why? To make sure your escape plans works, of course," Armanjani said, returning the cigar to its accustomed place as he slowly walked from the room.

"Yes, sir."

"And don't forget to also hit some American targets!" the major added, opening the door. "Anything will do, even a ship at sea! Just make them bleed! I want dead Americans on the six o'clock news! Understand?"

"Yes, sir! But what about—" Khandis was cut off as the door closed. Annoyed, he did nothing for a few moments, then returned to his bloody task, and started deciding who would live, and who would die.…

Devakottai, India

SOME TIME LATER, Bolan sluggishly woke in a marsh, cold mud seeping into his clothing.

He felt sore all over, as if every muscle had been individually beaten. His tongue was numb, it was a little difficult to focus his eyes, his teeth ached and both kidneys throbbed with pain. Those were the classic signs of getting zapped by a high-voltage stun gun.

Only his years of training had saved Bolan from going down for the count. The instant he realized that he had been shot with darts, he twisted sideways to break any attached wires just in case it was a stun gun. Better safe than sorry.

It had been a wise precaution, and even then, in spite of his best efforts, Bolan still received a powerful electric shock.

There were muffled voices in the distance, and bright lights moved through the tall weeds—guards with flashlights hunting for him.

Summoning what strength he could, Bolan painfully crawled deeper into the marshy runoff, the stinking mud quickly revealing that this was also the garbage dump for the base. The mercenaries had to have been too lazy to dig a pit, and simply dumped their excess refuse into the swamp. Apparently for years, Bolan noted, from the depth of the stained food containers, crumpled papers, tin cans and unrecognizable wads of rotted food. Black beetles crawled over everything, and one of those strange oversized rats sat on a rock nibbling on a chicken bone held tightly in its paws. With bloodred eyes, it watched Bolan struggle by, wary of the man, but clearly not frightened.

Angling away from the flashlights, Bolan saw some

trees to the right. More than a copse, but smaller than
a forest, he reasoned it had to be an orchard of some
kind. Wisely, he also veered away from that. The orchard would be the first place the mercenaries would
check, if they didn't have guards already stationed
there as perimeter sentries. Avoiding the trees would
only buy him a few moments, certainly less than a
minute of freedom, but every second counted as his
body struggled to recover from the massive shock. His
thoughts were disorganized and chaotic, memories of
childhood, old friends, past battles, baseball games
and his first meeting with Brognola, all mixing together into a useless hodgepodge. Utilizing a martial
arts technique to manage pain, Bolan concentrated
on his breathing and banished everything else from
his mind. There was only the mud and his breathing,
nothing else.

Long minutes passed as Bolan crawled behind a
rusty stove—only to step back at the sight of an enormous beehive inside. However, there was no buzzing,
and he relaxed with the realization that it was an old
abandoned hive. Battered, bruised, shocked, shot and
surrounded by trained killers, Bolan almost laughed
at himself for flinching from getting stung.

Straining to listen to the advance of the mercenaries, Bolan lowered his head to lap some rain water
from a small depression. That eased his sore throat,
and helped settle his stomach. The last thing he wanted
now was to be sick. Nobody could vomit quietly, so
it would be the last thing he ever did. He had to stay
silent and keep moving. That was the only hope of
survival.

Moving to another clear pool of water, Bolan drank
again, deeper this time, and felt a little of the fog in his

mind ease. Okay, back to work. Fumbling to check his weapons, Bolan wasn't overly surprised to find that the big Desert Eagle was gone, along with his belt knife and EM scanner. There was only the muddy Beretta and a couple of magazines.

Rinsing the weapon off in the water, the soldier then continued on to a splintery tree stump and rested for a moment amid the tangle of exposed roots.

Just then, a sharp whistle cut the night.

"He's over here!" a man called out.

Rolling over fast, Bolan saw the murky figure of a man holding a flashlight near the iron stove. Damn, that was less than a hundred feet away!

With no choice, Bolan drew the Beretta and swung down the front grip of the machine pistol. Holding his breath, he cradled the Beretta in a shaky two-hand grip and snapped off four fast rounds. The mercenary near the stove fell screaming, the flashlight crashing on the appliance and going out.

Instantly, the marsh became alive with gunfire, assault rifles, pistols and shotguns sounding off.

Keeping low behind the stump, Bolan counted twenty other people, which meant this was the entire mercenary team. That was both good and bad.

Knowing what was coming next, Bolan rolled over and over in the sticky mud, trying to cover himself as much as possible. Stopping near a soggy mattress, he grabbed a fistful of reeking garbage, and spread it across his face and chest, then went still.

Only seconds later there was the sound of a dull thump, followed by a prolonged hiss. Closing his eyes against the glare, Bolan heard the flare detonate in the sky, and saw his eyelids turned red from the bright light. Covering his face with a hand, he blinked several times quickly to get accustomed to the harsh illumination.

He heard the sound of running feet coming from numerous directions, the boots making sucking sounds as they were pulled free in the garbage field.

"There he is!" somebody shouted to the left, but the weapon fired to the right.

"No, over here! I see him!" another man shouted.

"Go, go, go!" added a third, and briefly their weapons chattered harmlessly into the sky.

Easing off his boots, Bolan scoffed at the trick when a rain of heavy objects thudded down across the field. He forced himself not to move as something impacted nearby.

As expected, it was just a rock, not a grenade. This was amateur stuff. Combat 101. Where had these people gotten their training? No real soldier would ever fall for these childish ploys.

The bright light of the parachuting flare died away, and Bolan stood the instant he was back in darkness. There was always the slim chance that the mercenaries had night-vision goggles, but from the rest of the equipment he'd seen, he didn't think they had those kinds of funds. The first thing anybody bought was better weapons. Second-rate guns meant that everything else was third-rate or worse. It was a gamble, of course, but he'd bet his life on far worse odds and survived. The trick was speed.

Briefly, assault rifles chattered, the muzzle-flashes pointed upward. Bolan tried not to smile at that. With the mercenaries spread across the marsh, they no longer had a clear field of fire. If the men shot randomly they would almost certainly hit one another, and that gave him a chance.

Padding barefoot across the marsh, Bolan made a lot less noise than the mercs in their boots, and reached a toppled refrigerator without getting shot. He had stepped on several sharp objects hidden in the mud along the way, but he ignored the minor pain and holstered the Beretta.

Two of the mercenaries were sloshing through a deep puddle, holding their weapons high overhead to keep them dry. Bolan let the first one pass unmolested, then charged out of hiding. As the second man came out of the puddle, Bolan lunged forward to grab his head and savagely twisted to the left, then the right. The neck broke with a snap, and the mercenary shuddered into death.

Grabbing a knife from the belt of the corpse Bolan threw it with all of his strength. Caught in the act of turning, the second mercenary got the blade full in the throat. Gushing crimson, he tried to shout for help, but could only manage a watery gurgle, so he yanked out the blade. Immediately, the man began to convulse, drowning in a torrent of his own blood.

As he dropped to his knees behind a refrigerator, Bolan moved in fast and recovered the knife. Going behind the mercenary, the soldier reached around to grab his jaw as a guide in the darkness, then rammed the knife into his head directly behind the left ear.

Instantly, the mercenary went still and died. The Navy SEAL had nicknamed that location in the human skull Death's Doorway, and there was no faster way to take a human life. However, while Bolan didn't torture his enemies, this maneuver was done merely to keep the man silent and not reveal his location to the others. Bolan was a soldier, not a saint.

Easing the warm corpse to the ground, he quickly

took a Glock pistol, some spare magazines, a canvas ammunition belt and the AK-47 assault rifle. There were no hand grenades, but he did find two 30 mm shells for the grenade launcher attached under the main barrel of the Kalashnikov, along with a half-eaten candy bar.

He ate the bar as he checked over the assault rifle for any damage or mud, then thumbed a fat 30 mm shell in the launcher.

Taking a calming breath, Bolan steadied the assault rifle, then turned fast and emptied the entire magazine into the night.

Several voices cried out in surprise, then pain, and a couple of the mercenaries started wildly shooting back. Another followed suit, and suddenly the marsh was alive with crisscrossing rounds, tracers stitching through the darkness.

Dropping low, Bolan heard the weeds patter from the passage of the 7.62 mm rounds, then something white-hot grazed his shoulder, and a another slammed into his back with stunning force.

Falling face-first into the mud, Bolan jerked back as a shard of broken glass sliced open his cheek. Forcing himself not to speak, the soldier rose to his knees, listening to the bursts of gunfire, gauging distance and directions.

Furiously, a man shouted something in Hindi, and the shooting stopped. Assuming that was the leader of the mercenaries, Bolan aimed in that direction and sent off a short burst. The same voice cried out in painful surprise, and an AK-47 briefly chattered, the muzzle-flash arching up into the starry sky before terminating.

Instantly, everybody started shooting again.

Deciding this was the time to move, Bolan took

off to the right, heading for the distant highway. With luck, he could flag down a car and get away before the mercenaries got their act together and started to sweep the marshland in an organized manner.

Staying low, Bolan padded across the mud. Unexpectedly, a man rose to his right, and the Executioner paused to make sure it was a mercenary before taking him out with a burst from the Kalashnikov.

Angry voices were shouting from different locations across the marsh, and the gunfire was taking on a more precise pattern, probing in one direction before moving on to another. Bolan was grazed twice more and felt something hot go through his hair. That sent him into the mud, and crawling fast. That had been way too close for comfort. Somebody was either very good or very lucky.

Reaching the edge of the marsh, Bolan saw a Hummer parked on the berm of the highway with two men standing outside, one of them was cradling a Russian assault rifle while the other toted an American-made M-60 machine gun. They hid the weapons as a car drove past, and Bolan hoped the noise would disguise any sound he made as he crept along the edge of the marsh until he located a drainage ditch.

Because he was only able to move when traffic drove past, it took Bolan an inordinate length of time to locate a small culvert and wriggle inside. Trying not to breath in the fetid smell of decaying waste, he finally came out the other side.

Slowly rising behind the mercenaries, Bolan debated his next action, then started boldly across the open pavement, the Kalashnikov and Beretta at the ready. This was going to be close.

Triggering the grenade launcher, Bolan sent the 30

mm shell into the back of the larger mercenary carrying the M-60. The range was much too short for the warhead to arm, but the shell smashed into the mercenary like a cannonball, shattering his spine. With a jerk, the man dropped onto the pavement, shaking wildly.

Snarling a curse, the second man spun, his Kalashnikov spitting fiery death.

Diving to the side, Bolan rolled under the Hummer and shot the mercenary in the foot. Screaming in pain, the man fell, and Bolan ended his misery with another round to the middle of the forehead.

Voices shouted from the marsh, and a radio clipped to the belt of the dead man began to crackle loudly.

Ignoring that, Bolan retrieved the M-60 from the convulsing mercenary, then rapped the weapon's butt against the guy's head. With a sigh, the criminal went still.

Quickly checking the big M-60, Bolan started shooting into the marsh, white-hot tracer rounds stitching through the inky night. Starting at the far end, the soldier burned through an entire belt to try to drive the mercenaries back to the junkyard, a place they would naturally think of as a safe haven.

As the belt became exhausted, they boiled out of the weeds, Bolan tossed away the heavy machine gun to raise both of the Kalashnikovs and cut loose in a prolonged barrage. The double volley of 7.62 mm rounds ripped the mercenaries part, their limbs flailing about like drunken puppets.

When the assault rifles cycled empty, Bolan dropped them and pulled out the Glock. Bracing the pistol on top of the front hood of the Hummer, he squeezed off single shots, blowing the survivors away one at a time.

As the last man fell, Bolan bolted away from the Hummer. He'd barely got clear when there was a flash of light from the roof of the garage, and a rocket streaked in to annihilate the Hummer in a strident explosion, chunks of men and machine rising high on a roiling fireball.

Kneeling to steady his aim, Bolan drew the Beretta and emptied the entire magazine. The chattering stream of bullets peppered the distant garage, apparently without result. But as he reloaded, a man rose into view holding a Carl Gustav rocket launcher. As the mercenary aimed the rocket launcher, Bolan cut loose with the contents of his last magazine. The mercenary staggered from the incoming rounds, then sagged and launched the rocket straight into the sky.

As the rocket streaked harmlessly away, the backwash engulfed the rooftop, blowing off the man's legs and setting his clothing on fire.

Shrieking pitifully, he feebly rolled about until going off the edge of the garage and falling directly onto the pile of rusty saw blades.

A split second later, something inside the garage detonated, spreading out a fiery corona. Another explosion closely followed, then several more, some louder, some weaker, then the entire building erupted. Bodies, furniture and vehicles formed a hellish geyser into the sky, ragged lumps and chunks arching away to pelt down into the marsh.

As the stores of ammunition inside the garage began cooking off, Bolan wearily walked to the wreckage of the Hummer and began to search for a medical kit, more ammunition, or anything else usable. His best guess was that all of the mercenaries had been killed, but until that was confirmed, he would stay alert.

In the far distance, Bolan could hear a siren wailing and forced himself to start for the marsh again.

Suddenly, a pair of headlights appeared, sweeping the Hummer as a Rhino came jouncing off the highway heading directly his way. Checking the load in the Glock, Bolan took cover behind the Hummer. He wouldn't shoot the police or firefighters, even at the risk of his own life. However, their car tires were another matter entirely.

As Bolan drew a bead, the Rhino barked to a rocking halt on the grass, then the horn sounded in a fast series of honks: three, two, one, then three again.

"About time you showed up," Bolan muttered, trying to put the Glock into a holster designed for a Beretta. When it didn't fit, he merely tucked it into his belt.

"Got here as fast as we could," Kirkland announced, climbing out from behind the wheel with the Webley in his grip. Montenegro's Neostead was slung across his back, and a canvas ammo bag hung at his side.

"Matt, are you all right?" Montenegro asked, stepping out of the vehicle. The heavy XM-25 grenade launcher hung at her side from a nylon strap.

"Never better," Bolan said, walking forward. "How did you find me?"

"We met a helpful fisherman, followed your trail, then listened for World War III," Kirkland said. "That's always worked before."

"Can't argue with success."

"Lord Almighty, did you escape through the sewage system?" Montenegro asked, holding her nose. "I've known week-old corpses that smelled better than you."

"I am a mite ripe at that," Bolan admitted.

"More importantly," Kirkland asked intently, "did you get what we need?"

"Almost," Bolan replied in blunt honesty. "But the phones got smashed along the way."

"All right." Montenegro sighed, adjusting the heavy XM-25. "Is any of their communications equipment still intact?"

"I doubt it highly," Bolan snorted, glancing at the burning wreckage.

"Only one way to know for sure," Kirkland said. "Let's go hunting."

"This way," Bolan said, starting off at a stiff walk.

"Freeze right there, mister!" Kirkland bellowed.

Stopping motionless, Bolan looked around, positive that the man had spotted a land mine or a trip wire.

Instead, he bent down to look at Bolan's bloody feet and removed his own boots.

"Put them on," he stated. "A limping man only slows the rest of the platoon and gets everybody killed."

Bolan started to object, then saw their expressions and did as requested.

"Better?" Kirkland asked, wiggling his toes in his socks.

"Better," Bolan admitted, then added. "Thanks."

"Keep them," Montenegro added. "You'll be cursing our names after we clean those and put in some stitches."

"Yeah, been there, done that," Bolan said with a shrug.

Sweeping into the junkyard in a standard three-on-three defense pattern, they made it to the burning garage in only a few minutes.

The base was dotted with numerous small fires, and

in the distance the mountain of crushed cars was still shifting and creaking into its new position.

"I love your work," Kirkland snorted. "But you were probably right, we're not going to find anything intact here."

"Unless," Montenegro said, then suddenly fired the XM-25.

Far across the junkyard, standing brazenly on top of a pile of crushed cars, a man holding a flamethrower cried out as the heavy shell slammed into his belly. The impact spun him, and sent him tumbling over the other side.

"Why'd you shoot him?" Kirkland demanded.

"To stop him from shooting us," she replied. "Are you unclear on how this whole battle thing works?"

"I think he meant that we could have used somebody alive to question," Bolan answered, then went silent.

"Something wrong?" Kirkland asked, Neostead sweeping the fiery yard for any suspicious movements.

"Listen," Bolan whispered.

The others stopped talking, and a few seconds later there came a low moan of pain from the mound of used tires.

Staying in formation, they checked for traps, then shifted a few of the tires. Buried underneath was a man in bloody clothing, an AK-47 at his side, the barrel visibly bent.

"Hi, there!" Kirkland said with a smile. "Looking for some reliable retreads?"

With a snarl, the wounded mercenary pulled a knife out of his sleeve, but Montenegro kicked it free. It sailed away to land with a clatter amid the tractors, and rusty plows.

"Now that the preliminaries are over..." Bolan said, working the slide on the Glock.

At the familiar sound, the mercenary sneered in repressed fury and started for the assault rifle, then stopped and cut loose with a long string of Hindi, followed by German and then French.

Kneeling, Bolan lowered the muzzle of the weapon against the man's left eye. "Enough of that," he ordered. "I heard you speak English before when I did a recon." It was a lie, but the man had no way of knowing that, and most people in India spoke a little English.

"Yes, yes, I speak," the man growled, shifting uncomfortably on the filthy ground.

"Give me the name of the person who hired you to do the recon in Sri Lanka," Bolan demanded.

"And please don't say that you don't know," Kirkland said, low enough to make the other man strain to hear the words. "Because otherwise you're useless to us."

"Useless," Montenegro repeated, lowering the big muzzle of the XM-25.

For a long moment, the mercenary said nothing, his eyes darting about the ruin of the junkyard, the dead bodies and then all of the weapons pointing his way. "Merc," he growled in heavily accented English, gesturing at himself with a thumb. Then he made an international gesture by rubbing two fingers together.

Surprised, Bolan eased his stance. He wanted to get paid for the information? Once hired to do a job, a professional would never stop until the job was done. On the other hand, his job was done, so...

"Deal," Bolan said, removing the gun barrel.

"I do like a man without principles," Montenegro

said, pulling out a thick wad of euros, and tucking it into the shirt pocket of the mercenary.

Unexpectedly, Kirkland then rolled him over and took his wallet in exchange.

Clearly confused, the merc stared as Kirkland removed all of the identification cards inside and tossed the empty wallet back to the man.

After a moment, the merc nodded in understanding. "I speak truth…or you go back."

"Come back," Montenegro corrected gruffly.

Minutes passed, and nobody spoke, the silence becoming more intense with each passing moment.

"Start talking or start dying," Bolan stated in a graveyard voice.

Inspecting the amount of cash in his pocket, the wounded mercenary sighed, then spoke a name: Roger Sullivan.

CHAPTER ELEVEN

The Sea of Japan

It had started as a beautiful day, but now the sky was heavily overcast, the roiling clouds dark and low. The ocean below was calm and serene. There were a few low swells, and a gentle breeze coming in from the northwest. Aside from the colossal U.S.S. *Esteem* there were only a few other vessels in sight, mostly fishing trawlers, and a few pleasure boats skimming along the waves.

The nuclear generators and electric engines of the U.S.S. *Esteem* revved toward overload as the colossal aircraft carrier desperately raced toward its home port of Yokohama. The armored prow of the vessel didn't plow through the waves, it crushed them aside, the aft propellers kicking up a frothy wake that spread outward for hundreds of yards. Along both sides of the vessel, deadly Phalanx autoguns scanned the area with their radar beams probing for any incoming danger.

Hundreds of sailors were scrambling to get the last couple of jetfighters onto the waiting elevator. The motorized trawl normally used to move the aircraft into position had unexpectedly blown a fuel gasket, and instead of waiting for the second trawl, the grim sailors swarmed over the jets like ants, using sheer muscle power to push, pull and drag the F-18 Super Hornets toward the waiting elevator.

The hydraulic lift was already loaded with an Apache gunship and a Tomcat, but the crew was grimly determined to get one more jet safely below before all hell broke loose.

"We don't even know if this is going to help!" a sailor groused, putting his back into the task.

"However, we do know this baby is a sitting duck on the flight deck!" a lieutenant replied gruffly. "So, more muscle, less lung!"

"Yes, sir!"

There had been no official announcement from the White House, the Pentagon, or the Pacific Fleet's commander, but they all watched television. For some unknown reason, lightning was systematically destroying military and civilian targets around the world. American, Russian, French, British: it made no difference, people were dying in droves, and the grim crew of the *Esteem* had absolutely no intention of joining the ranks of the dead just yet.

The minute dark clouds formed overhead, the captain began shouting orders over the PA system, and everybody scrambled to get the jets quickly off the flight deck and safely inside the carrier.

Theoretically, the crew and jetfighters were both safe enough; the ship's steel deck was eighteen inches thick, the armored hull over three feet thick, proof to anything short of a nuclear torpedo. However, while lightning strikes had been considered in the original calculations, multiple strikes coming in nonstop for minutes at a time certainly hadn't.

But since there was no way of knowing if their standard antilightning safeguards were sufficient to the task at hand, the captain and crew were playing it safe and trying to clear the flight deck. The standard complement of eight jetfighters, full of fuel and high-explosion munitions, normally the greatest defense of the *Esteem,* were now its deadliest threat.

On the bridge of the aircraft carrier, the captain watched the display screens with an intensity normally reserved for combat. The radar screens were clear, and sonar showed that there was nothing below the waves but a pod of whales and a few dolphins.

"Engine room, go to a 110 percent," the captain said in a deceptively calm voice.

"Sir, that is strongly not recommended," the chief engineer replied over the intercom.

"Neither is sinking."

"Sir—"

"I said now!" the captain interrupted in a dangerous tone.

There was a brief pause. "Aye, aye, sir," the woman replied.

A few seconds later, the dials and gauges on the control board rose, and the speed of the aircraft carrier ever so slightly increased.

"Think that'll do it, Captain?" the executive officer asked tersely, looking through a window at the sky overhead.

"I'll tell you when we reach port," the captain growled, as a gentle rain began to patter against the windows of the bridge.

Instantly, a klaxon started to sound, then every klaxon cut loose at full volume. Next, a siren began to wail, closely followed by the rarely used collision-warning bells. The simultaneous cacophony bordered on deafening, echoing and reverberating through every level of the massive vessel.

"Red alert!" the captain announced over a PA system. "Repeat, red alert! The rain is here! All hands belowdecks. This is not a drill. Repeat, this is not a drill! All hands belowdecks!"

Thunder boomed as lightning lanced down from the clouds to hit a group of sailors. As their stunned comrades struggled to recover from the numbing strike, another bolt crashed into the Super Hornet on the deck. The fuel and ammunition stores detonated like a bomb, the blast clearing the deck of everybody, broken bodies flying over the side to splash into the sea.

Static electric charges crackled along the metal hull of the carrier, burning out lightbulbs, making the crash net jerk upward into position, and burning out the sirens and horns until a strange silence covered the bloody flight deck.

As another bolt hit, two of the Phalanx guns blew apart into fiery shrapnel, but the rest stuttered into halting operation. Without targets, the computerized Gatling guns wildly sprayed out streams of 20 mm shells into the sea and sky. Then, firing randomly, they hosed the deck of the carrier, the shells annihilating everything in sight: men, machines, even blasting a string of jagged holes across the lower sections of the bridge.

"What are they shooting at?" a sailor yelled, wiping the rain from her face.

"How do I know?" her companion replied, clenching both fists while hunching his shoulders.

With a lurch, the elevator began to descend into the dark bowels of the great ship. Set askew, the blades of a wrecked Apache were sheared off as it dropped below the flight deck, then the wing of a burning Hornet was nipped off, aviation fuel gushing out like pale blood.

"All hands, emergency fire procedures!" an ensign yelled, as the fuel rained down from the elevator to splatter on the interior deck, and rapidly spread out in every direction.

As the sailors rushed for the water hoses, thunder rumbled in the distance, closely followed by the crash of lightning. Everyone flinched at the noise, and several officers irrationally started to draw sidearms, only to slam them back into their holsters. What good was copper-jacketed lead against lightning?

With a fast series of dull clunks, the huge elevator arrived and locked into place.

"Hit it!" the ensign bellowed, twisting the nozzle on a quivering fire hose. Instantly, a rock-hard torrent of salt water blasted out to push back the expanding pool of burning fuel.

A dozen more sailors did the same, the combined wash clearing the deck, and forcing the Hornet and the Apache across the elevator and over the edge.

Suddenly, the entire carrier trembled as if it had struck a submerged reef, or been hit by a torpedo. Before anybody could react, the overhead lights flared painfully bright, then died away completely, leaving the sailors in total darkness. Then the ship trembled several more times, and a powerful explosion erupted above, closely followed by the agonized shrieks of dying sailors. It was a terrible sound that once heard could never be forgotten.

Immediately, everybody started to dash for the exit. The ensign blocked the way, and shook his head. There were enough hands on deck to aid those who could be rescued, and any more would simply get in the way or, worse, become victims themselves from additional lightning strikes.

As the screaming died away, nobody spoke or moved for long minutes. Aside from the rain pelting into the sea, there were no other sounds. The air vents were silent, the elevator had stopped inches away from the flight deck, and even the ever-present background vibration of the main engines was gone. Their beloved ship was dead and completely without power—fifteen miles off the coast of North Korea.

A few seconds later, the emergency lights crashed into operation, the bright white beams crisscrossing the darkness to highlight fire equipment, weapons caches, medical supplies and exit doors.

"Okay, back to work!" the ensign shouted through cupped hands.

"Should we send somebody down to check the reactor, sir?" a young sailor asked, licking dry lips.

"That might not be a bad idea," another sailor said, nervously cracking his knuckles.

"Yeah, maybe so," the ensign admitted grudgingly.

Without warning, the entire aircraft carrier shook several more times, the lightning strikes come even faster than before. Everybody stiffened as they felt a faint electric tingle surge through their rubber-soled shoes.

"Now what in the world… oh, shit. Kill the water!" the ensign yelled, casting away the gushing hose. "Kill the fucking water right now!"

The ship was hit again, and static charges crackled up the streams of water to reach the inner bulkheads. Unexpectedly, all of the battery packs for the emergency lights exploded, and darkness returned.

Then an F-14 Tomcat jerked alive. As the turbo-engine surged with mounting power, it started to roll out of a repair stall, the aft flame melting the tools on the wall.

Everybody raced toward the runaway aircraft, but several sailors were knocked down by the expanding wings. A pilot tried to claw his way up to the cockpit, but he was thrown to the deck as the Tomcat swung about randomly, the fiery exhaust washing across a fully armed Apache gunship.

At the sight of the burning gunship, everybody ran for their lives. However, they only got a short distance before the fuel in the missiles, the rockets and the hundreds of pounds of ammunition in the hoppers ignited. The entire deck was filled with a searing fireball of gargantuan proportions.

Trailing dark smoke and starting to tilt, the U.S.S. *Esteem* continued on its original course from sheer inertia. But, quickly decelerating, it began to drift with the incoming tide, heading straight for the fortified coastal city of Hŭngnam, and the main battle fleet of North Korea....

Lavagh, Ireland

A COOL MIST FILLED THE mountain valley. A thick forest of pine trees covered the irregular landscape, masking the many cliffs, crags, swamps, caves and foothills.

Dawn was starting to break over the mountains when the Black Hawk helicopter started its descent into a small clearing. The flight from India to Ireland had taken the entire night. Hal Brognola had contacts in the Indian military, and he'd arranged to have the team flown to RAF Lakenheath. The Black Hawk was a U.S. Army asset and was on loan.

"Excuse me, Evil Kenivel, there's not enough space for the blades!" Kirkland growled, holding on to a ceiling stanchion for dear life.

"No backseat flying!" Montenegro replied curtly from the pilot seat, both hands busy on the controls.

As gentle as a snowflake, the military aircraft landed on the lush grass, and she killed the engines. "Thank you for flying Air Montenegro. Please remember to tip your air hostess, and return your seat to its upright position."

"Are we there yet?" Bolan asked, yawning and stretching, pretending to have just wakened.

"Nope, they took us out with a Redeye," she replied, removing the helmet. "Sorry, we're dead."

"Funny how much that feels like visiting Chicago."

"Hell has many names, Matt." She laughed, running fingers through her hair to loosen the compacted curls.

"Any radar contact?" Kirkland asked, pressing his face to the bulletproof window to look outside.

The world below was lush, green and wild. There were no structures of any kind in sight, only sylvan fields of grass, dotted with tufts of heather, and pine trees large enough to support the roof of the world. It was more like something from a fairy tale than reality. Kirkland smiled at that. It was no wonder the Irish loved the country so much, it truly was beautiful. Although, as a Scotsman, he much preferred the rocky Highlands across the Irish Sea.

"None," Montenegro answered, locking the blades into position. "Nobody knows we're here unless they saw us land."

"Not impossible considering the pilot."

"You used to love how I made things fly," Montenegro said, seductively batting her eyelashes.

He grinned. "Sorry, can't remember that far back. How many years was it again?"

"I am armed, you know."

"Play nice, you two," Bolan muttered, using a new EM scanner to check the vicinity. "Okay, it looks like the only mag-fields are cable television, power lines and some cell phones."

"Excellent. Then let's go chat with Roger-dodger," Montenegro said, sliding a clip of rubber bullets into her Glock machine pistol.

"Be sure also to bring something a little more unfriendly," Bolan suggested, checking the magazine of rounds in his own Beretta.

"Not a problem," Montenegro replied, easing a magazine of steel-jacketed hollowpoint rounds into her other Glock.

"Ditto," Kirkland said.

The team had come to Ireland to call on Roger Sullivan, the man the wounded Indian mercenary claimed had hired them to recon the White Tiger base.

Sullivan was a former IRA assassin, infamous for his many bombings of military personnel while they were off duty. After the Belfast Treaty had been signed, Sullivan had turned freelance, and he now brokered jobs for mercenaries around the world: Sri Lanka to India to Ireland. Wheels within wheels was pretty standard for this sort of operation, and where it would take them next was anybody's guess.

The goals of a client were of no interest to Sullivan. He honestly didn't care if you wanted a church blown up or a child molester executed. Anybody and everybody was fair game to him, as long as the client paid in full and on time.

Just another mercenary, Bolan mentally noted,

checking over his garrotes and knives. These snake charmers seemed to specialize in hiring disposable personnel. That said something important about them, but he wasn't quite sure what that was yet.

Bolan knew that most civilians had the notion that a mercenary could be bought off hitting a target. That was completely wrong. If a mercenary could be stopped that way, then nobody would ever hire them to do anything. Sullivan, and others of his ilk, were oddly honest, in their own bizarre way. The man would always keep his word, if only to make sure he got hired again in the future.

Oddly, everybody in this line of business knew how to contact Sullivan. The man had a webpage. But not even Brognola knew where Sullivan was physically located. However, Bolan did. Roger Sullivan resided at Glen Moor Castle in Ireland, a genuine medieval fortress located on top of an unclimbable mountain peak in an isolated valley. It wasn't the least-accessible place Bolan had ever tried to infiltrate, but certainly it was one of the top ten.

"Where is the place?" Kirkland asked, looking through the telescopic sights around the helicopter.

"A mile down the road, past the next waterfall," Bolan said, checking the bandage on his ribs.

"Got it," Kirkland said, adjusting the focus. "Damn, it's big!"

"Ever heard of a small castle?" Montenegro snorted.

"Only a white one."

The gargantuan castle stood crumbling on a rocky escarpment. There were battlements, a drawbridge, a barbican and even a water-filled moat.

Seeming like something out of a fantasy movie, the ancient stone blocks of the castle were covered with moss and a million leafy creepers. The place looked as if a stiff wind could knock it over easier than a pile of dry autumn leaves.

Which was proof that looks were often extremely deceiving, Bolan noted.

"Heat source on the second floor," Montenegro reported, fine-tuning the controls on the infrared scope. "Nobody seems to be moving around, but there are a lot of oddly-placed hot spots. My guess would be electric wall-heaters."

"To confuse any infrared scanners?" Bolan asked.

"Exactly."

"Fairy-tale castle, my ass, this is a goddamn military hardsite," Kirkland stated, sweeping the battlements with the Black Arrow's scope. "Damn, I love this weapon!"

Montenegro smiled. "And I thought your favorite was hanging between your legs."

"One is for fighting, and one is for fun."

"Which one of those is the rifle?"

"Come closer and I'll show you," Kirkland said, easing out the boxy magazine to check the load. Five cigar-size bullets lay inside, shiny with fresh oil.

"Hey, Matt, your feet feeling good enough to do some running?" Kirkland said.

"Never better," Bolan said resolutely, stomping his new boots.

"But if we give a shout, come in blazing," Montenegro added grimly.

"I got your six," Kirkland growled, levering in a 700-grain round. Then he cursed. "What time is it?"

"Zero-six-fourteen," Montenegro replied, tuning the transceiver on her belt. "Why do you want to know?"

"Because the goddamn castle is a tourist site!" Kirkland replied furiously. "There's a sign out front listing details. The first tour starts at zero-nine!"

"That's over two hours from now!" she scoffed, tucking in earbuds. "If we need longer than one hour to bust this dump, then we might as well surrender and go home."

"Thirty minutes, max," Bolan countered. "And we'll need some kind of a disguise. Any cardboard boxes in here? A wicker picnic basket would be even better."

"In this ride? Sorry, nothing like that," Kirkland apologized. "But there are some heavy blankets tucked under the rear seats."

"Ponchos?"

"Better than nothing, old buddy."

Going to the aft of the Black Hawk, Bolan unearthed the blankets and grunted in satisfaction. "These will do," he said, cutting a hole in the middle of each.

Sliding the blankets over their heads, Bolan and Montenegro saw that their weapons were fully covered.

"Not much of a disguise," Montenegro snorted. "Then again, the mist is chilly, and we only need these long enough to get close."

"Okay, let's go, Heather. Bill, sharp watch for non-combatants."

"Roger wilco," Kirkland subvocalized into his throat mike.

Leaving the Black Hawk, Bolan and Montenegro stayed off the main road, and moved through the cool forest, ever-watchful for pitfalls, land mines and other traps. However, the area surrounding the castle was clean, without even so much as a hidden video camera.

"Sullivan is hiding in plain sight, protected by civilians," Kirkland whispered in their earbuds. "The armor of criminals has always been our own value on human life."

"You know my opinion on the matter," Bolan stated.

Montenegro nodded. "If you act against society, then you no longer have a moral claim to the protection of that society."

"Behave like a mad dog, and you'll get gunned down like a mad dog," Kirkland said over the radio link. "I have no real problem with that, Matt."

"Many do," Bolan said, his tone a mixture of feelings, mostly irritation and disappointment.

About a hundred feet from the castle, they came out of the woods, their hair and blankets soaked with moisture from the leaves and nettles. Strolling boldly to the front door, Montenegro stood guard while Bolan used a keywire gun on the front lock. He shot the lock full of stiff wire, gave a twist and the door silently opened on well-oiled hinges.

The interior of the castle was cool and dark, the early-morning light making the stained-glass windows softly glow, but not really providing illumination. Velvet ropes closed off sections where the public wasn't allowed to venture, and there were electric ceiling lights, the beams pointed at suits of armor, oil paintings and other historical artifacts.

"This really is a museum of sorts," Montenegro marveled, both hands tucked out of sight under the wet blanket.

"And dusty," Bolan replied. "The sign out front says there are daily tours, but nobody has cleaned this place in a month, maybe more."

"You think it's a dead drop?" she asked, scowling, keeping alert for hidden cameras.

"Let's find out," Bolan whispered, removing a velvet rope to start up a long flight of stone stairs.

The carved wooden door at the top of the stairs was securely locked, but the keywire gun did its usual job, and they were through in only a few seconds. However, as he stepped through, Bolan drew his Beretta at the sight of a towel that had been stuffed under the door.

"To hold in gas or keep out smells?" Montenegro asked, swinging up both of her Glocks. Then she scowled as the smell hit. It was the reek of old bologna and pennies—the smell of an old corpse.

"This way," Bolan said, following the stench down a side corridor to another locked door.

Inside, the room proved to be a small washroom with an old-fashioned clawfoot tub situated in the corner near a fireplace. Held in place by duct tape, a heavy plastic sheet covered the tub, the center distended from the pressure trapped inside.

Removing their wet ponchos, Bolan and Montenegro cut off strips to bind around their nose and mouths, before slicing open the plastic.

As expected, a decomposing human body lay sprawled in the tub, several black holes in the face proclaiming the cause of death.

"That him?" Montenegro asked with a scowl.

"I can't tell after this much decomposition," Bolan said, holstering the Beretta.

Removing his watch, the soldier slid a hand gently under the gelatinous corpse and searched until he located a wallet. There was a disgusting sucking noise as he pulled it free, dripping a thick, viscous fluid.

At the sink, Montenegro already had warm water running, and Bolan thankfully rinsed off the grisly object before finally easing open the ooze-soaked leather.

"These belong to Roger Sullivan," he announced, studying the identification cards. "Could be fakes, however."

"Let's find out," Montenegro countered, going back to the corpse. Pulling out a Gerber knife, she slashed open the left leg, the jellied flesh falling away to reveal a steel pin in the left hip and a titanium knee.

"That's Sullivan," Bolan stated, tossing the wallet into the sink. "I shot him in that knee a decade ago."

"I did the hip," Montenegro added with a touch of pride. "Tough man to kill."

"Somebody got the job done," Bolan said, rinsing his hands under the stream of water.

"Which means the mercs were hired by terrorists pretending to be Sullivan," Kirkland growled. "Somewhere in this castle will be a radio relay, so that the terrorists can hire whatever personnel they need for a mission while staying deep under cover."

"Then this is a trap," Montenegro said with a hint of a smile.

"Always thought it might be," Bolan said, leveling both of his weapons. "Bill, any new hot spots?"

"Are you kidding?" Kirkland replied. "Once you slit the sheet and the decomp gas escaped, the whole castle went live! There are video feeds all over the place!"

"The terrorists want to see who is after them," Montenegro said, holstering a Glock. "We're going to try for a piggyback?"

Bolan nodded. "If Sullivan was dead, as I expected, it would be our best chance to find the bastards."

"Sounds good to me." Kirkland chuckled, then cursed. "Just watch your ass! The best way to learn about who is coming after you is to see them in action... Goddamn it, here come the tourists!"

"Keep them back while we hunt for the radio relay!" Bolan commanded, pulling out an EM scanner. "Don't let them get inside under any circumstances!"

"Not a problem!" Kirkland said, and there came the boom of the Black Arrow. "Okay, I just removed both of their front tires. The car crashed into some bushes, and now a man and a woman are running away like their asses were on fire."

"Nothing subtle about our William!" Montenegro said, kicking open the washroom door.

For almost an entire second nothing happened. Then the door at the far end of the corridor exploded into splinters as a machine gun cut loose.

Already in motion, Bolan and Montenegro got behind a stone wall just before the arrival of the stuttering stream of rounds. The bullets raked across the washroom, denting the iron bathtub and splattering Sullivan across the tiled walls. Moving back and forth, the 9 mm bullets shattered the window and mirror and broke chunks off the porcelain sink.

"That's an auto-sentry gun!" Montenegro muttered, tightening her grip on the two Glocks. Then she lowered her voice and added, "I hate those damn things."

In the distance, police sirens began to wail.

"Any way of telling if it's being operated by a computer or remote control?" Bolan asked tersely, as another barrage hammered the lavatory.

"Sure," she replied, grabbing a towel off a rack and tossing it across the doorway. Instantly, the gun fired, tearing the towel into shreds before it fluttered to the floor.

"It's computer-operated," Montenegro announced. "Which means we can easily take it out, but there's no live feed for us to trace! Bill must have misread the scanner."

"Like hell I did!" Outside, the Black Arrow boomed twice, and the police siren went silent. "Okay, I bought us a few minutes," Kirkland said. "But the local constables will send in a SWAT team next wearing full tactical body armor and riding in an APC. These Irish cops don't play games. So move it or lose it, people! We have just officially run out of time."

"Agreed. Get the Black Hawk ready to go!" Bolan commanded as the machine gun fired again. "Heather, where would you hide a video camera to see who the gun killed?"

She frowned in thought, then scowled. "Aw, fuck me running! The only place you could be sure of getting a clear picture would be from inside the corpse!"

"I was afraid of that," Bolan muttered, pulling the pin from a grenade. Moving as fast as possible, he tossed it through the doorway and the auto-sentry gun fired.

As the lethal sphere rattled along the floor, Bolan wiped his mouth with the back of his hand, then the grenade cut loose, the blast shaking the walls and ceiling.

Tossing another towel, Montenegro ascertained the auto-sentry gun was dead, but tossed a second grenade down the corridor just to make sure. However, Bolan was already up and moving across the bathroom. The grenade exploded just as he reached the tub.

Grabbing the side, the soldier braced himself and heaved. Made of solid cast iron, the antique tub was incredibly heavy, but he got it moving upward.

As it came off the floor, the ghastly ruin inside sloshed out, then Sullivan tumbled free. Partially dissolved, the rotting corpse broke into numerous sections, the head cracked apart and a small video camera rolled into view.

Pulling out a tool kit, Montenegro started to move closer, but Bolan continued raising the tub until it flipped over and crashed down to completely cover the body.

A split second later, there was a muffled explosion from under the tub, and it heaved upward, only to come crashing back down again.

"Damn, that was close," Montenegro said, kicking some sticky human residue off her boots. As a finger rolled into the corner, an explosion sounded from somewhere above them.

"Heads up! All of the live feeds just stopped," Kirkland reported crisply. "I think they blew up the relay."

"Damn, that was fast," Montenegro cursed. "Whoever is running their tech knows his stuff."

"Think they got our pictures?" Bolan asked.

"They got a good view of me," Montenegro snarled, pulling out a cell phone.

As she started to text a message, Bolan heard thunder rumble in the distance. His combat instincts flared at the coincidence, and he grabbed the phone from her hand and smashed it on the floor, then crushed the components under his boot. His numerous cuts voiced their strong objection about that, but Bolan kept going until the phone was totally destroyed.

"What in hell did you do that for?" Montenegro demanded furiously. "My Florida driver's license has my picture on it! I have to warn my people to get out of the gym!"

"Only after we're far away from here," Bolan countered, striding from the room. "Then we'll stop and you can use a landline. But from this point on, no more cell or sat phones!"

"Why not?" Kirkland asked.

"Call it a hunch," Bolan replied, starting quickly down the granite stairs.

Only a few minutes later, Bolan and Montenegro were back at the Black Hawk. Montenegro started for the pilot chair, but Kirkland was already there, revving the engines to full power. With a shrug, she took the copilot's seat, and Bolan climbed into the rear.

As the helicopter lifted off the ground, a long peal of thunder rumbled in the cloudy sky, and lightning slashed down to slam into the castle. Massive stone blocks flew off the walls as a fast series of bolts struck the Irish fortress, shattering the towers, cracking apart the battlements and setting countless fires.

"Bill, get me to a landline, right now," Montenegro said in a tight voice, clenching her hands into fists.

"There's a shopping mall only ten minutes away," Kirkland replied, swinging the helicopter around. The pitch of the blades changed sharply as the chopper accelerated in the new direction.

Behind them, lightning flashed brightly as it continued to destroy the castle.

"Try and make it in five," Bolan advised, removing his own phone and smashing it to pieces with the butt of the Beretta supplied to him by Brognola's Indian contact.

CHAPTER TWELVE

The Atlantic Ocean

The door to the command room was slammed open and an unshaven Major Armanjani entered wearing only a bathrobe and slippers. "What's wrong?" he demanded, tightening the belt to his silk robe.

"The castle was activated," Dr. Khandis reported, working the control board.

That startled the major, but he tried not to let that show. "Destroy it," he commanded in an even tone.

"Already done," Khandis replied, flipping some switches. "I blew the relay and leveled the place with the Scimitar."

"Excellent work," Armanjani said, walking closer to inspect the monitors. On them were several pictures of a man and a woman.

"Are these the intruders?" Armanjani asked with a scowl.

Still typing, Khandis nodded. "Yes, sir. I'm running the pictures through the internet using a boolean search protocol, but I have no confirmation on their identity yet."

"They might just be common thieves," Hassan commented from where he sat.

"Not with that knife she has," Armanjani stated.

"It is a Gerber, very expensive, and a favorite of U.S. Special Forces."

"And us, too," Nasser said, pulling a blade from behind her back. "The knife proves nothing, sir."

"But those cuts do," Hassan countered eagerly, his eyes shiny with excitement. "See there? She opens his left knee, then his right hip. Each time exposing surgical repairs."

"They knew about the wounds," Nasser said in sudden understanding. "Were these things common knowledge? Something Sullivan bragged about to his friends when he was drunk?"

"No, he was very close-mouthed about anything personal," Armanjani stated with conviction. "Plus, he did not drink or indulge in most of the more common vices. That was why I chose him to be our puppet."

"Of course, most wise."

Scratching his head, Hassan asked, "Sir, could these be the people who gave him the wounds?"

"That is highly doubtful." Armanjani laughed. "More likely they're British SAS agents who specialize in hunting down known Irish criminals."

Unexpectedly, a bell began to loudly clang.

"Fire alarm?" Hassan asked nervously.

"Intruders!" Armanjani snarled, as there came the crackle of an assault rifle. A man screamed, and a body fell past the porthole. Going for his hip, the major grabbed only cloth. "Lieutenant, give me your weapon!"

"Yes, sir," Nasser said, passing over the Tariq.

As the assault rifle sounded again, the major checked the magazine, and Nasser went to a gunrack to grab her XM-25.

"Doctor, keep working and lock the door!" Armanjani ordered brusquely. "Let nobody enter, even me, until you know for absolutely certain the ship is secure!"

"Yes, of course," Khandis said quickly. But the others were already gone, sprinting down the passageway.

Following the sounds of gunfire, Armanjani almost stumbled over a body. He cursed to see it was one of the older men, a friend from before the war. His throat was slashed from ear to ear. His Tariq pistol was still holstered at his side, but the spare ammunition magazines were missing. The intruder had brought along a weapon, but no ammunition?

"Not an invader, a cursed stowaway!" Nasser snarled, just as bullet zinged past. She dropped to the deck, and Armanjani fell, clutching his wounded shoulder.

Swinging around his shotgun, Hassan cut loose with several shots, the barrage of lead pellets throwing off a fireworks display of sparks as they ricocheted off the steel walls and deck.

Rolling to her feet, Nasser triggered the XM-25. The shell streaked away, and a powerful explosion filled the far end of the corridor. The lights crashed, smoke billowed and a man bitterly cursed.

Charging that way, they found fresh blood on the floor, but the intruder was gone.

"Damn, he's fast," Hassan muttered, thumbing fresh cartridges into the shotgun.

"Be faster!" Nasser snarled, charging after the crimson trail.

Taking the stairs to the main deck, Nasser and Hassan dove out of the way as a hail of rounds drilled past them. Rolling to the sides, they came up again with

both weapons firing. Just for a moment, they saw a
figure on top of a cargo container, then he was gone.

Charging in straight, Nasser made it to the ladder
that led to the elevated rear of the ship, while Hassan
proceeded to go systematically from cover to cover, always shooting in short bursts to conserve ammunition.

Standing in the open, Nasser frowned. Nice, orderly,
precise and much too damn slow!

Suddenly, a ferocious roar of heavy machine-gun
fire erupted from above, and she looked up to see
bloody Armanjani standing in the open doorway of the
bridge. He was with six other members of Ophiuchus,
and awkwardly cradling a 7.62 mm RPK machine gun.

Immediately, a pistol fired twice, and one of the
soldiers cried out to topple sideways over the gunwale.

"Abdul!" another soldier cried out, reaching after
his friend.

The unseen shooter fired again, and another soldier
staggered backward, a red geyser of life pumping out
his ruined throat.

Mercifully shooting the dying man in the heart to
end his pain, Armanjani then unleashed the Russian-
made RPK, the spent brass rattling along the deck,
while hot lead ricocheted wildly between the stacked
containers.

"Blue dog, blue!" Nasser shouted.

Nodding, the major pointed at the other men, and
they quickly fanned out, firing nonstop.

Trapped by the unexpected assault, the invader was
driven out of hiding and burst into view for a moment.
Dressed in the uniform of Ophiuchus, he was a young
man, slim with black curly hair, and he carried two
Tariq pistols.

Instantly, everybody cut loose. He fired back in a

syncopated hail, killing two more soldiers and wounding others. Shooting from the hip, Nasser missed with a shell from the XM-25, then Armanjani attacked with the RPK. Hit several times in the chest, the invader was forced backward by the hail of 7.62 mm rounds until slamming against a cargo container, his head audibly cracking on the painted steel. Shuddering, he slid to the deck, both guns falling from twitching hands.

Firing as she ran, Nasser sent both of the weapons skittering across the deck and straight through a wash port into the ocean.

"Filthy pig!" Hassan growled, grabbing the unconscious man by the hair and hauling him upright.

The invader mouthed something unintelligible, a string of spittle drooling from slack lips.

"He's out!" Nasser declared, lowering her weapon.

"I don't care!" Hassan announced, slapping the man across the face with a pistol. The blow sent the man spinning around to land in a crumpled heap.

"Enough! Check him for traps," Armanjani commanded, keeping his distance, both hands wrapped tightly around the machine gun. The barrel never wavered from pointing at the intruder.

"Yes, sir." Slinging the shotgun over a shoulder, Hassan drew a knife and began to cut open the invader's shirt, carefully avoiding the seams and buttons. Those were where most people hid the trigger for a personal self-destruct.

Nobody was overly surprised when Hassan found a PSD strapped to the upper arm of the invader. Resembling a decorative leather band, the buckle contained a small charge of high explosive, just enough to blow a hole in the major artery located less than an inch away, just inside the armpit.

With a scowl, Hassan deactivated the PSD, then cut away the belt, uncaring of the slashes he made in the man.

"Should I kill him now, sir?" Hassan asked, reaching down to press the point of the knife into the throat of the unconscious man until a bead of blood formed. "I can do this slow and hard…"

"Perhaps later," Armanjani said, resting the RPK on his good shoulder. "But for the moment, I want him alive for questioning."

"Haul him to the interrogation room!" Nasser commanded.

With Armanjani leading the way, the other soldiers carried the invader through the maze of containers and down into the hold of the ship.

"Sir, do you think that the auction may have been compromised because of this?" Nasser asked with a dour expression. "We have no idea if the spy got off a message to his confederates before being discovered."

"That possibility has occurred to me," Armanjani replied, stuffing both hands into the pockets of his robe.

"We could always move to another location," Nasser suggested, taking a corner.

The major smiled. "True, but instead we will allow the auction for the Scimitar to proceed as planned."

"Sir, it could now be a trap!" Khandis exclaimed, clearly puzzled.

"I am counting on it," Armanjani said.

Since no further details were forthcoming, Khandis grudgingly accepted the rebuff. To date, everything had worked out exactly as Armanjani planned, so he would accept the major's word that the situation was under control, and wait to see what happened.

In a large, empty room, soldiers lashed a thick rope around the wrists of the invader, then tossed it over a beam. They hauled the man upward until his boots were dangling inches off the deck.

"Strip him," Armanjani commanded.

Staying alert for any more PSDs, the soldiers used straight razors this time, the clothing carefully removed and piled to the side.

Under the shirt was molded body armor unlike anything they had ever seen, and that was it. There were no dog tags or tattoos. There was no cell phone or transceiver. His clothing had no labels, there was no wallet, only a large sum of cash in euros, U.S. dollars and Swiss francs.

"This is a spy," Nasser said in disgust.

"Of course, but for whom?" the major asked, walking around the limp prisoner. "His manhood is not mutilated, so he is not a Jew."

"Many Americans and British also do the abomination," Hassan stated.

"Wake him," Armanjani said in a low voice. "And do not be gentle."

Nasser stepped forward and delivered several stinging blows across the prisoner's face. Almost instantly, he awoke.

"Better," the major said, with a cruel smile. "Now, tell me what you were after on this vessel, or else death will come only when I no longer find your screams amusing."

The naked man breathed hard for a few moments, then laughed contemptuously. Slamming his mouth shut, he ground his teeth hard enough to break off small chips.

"Stop him!" Hassan yelled, unsure of what else to do.

Several of the men present reached for the prisoner and tried to force open his mouth, then quickly let go as a white foam fizzed out from his graying lips. Bucking and convulsing, the prisoner shook all over, then went still.

Reaching up, Hassan checked the man's throat for a pulse. "Dead," he reported, wiping his fingers clean on his shirt.

"Must have been some sort of poison," Nasser muttered, sniffing at the mouth of the corpse. "Yes, bitter almonds. He used cyanide with some sort of accelerant. This is an old Nazi trick to escape being tortured into divulging important information."

"He was a Nazi?" Hassan asked, puzzled. "They still exist?"

"They do, but this was no German fanatic. Just the opposite, in fact. This smells of the Mossad," Armanjani said. "Dispose of the Jew, and clean the room before—"

Suddenly, the chest of the corpse exploded, pieces of flesh and bones smacking into everybody.

"By the blood of—" Nasser wheezed and coughed. "Wh-what just happened?"

"I have no idea," Armanjani growled, going over to a bleeding chunk of flesh.

"Medic! Medic!" Hassan bellowed, ripping off his shirt.

Lying on the floor, four soldiers were covered with deep gouges, white pieces of splintered bone sticking out of their bodies and gushing hot life.

Rushing to their aid, the others did what they could

under the circumstances, but each man soon died, the deck awash with their warm blood.

"Four more of my men," Armanjani whispered, slowly standing. "Somehow, he got on board, shot three of us, and even when dead, he took out four more. Seven in total!"

"Sir, I…" Nasser started, then quickly stopped at the raging fury in the face of her commander. She had never seen him this angry.

Going to a wall phone, the major lifted the receiver. "Give me the control room," he growled in a barely human voice. "Khandis? Forget Ireland, attack Israel. Hit them hard! Use the very first storm available and start burning down their hospitals, maternity wards, preschools, playgrounds. Slaughter their children!"

He started to hang up the receiver, then paused to listen intently, his face undergoing a strange change.

"What do you mean this is the dry season?" Armanjani snarled. "But…all right then! Find me other Jews… No, I don't know where! Try the United States. This will kill two birds with one stone! Find the Jews, and make the streets of American run red with their blood!"

Donegal, Ireland

BOASTING INDIRECT LIGHTING, slide-walks and bizarrely decorated in chrome and steel, as if it were a starship from the next century, the Charing Cross Mall was about as far away from the noble Celtic roots of the proud nation as it was possible to get without appearing to be from another dimension or, worse, British.

Sickly sweet elevator music played over the PA system, the blanched versions of American gangsta rap and German techno. In perfect counterpoint, parked outside the glass doors of the entrance to the mall, a local radio station had a promotional truck staffed with amazingly busty girls who were passing out free T-shirts while an enormous pair of speakers boomed classic Swedish disco.

The crowds were bustling with activity, full of aimlessly strolling teens, families hunting for bargains and more than a few military personnel on leave, both soldiers and sailors. Although they wore civilian clothing to try to blend in, their new crew cuts told the truth. Everybody seemed relaxed and was enjoying the atmosphere. The few snatches of conversation were banal and full of the details of ordinary life; work, chores, sex, money and love.

Sitting at a small Greek café, Bolan and Kirkland were working their way through a stack of lamb souvlaki, while Montenegro was sitting inside a phone booth just finishing her transatlantic call.

"Did you see that place near the water fountain?" Bolan said.

"You mean the one selling deep-fried candy bars?" Kirkland said, topping off a glass of beer. "Who would eat one of those crazy things?"

As a mall security guard strolled into view, both men stopped talking and concentrated on their food. The guard was a young man with old eyes, and heavily armed with a Smith and Wesson .45 pistol, an MP-5 submachine gun and a military stun gun. Northern Ireland had been the victim of many terrorist attacks, many of them the work of its own people, and guards such as this one were commonplace. Nobody paid the man the slightest attention. His presence was the price of peace, and only the criminals complained.

"Sorry we let you down, Matt," Kirkland said out of the blue. "I owe you better."

"Come again?" Bolan asked.

"Heather and I, we're not exactly delivering our A game," Kirkland stated. "Oh, the raid on the White Tigers delivered a solid lead to Sullivan, but the castle was a total fiasco!"

"It was just a dead end," Bolan stated. "Nothing more. Never knew a mission that didn't take a few wrong turns."

"But we learned nothing at the castle," Kirkland insisted, "and now the terrorists have pictures of you and Heather. I'd call that a disaster, not a setback!"

"Could have been worse."

"How?"

"Nobody died."

"Not yet, anyway."

"Okay, everybody is safe," Montenegro announced, walking over to the table.

"No lightning strikes yet?" Bolan asked, watching a mall security guard stroll past.

She smiled. "The sky is clear! So far, anyway."

"Good to hear," Kirkland said with a nod.

She smiled. "Damn straight." Sitting down, Montenegro grabbed a souvlaki and started eating with gusto. "Good lamb."

"I've had better in Syria," Kirkland said, trying to generate some enthusiasm. "But honestly, not by much. Irish women really know how to cook!"

"And not just in the kitchen," she boasted with a wink.

Both men laughed, but Montenegro could tell their hearts weren't in it. Clearly, she had interrupted something going on between the two of them, and just as obviously they didn't want to talk about it.

However, she could guess that it had to do with their failure to learn anything of value at the castle. Montenegro was pretty angry about that herself, but the martial arts taught self-control, and she would never let them see her mounting frustration. So much work, so many lives, and they still knew nothing about their enemy, not even a name!

"By the way, Matt," she continued, "there was a message for you with my receptionist, Sherry."

That caught his attention. "For me by name?"

"No, for Roger Dupree," she said, sprinkling salt on the French fries. "Your friend Hal said to call."

"Be right back," Bolan said, quickly rising and going to the nearest pay phone.

A few minutes later, he returned.

"Has there been a new attack?" Kirkland asked in a low voice.

"Several," Bolan replied. "But more importantly, a group calling itself Zeus was going to hold an auction for the lightning weapon at Port Royal in Jamaica."

"Was?"

"They just canceled."

Montenegro frowned. "Think we scared them off by hitting the castle?"

Kirkland snorted. "Not a chance in hell."

"Agreed. That's not how I read these people," Bolan answered slowly, laying aside the rest of the souvlaki. "Something went wrong on their end, something big, and now Zeus, or whatever their real name is, is regrouping before continuing the attacks."

"Whatever the reason behind it, this buys us some time," Montenegro said thoughtfully, adding sugar to a foam cup of steaming tea. Coffee was available on the menu, but from experience she knew that what the people in the British Isles called coffee was vastly different from what was served in America.

"Okay, what's our next move?" Kirkland asked, cleaning his hands on a napkin.

"We need access to a top-notch hacker," Montenegro answered. "Try and find out if anybody has ever done research into trying to control the weather."

"Every nation has given that a shot," Kirkland replied gruffly.

"True. But only one country had some small degree of success," Bolan said unexpectedly. "I've come across this type of thing before. There were several promising papers on the subject published by a Dr. Kazim Khandis from Iraq."

"Great!" Montenegro grinned. "Let's find the guy!"

"We can't. He's dead."

"Damn. When?"

"Killed during the Iraqi War."

"Interesting," Kirkland said, giving the word extra syllables. "What's the status of his lab and home?"

Bolan grinned. "Both of those were also destroyed...on the same day."

"Any chance those were right next to each other?"

"Opposite ends of town. Miles apart."

"So he's alive," Montenegro stated.

"Most likely, yes. Some of his staff and lab assistants escaped alive," Bolan added. "Unfortunately, they were on board the 747 that went down in the first attack."

"So the opening volley was to clean house? Smart."

"*Ruthless* is a better word."

"How do you know all of this?" Kirkland demanded, leaning forward to rest both arms on the table. "Hal?"

"Yes."

"Do you trust him?"

"With my life," Bolan said with conviction. "Now, here's the real kicker. According to the Mossad, it's believed that Dr. Khandis was the technical adviser for something called Ophiuchus."

"Come again?"

Bolan pronounced the odd word slowly. "It's Hellenic Greek for 'serpent bearer.' The sign was removed from the zodiac in the Middle Ages because of the overt sexual symbolism of a naked man holding a large snake."

"Wow, I had no idea there was a sign in the zodiac named after me," Kirkland said smugly, hitching up his gun belt.

"Wow, there's an astrological sign called asshole?" Montenegro asked in feigned surprise.

Extending a finger, and cocking back his thumb, Kirkland took careful aim, then shot her in her rear.

"Back on topic, Saddam Hussein didn't take a crap without an armed escort," Montenegro said, trying not to smile as she sipped the tea. "Who was the military liaison for Dr. Khandis?"

"Some lieutenant," Bolan said with a shrug. "But the officer in charge of security for the weather lab was Major Zafar Armanjani."

"The scourge of Baghdad?" Kirkland asked in surprise. "Holy crap. He was one of the head honchos of the Republican Guard! How do we find this guy?"

"According to the CIA," Bolan replied, "the major often did wetwork for other Arab nations without the knowledge, or permission, of Saddam Hussein. He used the alias Amir Bull."

"Never heard of him," Montenegro said slowly.

"Unfortunately, I have," Kirkland stated. "After the war, Amir Bull became famous as a turkey doctor for Swampfox."

Bolan scowled. *Turkey doctor* was slang for an expert at torture. He had met several such people over the years. Whenever possible, he left them in a great many small pieces.

"Major Armanjani was a TD for Barrington's Bad Boys," Montenegro said. "If he's in control of this weapon, God help us all."

Bolan fully agreed. Edgar Barrington was a self-made billionaire, and the sole-owner of Swampfox, a company that hired out as security to guard convoys, recover kidnapped business executives and such. During the recent troubles in the Middle East, Swampfox was hired by politicians to help protect museums and food convoys. In reality, they stole everything not nailed down and killed anybody who got in their way, even U.S. soldiers.

"Swampfox," Bolan said in a tone normally reserved for describing something recently stepped in. "They give mercenaries a bad name."

"Any chance we can confirm that Armanjani is at their home base in Alabama?" Kirkland asked hopefully. "Hack their laptops or piggyback their cell phones?"

"No way. Barrington is a technophobe. His organization doesn't even have laptops, much less a supercomputer," Bolan replied. "Everything is on paper, or locked in steel cabinets."

"Then we'll have to do this the old-fashioned way."

"Kick down the door and slap some people around until they talk?"

"Exactly."

Kirkland shrugged. "I have no problem with that."

"Same here. Hopefully, it's the dry season."

"Better check the weather service to see if there are any storms in the area," Montenegro added sagely.

"Not yet," Bolan said, putting a tip on the table. "But trust me, one is on the way."

CHAPTER THIRTEEN

Southern Indian Ocean

Glancing up from where he stood feeding documents into a shredder, Major Armanjani frowned. "What did you just say?"

"The entire South Korean fleet has moved to surround the American carrier we damaged," Khandis reported, glancing at a scrolling monitor on the console.

The major scowled. "Surely, you mean the North Korean fleet?"

"No, sir." Dr. Khandis sighed, pointing at the monitor. "It is the South. Plus, an entire wing of Chinese jetfighters have arrived to join the British helicopters and a French submarine to escort the *Esteem* into international waters, just in case the North Koreans do something stupid."

"Incredible," Armanjani muttered, turning on the shredder. The papers vanished into a spray of confetti that sprinkled into a burn unit and flashed into ash.

Bitter rivals helping each other. The major had never imagined that such international cooperation was possible, and certainly not between bitter rivals like America and China! Perhaps there really was something about the ocean that bound sailors together into a sort of brotherhood. Oh, he had heard stories about such things happening before and had simply not put any credence into the tall tales. Clearly, he was wrong.

Unfortunately, that put a serious crimp in his plans. By now, North Korea should have sunk the *Esteem,* and America should have retaliated with their long-range bombers. But that plan was now moot. The ruthless dictator of North Korea was insane, but not stupid. No nation in the world wished to face a united America and China.

"Are there any storms in the area?" Hassan asked, feeding blank sheets of linen paper into a chattering printer. The documents tumbled from the bottom covered in Cyrillic and bearing the logo of the Russian Central Military Command.

"Nothing. Visibility is unlimited," Khandis reported crisply, his hands flowing across the controls of the console. "Our satellites show no clouds near the Korean peninsula."

"What about fog, forest fires or earthquakes?" Nasser demanded, hanging some Russian uniforms in the closet. "Is there anything we can use to invoke a lightning strike and attack the rescue vessels to try to trick them into fighting with each other?"

"Nothing."

"Then ignore the ship," Armanjani said with a shrug, turning off the shredder machine. "This one small failure does not change our plans."

"As you say, sir," Hassan muttered, stuffing the documents into manila folders bearing the seal of the Kremlin. As a soldier, he disliked subterfuge, but grudgingly admitted it had some small use in battle.

It was now painfully obvious to the sergeant that the announcement of the White Tigers had obviously been a fake to lure Ophiuchus out of hiding.

Stuffing the folders into a file cabinet, Hassan scowled. Unfortunately, the trick worked, and there was now a very strong possibility that somebody had piggybacked their video signal from the castle in Ireland and an armada of enemy vessels was now rapidly converging on their present location. The Scimitar was very powerful, even more powerful than a nuclear bomb as there was no radioactive fallout, but right now, speed and misdirection were their best defenses.

Muttering a prayer, Hassan locked the cabinet, then twisted the key to snap it off in the lock. Once Ophiuchus was securely installed at its second base, he thought, the foolish West would pay dearly for its foul transgressions.

Crumpling a Russian newspaper into the wastebasket, Armanjani tried not to smirk. All across the *Red Rose,* the rest of the crew was destroying every trace of the group's presence, and then replacing it with hard evidence that Russia was behind all of the lightning strikes. There was even a smattering of trace DNA scattered about the huge vessel. The tissue scraps, hair and blood had been forcibly gathered from assorted drunks, prostitutes and small children, on his last trip to Moscow.

"How is our time?" Armanjani demanded, removing a pair of latex gloves and stuffing them into a pocket.

"Almost at the one-hour mark, sir," Nasser replied, adjusting the clock with Cyrillic script on the wall.

"Excellent! Then please…" But the major was interrupted by a hooting siren. "Report!"

"Sir, our main targeting satellite is gone," Khandis announced.

"Was it shot down, or is this an electrical malfunction?" Nasser demanded, nervously biting a lip.

"Unknown," Dr. Khandis replied. "Switching to secondary systems."

Nobody spoke as the scientist spent several minutes working the console. However, the central monitor remained blank.

"Well, Doctor?" Armanjani demanded.

"The cause of the disruption is still indeterminate," Dr. Khandis answered slowly, then jerked up his head. "But a Canadian spy satellite is approaching our former vector, so I would strongly advise leaving this location as fast as possible!"

Breathing deeply, Armanjani said nothing for a long minute, then he finally nodded. "Accepted," the major growled, pulling out a small control box.

When he pressed his thumb against a glowing square, the rest of the switches became illuminated. Armanjani began flipping switches in a seemingly random pattern. There sounded a low buzz and the box went dark. The major tossed it away just before a spurt of dark smoke jetted from its side. The box hit the wall and broke apart, the melted components scattering across the room.

"Let's go! We now have five minutes to get clear," Armanjani announced, striding for the door.

Moving swiftly through the maze of corridors, the four people reached the main deck just as a waiting Black Hawk helicopter revved its engine to full power.

Quickly climbing inside, the major and his people strapped themselves in, and the pilot immediately lifted off to angle sharply away from the cargo ship.

"Major, what about the ship's crew?" Hassan asked

in alarm, turning to stare at the mountain of rectangular steel containers rising high above the huge vessel.

"Sadly, there was no time to get them out," Armanjani replied gruffly, sliding on a helmet and activating the attached mike. "Black dog. Repeat, Black dog, black!"

Almost instantly there was a muffled explosion from under the surface of the ocean, and the saltwater began to bubble furiously around the *Red Rose*.

Starting to list, the cargo ship shuddered as several explosions erupted, followed by several more, each louder than the one before. Jagged chunks of the steel hull were blown away like flaming meteors as black smoke poured from every hatchway and out of every shattered porthole.

Crumpling apart, the bridge collapsed to crash across the helipad. Then each of the lifeboats violently exploded, the blasts sending out wild coronas of broken oars, burning wooden planks and dense billowing smoke.

Four more Black Hawks lifted from the *Red Rose* as the colossal ship began to list to the side, the hundreds of thick chains holding the stacked containers in place loudly groaning as they started to stretch. A cargo container situated near the top slipped free from the restraints and tumbled into the ocean, the impact smashing it apart. A second container came loose, then another, as the weakening chains began to snap like overextended rubber bands, the loose ends whipping about to hammer open other containers, dent the deck and flatten the flexing gunwale. Rivets popped free like a hail of bullets, spreading the destruction as they ricocheted off the containers and the writhing deck.

Just then, a powerful detonation ripped open the

stern, the hull spreading wide to admit the rushing ocean. When the cold water hit the hot engines, there was a stentorian blast that split the *Red Rose* asunder from stern to bow.

As the speeding Black Hawk raced for the horizon, the floundering vessel broke apart to disappear below the waves, leaving behind only greasy oil to stain the choppy water.

"God be merciful, what a terrible way for them to die," Nasser said softly, deliberately not looking at anybody particular.

"I am not cruel, Fahada," Armanjani said, sitting back into the copilot's chair. "As the scuttling charges ignited, sleep gas was released into the rooms. The crew felt nothing as they perished."

Keeping her own counsel, the lieutenant said nothing. There was, of course, absolutely no way to confirm such a thing. Feeling a swell of sympathy, Nasser fought back the urge to say a prayer for the dead, wisely deciding that this was neither the proper time or place.

"Look, sir, somebody is alive down there!" Hassan cried out, craning his neck to point out a window behind the speeding helicopter.

"Go back!" Armanjani commanded gruffly, pulling a pair of binoculars from an overhead bin.

As the pilot swung the helicopter around, the major adjusted the focus of the binoculars and soon found a small group of swimmers. Struggling to escape from the powerful undertow of the sinking vessel, the sailors were bobbing about in the choppy Atlantic supported by their ridiculously oversize life jackets.

"How close are the other helicopters?" Armanjani demanded, glancing about the sky. He found the other Black Hawks.

"Too far away to reach them in time," Nasser said in a neutral tone. "And we can't carry all of them." She wasn't offering a suggestion or giving advice, merely stating a cold, hard fact.

"Yes, I see," Armanjani muttered, his face a mask of stone. "So be it, then. We have no choice."

Swiveling around, the major activated the GIAT 12.7 mm coaxial chain gun and coldly strafed the struggling figures in the water with high-velocity lead. As the waves turned red, the sailors stopped moving, and the major released the controls as if they were unclean.

This unplanned slaughter of his own troops made the man feel physically ill. There had certainly been enough helicopters for them to use for an escape. They had to have been delayed for some reason, going back to the barracks to retrieve personal items, or in the mounting confusion, they simply got lost in the maze of containers. It was a terrible waste. But then, bad timing had always killed more soldiers in combat than enemy gunfire. Strange, but true.

"Where now, sir?" the pilot asked, steadily maintaining their original course.

"Head for base," Armanjani directed, briefly checking the glowing GPS on the dashboard.

"Roger. Do I fly there directly, sir?" he asked, angling the helicopter into the new direction.

"Of course not!" the major snapped irritably as the other Black Hawks assumed formation around them. Then his tone softened. "Head north by northeast for three hundred kilometers, then turn due west. I have contacts that can help us with refueling and layovers. It is going to be a long journey."

"Once we reach the coast, head north for Penzance,"

Nasser added, pulling a folded map from a pocket and spreading it across a knee. "Be sure to stay at treetop level! Keep well below their radar, and do not use your own under any circumstances. No radar, GPS or anything else. Understand?"

With both hands on the yoke, the pilot gave a curt nod. "Dead reckoning only, yes, sir."

"I can jam their radar for several minutes," Khandis offered, patting a bulky leather bag on the deck.

"Which would quickly summon a flight of RAF jetfighters from London," Armanjani snapped. "No, Doctor, we must stay low."

"Once inland, I will direct you across the moors," Nasser added succinctly.

The pilot scowled at the unknown word. "Moors?"

"Swamps. We own a small farm in the hills. Land in the apple orchard. There will be a delivery van waiting for us inside a barn. From there we drive to the base."

"Yes, sir! What are my orders if we encounter the military?"

"Ignore them. These helicopters are registered to the American NSA, which has a secret base near Menwithhill."

Reaching up, Hassan opened a storage unit and extracted a compact MP-5 submachine gun. "And what about the police?" he asked, inserting a magazine and working the arming bolt.

"Same thing, ignore them. The local constables think we're smuggling out the local cheeses to sell them illegally in France. So the last thing they want to do is interfere with our business," the major said.

"Because we employ their friends and relatives?"

"Exactly."

"Besides, we're not doing anything criminal," Hassan said slowly. "Only the French are for refusing to admit the cheese." The sergeant felt a rush of pride. How easily the major turned the police into his servants.

"Smuggling cheese. Is this a joke?" the pilot asked hesitantly, unsure if he should laugh or not.

Tolerantly, the major chuckled, feeling the tension ease from the pit of his stomach. "No, this is not a joke. There is a century-old feud between France and England over how to make cheese. Something to do with the pasteurization. Honestly, who can understand such people?"

"Not me!" The pilot laughed, then dared to add, "If it can be told, sir, why is our base here, and not somewhere deep in the Amazon jungle?"

Giving a snort, Nasser started to answer, but Armanjani cut her off with a wave. "What do you know about England?"

"Pale women, good beer," the pilot answered immediately. "They are friends of Israel, hate the Irish, are excellent sailors..." He paused for a moment, then smiled. "And it rains there constantly!"

"Near enough. The nation is overcast almost the entire year long," Armanjani stated, leaning back in the chair to gaze out the bulletproof window. "What better location for the masters of the Scimitar?"

Jacksonville, Alabama

DISPOSING OF THEIR WEAPONS before leaving Ireland on a commercial jetliner, Bolan and his team caught some much-needed sleep on the way back to Miami. Arriving on schedule, they drove to the storage units outside town to rearm, then grabbed a fast shower at Monte-

negro's gym. After Kirkland reclaimed the G5, they
flew directly to the Huntsville Airport. The three of
them took a cab downtown and purchased a brand-
new Hummer. They wanted something tough enough
to handle the rugged hills of the southern badlands, but
also needed a vehicle clearly identified as American
to avoid creating any bad feelings among the locals.

The Hummer fitted both of those requirements.
However, in that poor a section of the state a new car
of any type would have drawn unwanted attention, so
Kirkland bought a roll of duct tape at a hardware store,
and freely decorated the outside of the vehicle, making
it seem old and battered. Montenegro added to the effect by kicking some dents into the doors, and Bolan
shot it a few times, the bullet holes in the bumpers
proclaiming the passengers weren't people to annoy
with due provocation.

"Any coffee left?" Bolan asked.

"Check the thermos," Montenegro said, passing
over the container. "Been a long day, eh, Matt?"

"It's far from over yet," he replied, pouring a steaming black cup.

The brew was strong and sweet and banished the
fog in his mind like a magic potion.

"Better get sharp, boys, we're almost there," Montenegro drawled in a Southern accent, as they drove
past a long row of farm stands on the side of the road.

Finishing off his coffee, Bolan checked his weapons
and forged documents. His was wearing patched work
clothes: cowboy boots, denim pants, flannel shirt and a
leather biker jacket. The Desert Eagle was tucked into
a cheap nylon shoulder holster, and a massive Bowie
knife was sheathed alongside his Confederate flag belt
buckle. Chained to his belt, an old leather wallet car-

ried identification for a Daniel Coyote, along with all of the proper permits for him to carry a concealed weapon.

Kirkland was in similar clothing, denim and flannel, with a leather bomber jacket, a pair of aviator sunglasses jutting out of a pocket. He had added a bushy mustache, attached to his upper lip with heavy-duty glue to make sure that it wouldn't come off accidentally, and a tinted contact lens made his left eye seem cloudy. The big-bore Webley was holstered behind his back, and a .31 Russian pistol was shoved into his garrison belt.

Reeking of cheap perfume, Montenegro was dressed in snakeskin cowboy boots, dark nylons and a short leather skirt that revealed everything but her political opinions. A black bra was easily seen through her white shirt, and her long hair had been frizzed into a blond afro that made her resemble a summer dandelion. Much of her exposed skin was covered with lewd tattoos—fake—some of them expertly done, while others were crude and seemingly made in prison with a sharpened pencil, cooking oil and candle soot.

She carried both Glocks in a double shoulder holster, the handles riding just below the swell of her breasts. The weapons were partially hidden by a green-and-gold windbreaker bearing the logo of a famous football team.

Just then, the Hummer flashed past a billboard advertising the All-American Diner, only five miles ahead.

"All right, at this point it would be smart to use only our cover names," Montenegro advised, using a pocket compact to add more blue eyeshadow. "Barrington is no fool, and might have people hidden in the woods to scan approaching traffic for inappropriate conversation."

"Paranoids always have lots of enemies," Kirkland muttered, stroking his mustache with a finger. "Or my name isn't Victor Layne. Just call me Tor!"

"Bouncing a maser off the window would be useless," Bolan said, pretending to cough. "I've had a Humbug running since we left the car dealer."

"Smart. But they can still use a telescope," she said from behind the compact, "and a lipreader."

"At this speed?" Bolan countered, looking at the forest of trees flash past. "Then again, better safe than sorry..." He waited.

"Loretta Elizabeth Snodie," Montenegro said, using a pinkie to slightly smear her red lipstick. "But you can call me Larry."

"Larry?"

"Larry."

"Not Etta?" Kirkland insisted. "Or Liz? Liz is a pretty name."

She scowled. "Larry!"

"Daniel Coyote knows better than to argue with an armed woman," Bolan replied, checking the magazine in the Desert Eagle. This was a replacement. The other gun had proved too badly damaged to trust in combat without extensive repairs.

Dan Coyote...as in Don Quixote? Kirkland chuckled while shifting gears to switch lanes. "You're as subtle as a sledgehammer, Dan."

"Thanks, Tor. I'll take that as a compliment."

"So tell me, Loretta," Kirkland asked with a playful smile, "are we engaged, or just fooling around?"

Looking in the tiny mirror of the compact, Montenegro fluffed her hair and gave no response.

Glancing over a shoulder, Kirkland sighed. "Let me rephrase that. Are we lovers…Larry?"

"Of course not, silly! You're both my sweet cousins," she replied, tucking away the compact. "That leaves me free to try to seduce Barrington if it becomes necessary."

Bolan scowled. Edgar Barrington was the man in charge of Swampfox Security, the richest man in the state, one of the richest in the nation.

Swampfox had been formed originally merely to guard his factories and warehouses, but Barrington soon expanded its duties to breaking up strikes, smashing the offices of his competition, destroying unwanted environmental reports and dealing bloody justice to anybody who dared to steal from his many business concerns, or simply get in Barrington's way.

Trained by former Green Berets and armed with the best weapons on the market, the men and women of Swampfox Security were soon working around the world guarding diplomats and debutantes, marshalling Red Cross food convoys, and rescuing kidnap victims. For all intents and purposes, "Barrington's Boys" were mercenaries who refused to attack anything. They only defended. That sounded good on paper and got them a lot of work. But in the real world, they were stone-cold killers, experts at extortion, demolition and torture.

Unlike so many other legitimate private security firms, Swampfox worked for anybody who could pay their price, no questions asked: presidents, kings or warlords. But if their fee wasn't paid on time, they did whatever was necessary to maintain the company cash flow, often leaving a long and bloody trail of bodies in their fiery wake.

"Just watch your ass, coz," Kirkland whispered.

"That son of a bitch is crazier than a rattlesnake with rabies."

Taking a pair of cheap glass earrings from a pocket, Montenegro clipped them into place. "We'll ignore the fact that reptiles can't get rabies. Only warm-blooded animals can, you putz."

"Which is why he's so crazy," Kirkland said with a frown, then loudly added, "Honestly, Dan, why do I have to keep explaining these things to her?"

"Just stupid, I guess," Bolan said, allowing the thick Massachusetts accent of his youth to return in full force.

"And exactly which of us is stupid?" Montenegro asked demurely, a slim hand resting on a Glock.

"I take the fifth." Bolan laughed, then his face darkened as the diner came into view. Showtime.

CHAPTER FOURTEEN

Mousehole, England

Amid a whirlwind of loose leaves, the Black Hawk gently landed in the apple orchard. Shoving aside the hatch, Armanjani and the rest of his people quickly disembarked so that the pilot could immediately leave again. A few seconds later, the second Black Hawk arrived to disgorge twenty Ophiuchus soldiers, panting and sweaty from the tight confines.

"Merciful God, we were like sardines in a can!" a corporal groaned, twisting and turning to ease his cramped muscles.

"Move the bags into the truck!" Major Armanjani commanded, jerking a thumb toward the barn. "We have no time to waste after such a long journey. The red switch disarms the bomb in the fuel tank, and the ignition key is under the floor mat."

As the soldiers staggered away with the suitcases and equipment bag, the third Black Hawk landed to repeat the process, but this time the pilot turned off the rumbling engines.

"What's wrong?" Nasser snapped, a hand on the 9 mm Tariq pistol hidden under her loose shirt.

"Something happened to the last helicopter," the

pilot reported, giving a crisp salute. "They lost power and went down off the Channel Islands."

"Were there any survivors?" Khandis asked, turning to face the southeast. "Maybe we could—"

"No need, they're dead now," the major said bluntly, tucking a small remote control back into his pocket.

Utterly horrified at the callous execution, Khandis started to speak, but then caught a stern glance from Nasser. "Such a pity we lost so many good men," he said, touching his lips, then his forehead in a ritual blessing.

"Merely the fortunes of war, Doctor," Armanjani replied, doing the same in reply. "They were brave men who now are in paradise."

"However, we're not dead!" Nasser announced loudly, drawing her weapon to work the slide. The noise caught the attention of everybody, as she knew it would. Grief had a way of clouding the mind and slowing the reflexes. Fear fixed that problem.

"I want all of the luggage packed neatly into the rear of the truck!" she continued, the pistol kept in plain sight. "Make sure the license plates are for this year, and break out the grenades in case we encounter any trouble on the way to the base!"

"Lieutenant, I thought the English police did not carry guns," a private asked with a smirk. "What trouble could they cause us?"

"They have radios, fool!" Nasser shot back. "The death of a single policeman would result in an air strike by the RAF!"

Having personally seen the Royal Air Force in action during several wars and rebellions, the private went pale and nodded.

"All right, you heard the lieutenant and know the drill!" Hassan added. "Move!"

Surging into action, the soldiers got to work, and only a few minutes later, the barn door was pulled open, and a big Atkinson truck rumbled out to start driving through the neat rows of trees. Nasser was at the wheel, with Hassan in the passenger seat of the cab, and Khandis sitting uncomfortably between them. Armanjani and everybody else was in the back with the stores of weapons, including heavy machine guns and flamethrowers. Nobody was expecting trouble, but the major knew it was prudent to prepare.

"Any sign of detection or pursuit?" Hassan asked, craning his neck to watch the sky overhead through the dusty window. His Atchisson autoshotgun was on the floor for easy access, but lying across his lap was a Carl Gustav rocket launcher hidden under a wool blanket.

"Give me a moment," Khandis replied, attaching a portable radar unit to the dashboard. As the screen came alive, the glowing arm swept around to display no blips of any kind. "Negative. The sky is clear."

At that precise moment, they heard a low rumble of thunder and it began to drizzle.

"In a manner of speaking," Nasser said with a wan smile.

Thankfully, traffic was light at that time of the day, which was just as well. The roads of Cornwall were narrow, designed for farm horses and specifically made too small for the war chariots of the invading Roman Empire two thousand years earlier. These days that lead to a unique form of driving etiquette in which one car would pull over to the side to allow another to pass. The complex social rules of these maneuvers were incomprehensible to Nasser, so she always yielded to the other cars. This merited her countless friendly waves, and more than a few scornful laughs for being inappropriately timid.

"I hate the English," Khandis muttered. He had a steel briefcase handcuffed to his wrist containing the access codes for the Scimitar, along with several pounds of primed high explosive. He had heard terrible rumors on television about what Scotland Yard did to Muslim prisoners to make them talk, and he would much rather die in a clean explosion than be slowly taken apart by their surgeons or raped by other prisoners. Death before dishonor!

Oddly, the fact that Khandis had done the exact same thing to countless other men and women for the Great Dictator had no effect whatsoever on his indignation or demeanor.

"Lieutenant?" Hassan asked softly, glancing at the steel wall that divided the cab from the cargo section of the truck.

"Is something wrong?" she asked, slowing to let a Royal Mail truck rattle past. The driver waved his thanks, and she smiled in return, then flashed him the finger.

"Did...did the major blow up the helicopter that sank?" Hassan asked.

"Of course!" Nasser replied curtly, keeping both hands on the wheel. "Why do you ask?"

"Did he also do the same thing to the other Black Hawks that managed to get us here, but then left intact?"

Such an insightful question from the uneducated sergeant startled the lieutenant. "Of course not!" Nasser replied. "We'll need those for the negotiations!"

"What negotiations?" the sergeant asked, confused.

"I will tell you later," she replied.

Leaving the village behind, the truck rumbled into the countryside, and Nasser had to constantly check the map as she zigzagged into the hills and finally reached an abandoned stone quarry.

A faded legal notice on a weathered sign announced the closure of the Hercules Granite Mine decades earlier, and a rusty steel chain blocked the entrance. Pulling out a remote control, Nasser pressed a button and continued driving. The chain dropped into the ground just before the truck's grille.

"Hopefully, nobody saw that," Khandis whispered softly.

"The area is completely deserted," she replied, as the chain rose behind them once more. "That is why the major chose it as our hardsite."

Dropping into a lower gear, Nasser started driving down a switchback road and zigzagged around the quarry.

"This is mined, correct?" Khandis asked, trying not to look out the window. The sheer edge of the road was only inches away, and the bottom of the quarry looked impossibly distant.

"Of course!" Nasser replied, steadily tapping the brakes. "The remote deactivated the mines. They will rearm once we are past. Anybody trying to follow us would never reach the fifty-foot mark alive."

"That sounds more than satisfactory," he said, closing his eyes.

"Afraid of heights?"

"No, just of dying."

Eventually circumnavigating the spiral down the face of the quarry, Nasser shifted back into high gear upon reaching the bottom. Giving a wide berth to a rocky drainage pool, she drove into a dark tunnel and switched on the headlights.

In the bright beams, Khandis could see that tunnel was actually a mine of some sort, the rough walls supported by thick wooden beams to prevent a collapse. Wooden flooring had been added to facilitate moving equipment. The dusty boards creaked under the weight of the truck, but none of them snapped or broke apart.

Never having been to this base before, Nasser was suitably impressed. Clearly, the major had taken everything into consideration for their arrival.

The tunnel went on for over a mile, constantly angling off in different directions, where the ancient Cornish miners had stubbornly followed the elusive vein of precious metal.

"What did they dig for anyway, gold or silver?" Hassan asked, a touch of excitement in his voice.

"Tin," Khandis replied, watching the rock wall flow past his window only inches away. He had researched the area thoroughly.

"Why did they need that?" the sergeant demanded skeptically.

"Tin is a component of bronze weapons," Dr. Khandis replied. "Knives, swords and such. But after that came bronze cannons, which changed the face of Europe, and were used all the way to the Napoleonic Wars."

"Plus the American Civil War," Nasser added.

The doctor frowned in disbelief. "Really?"

"Absolutely!"

"Steel is better." Hassan sniffed.

"True. But the British could not make decent steel at

that time. Nobody could!" Dr. Khandis smiled. "That is, except for the Persians and the Spanish."

"Why not dig for gold, then simply buy weapons from other people?"

"Because whoever controls the weapons controls your freedom," Nasser stated in a no-nonsense voice. "Weapons are the essence of liberty! There is no other reasonable way to measure, aside from counting the dead."

As the sunlight from the mouth of the tunnel dwindled in her sideview mirror, Nasser used a different button on the remote control once more, and there came a fast series of soft explosions. Buried charges threw a thick layer of dirt and debris along the tunnel, masking their passage, and making the mine appear as if it hadn't been visited for decades. There was even a smattering of bat guano, as well as several desiccated rats.

"I dislike being underground," Hassan said softly, touching a long jagged scar on his arm from a childhood accident. The sand dunes of the desert often shifted as if they were alive and considered humans their natural prey.

The doctor laughed. "Aside from the ozone vents for my equipment, there are numerous exits. We can leave any time we wish, day or night."

"Really?"

"Absolutely! The major guarantees it," Khandis said, glancing briefly sideways.

Saying nothing, Nasser returned the look, and the two of them held a fast, silent conversation before returning to the task at hand.

Reaching a dead end, Nasser slowed the truck to a crawl and gently nosed the grille against the rough-hewn wall as she'd been instructed. A section of the rock depressed with a loud click, then the rest slid aside to reveal a brick-lined tunnel illuminated by halogen bulbs. On either side of the tunnel was a Remington .50-caliber machine gun behind a sandbag nest, bulletproof riot shields stacked against the wall for the operators to use during a firefight.

"Ben Franklin," Nasser said proudly.

"Excuse me?" Khandis asked.

"The major is a fan of the American revolutionary Benjamin Franklin," she explained lugubriously. "He often said that to achieve success, you must first plan for failure."

"Hmm, very wise. Are you sure Mohammed didn't say that first?"

"Sorry, no, it was Franklin."

Inching the truck carefully inside the new tunnel, Nasser paused to let the false wall close behind them, then proceed down the passageway until they entered a spacious garage. There were several more Atkinson trucks parked along the far wall, along with numerous motorcycles, several forklifts, and a British-made Warrior APC fully armed with a 7.62 mm machine gun and a 30 mm cannon.

"How did *that* get down here?" Hassan asked, sounding almost scandalized by the presence of a motorized fighting vehicle this deep underground.

"How do you expect?" Nasser snorted. "Piece by piece."

In a corner of the garage were neat rows of tanks of pressurized oxygen, and off by itself was a softly humming industrial air cleaner. All of the indicator lights were green, showing that the CO_2 filter didn't need to be replaced yet, nor the dust filter or humidifier grid.

Parking the truck near a gas pump, Nasser turned off the engine, but left the keys in the ignition. With the tunnel blocked, there was no place to drive the vehicle anymore. They were trapped down here until further notice.

As everybody got out of the truck, Major Armanjani strode over to a wall phone and lifted the receiver. "Status report," he snapped.

Walking over to an iron railing, Hassan glanced down into darkness. "What's this?" he asked, the words echoing off the bare rock.

"Drainage ditch," Khandis answered, rubbing the skin under the handcuff. "There is always some minor seepage from the surrounding rivers and lakes."

The sergeant went pale. "Could the mine flood?" he asked in a small voice.

"No, we have too many pumping stations as protection," Nasser answered, slapping the man on the back. "Our biggest problem is rats."

"Rats?"

"They love to chew on the power cables," the major replied. "But we fixed that by coating them with poison and laying out hundreds of traps."

"Good to know," Hassan said uneasily. Ever since first hearing about the plan, he had tried not to think about this part. He hated small places, and couldn't even tolerant being inside the tight confines of an army tank. The air in the garage seemed thick, and it was difficult to breath, but Hassan said nothing. A weakness shown was only an invitation to be attacked.

"Thank you," Major Armanjani said, hanging up the phone, then he turned and smiled. "Excellent news! We are getting inquiries about the Scimitar!"

As everybody congratulated the major, he strode

from the garage, and they fell into line. The terrorists exited into a different corridor, where brick columns had been added to support the ceiling instead of simple wooden timbers. The rough-hewn rock had been sprayed with gunnite to prevent any water seepage, and help maintain the environment.

"What is this?" Hassan asked, running a hand over the smooth gray material covering the walls.

"Concrete, of a sort," Khandis said. "But reinforced with steel filaments and epoxy."

"And you just spray it on, like paint?"

"Blast it on is more correct. The gunnite comes out of the hose at 140 kilometers per hour."

"Amazing," Hassan muttered, stroking the material. "Think of what our people could do with this back in Iraq!"

"Unfortunately, it's very expensive," Nasser countered.

"But oil is free!" Hassan smiled. "Well, almost. At least to us it is."

Since the situation was too vastly complex to explain, Nasser said nothing in reply. Silence was starting to become her default position.

Just past a humming hydroelectric power station, the major turned into a side corridor and soon reached a steel door. Pressing his palm against a glowing plastic square, Armanjani impatiently waited, tapping the toe of his boot. A few seconds later, there was an angry buzz, then the door unlocked and cycled aside.

As they walked into the control room, everybody had a brief flash of déjà vu. The control room was almost identical to the one on the *Red Rose,* except that the riveted steel walls had been replaced with gunnite, and there was no porthole, only another industrial air

cleaner as well as several potted plants, the ferns swaying gently in the breeze from the cleaner.

The air was cool and dry in here, the ceiling covered with bright halogen lights, which illuminated a
series of workbenches. There was a coat rack next to
a weapons cabinet full of AK-47 assault rifles, boxes
of ammunition and stacks of 30 mm grenades. Boxes
of U.S. Army MRE food packs stood stacked in neat
rows, more than enough food to feed the entire staff
for a month.

"Most impressive," Nasser said, brushing back her
hair. "We could stay down here for a month if necessary!"

"For years," Armanjani corrected. "But if all goes
well, we'll be leaving in two days."

"Has a sale been made already, sir?" Hassan asked
eagerly.

"Let's see," Khandis said, resuming his usual position at the control board. Making all of the equipment
identical was extremely clever. During an emergency,
he wouldn't have to search for a particular button or
switch. He knew exactly where everything was located. The man felt sure that he could operate the console in total darkness.

"Well?" Armanjani asked, going to the kitchenette
and starting to make tea.

"We *are* getting offers," Khandis said, adjusting
the controls. "But only a few of them are legitimate."

"Tell me the top five."

"The Mafia says that it is interested, but insists on
a face-to-face meeting, as does North Korea."

"The first is a trap, the second a lie," Armanjani
said in dismissal, starting to heat the water.

"Sir, they all want to meet in person."

"I have no problem with that. There is a nice little village in Portugal that will serve us well for just such a purpose. But I suspect the Mafia is a trap. They wouldn't have the funds."

"I see. That leaves only the Chinese Red Star and the Hammer of Saudi Arabia."

"They both have the funds for Scimitar, so both are potential customers." The major chuckled, carefully measuring the tea.

The Red Star was the infamous counterintelligence agency for the communist Chinese, and the Hammer was the nickname of the GIP—the General Intelligence Presidency, which was the main intelligence agency of the Royal Saudi government.

"What aren't you telling us, Doctor?" Nasser asked.

"Both of them wish a demonstration, something we announce in advance of the attack."

"They do understand that this is a weather-based weapon system?" the major asked.

"Of course, sir! But still…"

"What kind of money are they talking?"

"Red Star won't discuss that without a demonstration first," Khandis read from the monitor, "While the Hammer has offered an opening bid of fifty million."

"Euros, francs or dollars?"

"U.S. dollars."

"Bah, not enough," Armanjani replied, inspecting a mug. "All right, give them a demonstration, and get that price up to where it belongs."

"I'll assume you want something in America?"

"Where else?"

"Yes, sir. I'll bring up the feed now."

While the tea samovar began to bubble softly, Armanjani went to the wall monitor and studied the real-time weather patterns of the North American continent. There were good clouds over Ontario, useless as a target, but also decent rain storms near Kansas and Florida. However, there was nothing worth hitting there aside from some nuclear missile silos and NASA. He needed something big this time, something startling, that would garnish new coverage from around the world.

Just then, the weather patterns shifted into a new formation, and the major broadly smiled. "Hit that," he commanded, pointing at the target with a finger.

"Are you serious?" Khandis whispered, both hands poised above the keyboard.

"Burn it to the ground, Doctor! Hit it with everything we've got!" Armanjani growled, pouring himself a mug of tea. "And don't stop until I tell you to."

CHAPTER FIFTEEN

Jacksonville, Alabama

Flanked by a gas station and a car wash, the All-American Diner was unusually large for such a remote location. Bolan knew that was because the establishment didn't depend on drive-by traffic for its supply of customers. The diner was owned by Edgar Barrington and specialized in catering to the needs of his personal army. Rumor said that the cigars sold at the counter contained marijuana, and that there was a brothel in the basement. But neither the DEA nor the FBI had ever been able to prove the allegations.

Pulling into the parking lot, Kirkland braked to a halt away from the other cars and trucks. "All ashore that's going ashore!"

As Bolan got out of the Hummer, he heard bluegrass playing softly from a radio in one of the big rigs. The air smelled of diesel fumes and sweet dogwood, the combination taking him to happier times and places for a brief moment.

Taking her time, Montenegro climbed out of the Hummer. "Nice place. I like it!" she drawled, hoisting her bra into a more comfortable position. "Whadda they serve?"

"Food," Kirkland muttered dourly, slamming the door and locking it before heading up the front walk.

Knowing that anybody new would be noticed immediately, Bolan and the others had decided to use that to their advantage, and made sure they weren't very good at hiding their assorted weaponry.

Several of the truckers went silent as Bolan and Kirkland approached, then their attention switched to Montenegro and they openly grinned in frank appreciation.

"The boys seem to like your 44s," Kirkland whispered, politely holding open the door.

Walking past, Montenegro hit him with an elbow. "Dope, they're both 9 mm."

"He wasn't talking about your guns, coz," Bolan added, bring up the rear.

In spite of the number of cars parked outside, the diner was relatively empty. A few truckers sat at a small bar in the back knocking down beer and shots, while a burly giant was loudly slurping soup from a china bowl.

"Hey, folks, table or booth?" a waitress said in casual greeting as if she did the exact same thing ten thousand times a day. There was a pencil stuck behind her ear, and a worn plastic name tag on her breast said Dottie.

"A table far from the washroom," Bolan said, trying to sound exhausted as he stretched to pop a couple of joints.

"Been driving long?" Dottie asked with a knowing smile.

"All of my damn life." Bolan laughed, then he tried to appear embarrassed. "Oh, sorry, Dottie, no offense meant."

"None taken. I hear worse every fucking day," Dot-

is my cousin Victor Layne and my cousin Loretta Snodie."

"Hey, there. Roger Dupree."

Everybody at the table was suddenly alert.

"Come again?" Kirkland asked politely, a hand inching closer to the Webley.

"Dupree, Roger Dupree," the tall man said awkwardly. "Do you folks know me or something?"

"No, but we have a friend in Miami with the exact same name," Montenegro said slowly, deliberately not looking at Bolan.

Just a coincidence. Unnerving, but such things happen even to the best laid plans.

"Mind if a join ya?" Dupree asked.

"Have a seat," Kirkland said, pushing out a chair with his shoe.

"Thanks!" Dupree said, hunkering down.

Trying not to be obvious, he stole a glance at Montenegro, and she smiled in return, putting just enough voltage into it to generate some interest, but not cause a complete meltdown. Dupree responded by shifting his chair a little closer.

Introductions were made as Dottie delivered the coffee, plus a wicker basket of sweet rolls. It was clear that she wanted to speak further with Kirkland, but one look at Dupree, and she hurried away.

"What was that about?" Kirkland asked curiously, sampling a roll.

"Former girlfriend," Dupree said sheepishly. "We're really not supposed to date the staff here, ya know. But…" He made a vague gesture in the air.

"Boys will be boys," Montenegro supplied helpfully.

"After a tour, a man needs a little R & R," Dupree offered as an apology.

"Hey, you must be one of Barrington's Boys!" Bolan exclaimed, trying to sound excited.

"Bet your ass I am!" Dupree boasted proudly. "Anybody hauling iron in this part of the state is a brother, you better believe that. Even the cops. When did you folks join?"

"Haven't yet," Montenegro said, spooning some sugar. "But that's why we're here."

"Oh! You folks looking for work?"

"If Swampfox is hiring?" Kirkland said as a question, adding milk to his mug.

"Hell, yes! We always need a few more men on the line," Dupree said. "What with all of the crazy stuff happening in the Middle East."

Then he paused uncertainly. "However, the boss doesn't like ladies on the front line, and I'm not sure how well-fixed we are for nurses, cooks and such." Under the table, he patted her knee. "Sorry, Loretta."

"Not a problem, sweetie." Montenegro smiled.

"Etta here is one of the best smiths you'll ever see," Bolan said.

"You're a gunsmith?" Dupree asked in obvious delight and disbelief.

Munching on a honey bun, Montenegro smiled. "There are damn few guns that I can't rebuild or repair." Which was an outright lie.

"Can you prove it?" Dupree asked in a friendly challenge.

Drinking coffee, Bolan flexed his free hand, flashing five fingers, then two.

"Not a problem," Montenegro stated. "Your sidearm is a Glock 17, not the Model 18 machine pistol."

Reaching for a sweet roll, Dupree dropped his jaw. "How the fuck… I mean, shitfire…that is… I… sorry."

The man radiated embarrassment. "Loretta, how can you possibly know that? The 17 and 18 are absolutely identical! Glock deliberately made 'em that way!"

"I use the same gun," Montenegro said, gesturing toward the weapons tucked under her breasts. "And yours doesn't have enough wear on the barrel."

"Told you she was good," Bolan said, taking a sip of coffee.

"Damn!" Dupree laughed, reaching out to pat her wrist. "You're correct, this is a 17. Hellfire, girl, the quartermaster could really use a smithy like you at Gibraltar."

"Where? The Rock of Gibraltar?" Montenegro asked, searching among the artificial sweeteners for some real sugar. "Isn't that on the island of Malta or something? Like halfway around the world?"

"Not that one," Dupree laughed. "Gibraltar is just what we call our base out in the swamp. Man, you should see it! The place is a real hardsite. There's barb wire, video cameras, dogs, land mines, the whole magilla. We could hold off those idiots in the National Guard for years without breaking a sweat."

"Not much of a challenge there," Kirkland said, the National Guard tattoo on his arm feeling oddly uncomfortable under his shirt, as if it was itching to come out into public view.

"Yeah, you got that right!" Dupree chortled. "What do we care about those weekend warrior types? Hell, there's even a SAM bunker hidden in the..." He stopped short. "Sorry, not supposed to talk about that."

"Talk about what?" Bolan said puzzled.

Dupree furrowed his brow then smiled. "You're quick, Dan. Quick and smart. Damn, it was lucky bumping into you folks today!"

"For many reasons," Montenegro whispered, stirring the sugar around in her mug.

Grinning as if he had just won the lottery, Dupree squared his shoulders. "Now, you folks come see me on Monday! I'll take you straight to the boss myself!"

"And collect a nice bounty for the new recruits?" Kirkland asked with a knowing wink.

"Hey, a man's got to make a living," Dupree said, glancing at Montenegro. "Hope you don't mind waiting until then. What, ah, hotel you staying at?"

"Why can't we go now?" Montenegro asked, side-stepping the question. She wasn't overly worried about his amorous intentions. Southern men were an odd mixture of courtly knights and horn dogs. If Dupree went too far, she'd knock him unconscious and he'd have all the more respect for her as a proper lady when he woke in the hospital.

"Shoot, honey, there's nobody's at the base today!" Dupree said, gesturing around the empty diner. "The boss sends most of us out on field maneuvers every couple of weeks. Keeps us sharp." He shrugged, using both hands. "Just bad timing, I guess."

"Timing is everything," Bolan agreed.

"Why aren't you on maneuvers with everybody else?" Montenegro asked, looking the man directly in the eyes, while toying with her necklace.

"Somebody's got to stand guard," Dupree said proudly, his attention flickering back and forth. "I only came out for dinner. MRE packs will keep you alive, but—"

"But they're dogfood compared to our pork chop special!" Dottie announced, arriving with a tray loaded with steaming dishes. "Make some room there, people! These ain't daisies, you know!"

Quickly, the table was cleared and everybody dug into the food with gusto. The plates were almost overflowing—no skimpy meals at the All-American Diner.

The food was delicious, and nobody spoke again for a while until the initial rush ebbed. Then the conversation drifted away from business and into more neutral subjects: cars, guns and sports. By unspoken agreement among the men, their favorite topic, women, was strictly forbidden with a lady at the table.

As expected, Dupree kept flirting with Montenegro, until she decided the timing was right, then she pretended to misunderstand a compliment, and moved her chair away from the man in icy silence. Closing ranks, Bolan and Kirkland shifted positions to flank Montenegro.

Flustered, Dupree tried to regain lost ground but soon saw that the battle was over, and paid for the entire meal as a parting gesture before leaving the diner and climbing into a Range Rover.

As soon as the man drove away, Bolan and the others added a generous tip to the bill, then exited to their car, and drove off in the opposite direction.

"Okay, that got us the intel I had hoped for," Bolan said, steering with one hand, while turning on the Humbug. "Everybody is gone, and the base is down to a skeleton crew."

"Still won't be a piece of cake," Kirkland stated, furiously scratching his mustache. "We ghosting this time again? Shadows in the night?"

"We hit and git. All that matters is finding those files on Amir Bull."

"Now you're talking," Montenegro said, taking off the earrings and rubbing some circulation back into the aching lobes. It was a wonder that so many women got their ears pierced. "All right, I can jam the proximity sensors, sonar and land mines easily enough. I brought along enough equipment to invade the Pentagon. But what about those dogs he mentioned?"

"I hate shooting dogs in the first place," Kirkland stated, "and unless it's a clean kill they howl loud enough to wake up the whole state."

"There's a tranquilizer rifle in the back," Bolan said, turning onto a dirt road. "Along with some BZ grenades."

Surprised by that, Kirkland paused in the act of removing his contact lens. "Now, I thought the Army stopped making those years ago?"

"I know a guy who knows a guy."

"Don't we all," Montenegro said, unfolding a map of the state. "Okay, if we follow this road for another fifty miles, we'll come to the Tonawanda Wetlands."

"Swamp."

"Wetlands. There's an alligator farm near the entrance. We should be able to steal an airboat there and swing around the edge of the swamp until we reach Gibraltar from the far side."

"ETA?" Bolan asked.

"Depends on how good the security system is at the farm." She smiled.

"Do you really think they have any security," he asked, "aside from a thousand hungry gators?"

"No. So we should hit the base around midnight, maybe one o'clock."

"Groovy," Kirkland said, putting the contact lens back into a case. "By the way, how the hell did you know that Glock was a 17? They're identical to the machine pistol version."

"There was only one spare clip on his belt," Bolan

said. "An 18 goes through an entire clip in two seconds flat. Nobody but an idiot would carry only one spare."

"He might have been an idiot," Kirkland said, then turned to Montenegro, "and don't ask if I have any relatives down here."

"The thought never crossed my mind," Montenegro replied, unable to stop a smile.

A few miles later, Bolan saw a turnoff for the Tonawanda Wetlands. Heading that way, he soon spotted a billboard advertising Alie's Gator Farm! Cute, he thought.

Driving the Hummer off the dirt road, the Executioner parked inside a grove of banyon trees where the vehicle would be out of sight of any passing traffic.

"By the way, does anybody remember exactly how to kill an alligator?" Kirkland asked, testing the edge of a Gerber knife on the ball of a thumb.

"Very quickly," Montenegro said, sliding clips of armor-piercing rounds into both of her Glocks.

Packing their equipment into waterproof bags, the team discussed tactics while donning black ghillie suits, smearing on camouflage paint and putting fresh batteries into the UV lasers.

"Ready?" Bolan asked.

Kirkland smirked. "I was born ready."

"That must have been quite a surprise for your mother." Montenegro smiled.

"My dad, too!"

Leaving the Hummer unlocked and the keys in the ashtray, just in case they returned with armed troops in hot pursuit, Bolan and the others then eased into the bushes. Minutes later, an airboat drifted away from the wooden dock of the gator farm to disappear into the approaching night.

CHAPTER SIXTEEN

Cheyenne Mountain, Colorado

It was a beautiful day, the sun was shining, the sky was blue and there wasn't a cloud in the sky. However, inside NORAD the atmosphere was tense, and nobody spoke above a hushed whisper. The smell of black coffee was almost tangible, and everybody was armed.

The War Room was the heart of NORAD, the nerve center of the North American Aerospace Defense Command. The front wall was a triptych of screens. The left showed Europe, the middle screen showed the North American continent, and the left showed whoever was considered a threat. For thirty years, that had been the Soviet Union. Nowadays it was sometimes North Korea, sometimes China, and for a brief few months it had shown Iraq. Enemies came in many shapes and sizes.

The ceiling and walls were a flat black, the floor a dark reflectionless terrazzo. Banks of consoles curved before the three screens. There were a dozen of them in each line, and three layers deep. Busy technicians from every branch of the armed forces were working away at the twinkling controls, constantly whispering into their throat mikes to keep a moment by moment running communication to the duty officers, who in turn relayed the info to the Joint Chiefs of Staff and the White House.

The right wall was covered with clocks showing the precise time in every major city around the world. The left had a scattering of screens showing the worldwide weather, and the Stick, the indicator that showed the status of America. Only a few hours ago, the President had ordered it moved up to DefCon Two. DefCon Five meant open warfare. But as yet there was no known enemy.

Currently, a massive central monitor displayed a map of the world marking every known lightning strike where a death had occurred. White for civilians, red for military, green for politicians.

Since its inception, the War Room had always been noisy and busy, endlessly full of people coming and going, delivering reports. But that was good. Noise meant personal conversations, yawning, jokes. The louder the room was, the more peaceful and secure was America. At the moment, the War Room of Cheyenne Mountain was dead silent.

Located at the rear of the huge room, two generals and an admiral were standing behind the visitor railing where tourists used to come to gawk at the technological might of America. That wasn't allowed anymore for security reasons, but the facilities were still in place, and now congressmen and senators took tours and stood behind the railings while armed guards stood by and watched the movements of everybody and anybody inside the Hill.

"How's the *Esteem?*" an Army general asked, standing at attention behind the old visitor railing. Both hands were clasped behind his back.

"Out of danger," an Air Force general replied.

"North Korea got twitchy until the Chinese arrived, then they stood down and backed off."

"Meaning that we now have to thank the Chinese for their assistance?" a Navy admiral asked.

"I'm afraid so."

"Thank God it won't be me," the admiral muttered.

Suddenly, there was a strange flash of light on the monitor showing the main access road.

"What was that?" the admiral demanded with a scowl.

"Maybe just a glitch in the equipment," a brigadier general suggested, looking up from his clipboard.

Then it came again, out of the clear blue sky, a lightning bolt arched over the Rocky Mountains to directly hit a U.S. Army 6x6 driving toward the entrance to the underground base. The entire vehicle exploded as it was sent sailing away to crash in the decorative flowerbed edging the front of the massive underground base.

"Here we go!" the admiral bellowed, just as a dozen sirens started to howl a warning. But then, almost as quickly, the light came again, and the sirens were blasted off the poles around the base, one at a time, like firecrackers on a string.

"Primary satellite dish is gone, sir," an Air Force lieutenant reported calmly from her console. "Switching to secondary…secondary is gone. It exploded the instant it went live."

"All right, damn it, switch to the—"

"Gone, sir! As well as the next, and the off-site dish, and… We're blind."

A split second later, all of the monitors flickered and went dark.

"Son of a bitch!" the admiral growled. "All right,

use the underground land lines and switch control of the defense grid to Space Command."

"Sir, we… I mean, you don't have the authorization to do that," the lieutenant began hesitantly, then nodded. "Confirm, sir. Fuck the rules. Switching control now!"

"Good man," the admiral said in highest praise.

The Air Force general leaned closer. "He'll be dishonorably discharged by tomorrow."

"If we live that long," the admiral said. "Okay, America is saved. Now what about us?"

"What do you think? We fight!"

"How do you fight lightning?"

"Fire the northwest SAMS!" the Army general ordered.

"At what, sir?" a Marine corporal asked, both hands poised above the controls.

"At the storm, you fool! Lightning isn't alive, it can't think or dodge!"

Her face eased with understanding. "Aye, aye, sir!" the Marine corporal replied, her hands flashing across the console.

Only seconds later, eight missiles streaked up from the hidden battery. Almost instantly, lightning flashed down, and one of the missiles exploded in midair. As the stormy sky rumbled, another bolt slashed downward, and a second missile was destroyed, then a third, and fourth. But the rest penetrated the cloud cover.

"By God, it worked!" the Army general gasped. "Get that bunker reloaded, and start firing everything we have, in random patterns!"

Just then, a lightning bolt flashed across the clear sky to slam directly into the closed door of the underground base. Thicker than a man was tall, the truncated slab of metal quivered from the hit, but nothing more occurred.

Then another lightning bolt hit, closely followed by a dozen more, each bolt coming faster and with greater accuracy. Suddenly, a dozen meters on a control board flashed into the red, and whole sections of the internal power grid went dark. Then the monitor went dark.

"Switching to secondary cameras!" a major announced.

"The door is holding!" an Army colonel reported in a tight voice. "But the EM field is leaking through."

"Why, in the name of God?" the Air Force general demanded.

The major spun in the chair. "Sir, we're designed to withstand a direct nuclear attack. That only lasts a few seconds at the longest. Everything else is much weaker, shrapnel, heat corona...." He gestured. "But these bolts last for several seconds, that last one maintained for almost seven seconds."

A sharp pain went through the admiral's head. The world-famous, nuke-proof door to NORAD High Command wasn't tough enough to stop a lightning storm?

"What are our chances of survival if the front door fails?" a colonel asked.

"Zero point zero," a lieutenant replied brusquely.

The colonel grunted in acceptance. "Okay, start escorting the nonessential personnel into the escape tunnel!"

"We'll never get them all out in time, sir!" the lieutenant countered, then stood tall. "But I'll do my best!'

"Good man!"

Just then, lightning hit the front door again, the crackling bolt staying there for much longer than anybody thought possible. Then the monitor again went black.

"Switching to long-range cameras," the major said slowly, throwing a fast series of switches on the console. The screen came alive once more with a picture of the entire base. Then the picture zoomed in to focus only on the front entrance.

The titanic door was burned and battered, with wide gouges in the surface over a foot deep. The concrete apron in front was littered with glowing red droplets of molten steel. A charred corpse lay nearby but it was impossible to tell if it was a man or a woman, much less their rank or service.

"All right, fire one missile, repeat just one missile, every four seconds!" the Air Force general bellowed, gripping the railing. "And send out troops with cell phones through the emergency exit! Have them call for assistance from every air force base in the western U.S.!"

"We're going to need a shitload of missiles to last out this storm!" the Army general muttered, rubbing an old scar.

"And if the missiles don't work, sir?" a corporal asked with a worried expression.

"Then it has been my honor to serve with everybody here," the general said softly, the words carrying throughout the entire vast control room.

Tonawanda Wetlands, Alabama

THE ROAR OF THE AIR BOAT was nearly deafening as it streaked across the murky water. The flat-bottomed keel skimmed over sunken logs, alligators, sandbars, and flashed through thick forests of reeds and weeds.

The air was thick with earthy smells, most of them unpleasant, and insects swarmed around the hurtling machine as if they knew in advance that bloody meals always accompanied such a fearsome racket.

Still riding high on their hearty meal, nobody felt like grabbing a few winks, so Bolan and the others discussed in detail how to find the secret files, and what to do with Edgar Barrington afterward. Montenegro favored turning him over to the FBI, while Bolan had a vastly different idea.

"There's no chance we'll get any assistance from the local police," Kirkland stated. "I'm not even sure that the governor could send in the National Guard against Barrington. He's too well connected."

"And that's not even considering that fact that the bastard has more guns and helicopters than the FBI," Bolan said. "He even has a tank."

"A Panzer, perhaps? Or maybe a nice Sherman?" Kirkland asked hopefully.

"Nope. He has an Abrams M1A, and in full working condition. Officially, it's an exhibit for a military museum."

"An Abrams." Kirkland sighed. "That'll get the job done, sure enough."

"Brognola could call in the Air Force for a bombing run, but there could be innocent civilians inside the compound."

"Besides, it would reveal too much to Major Armanjani if he heard about it on the news."

"My, my, Barrington really has carved himself out quite a nice little kingdom in this fetid swamp," Montenegro said thoughtfully.

"Sure has," Bolan agreed, checking the magazine in the Desert Eagle. "Now let's take it away from him."

Skirting along the edge of the swamp, or the wetlands as the U.S. government preferred to call the place, the team spotted dozens of burned-down shacks, what remained of the structures riddled with bullet holes.

"It would appear that Edgar does not like neighbors," Kirkland stated, slathering more insect repellant along his arms and across his nape.

"Considering what he does for a living, would you?" Montenegro retorted, trying to ignore how her hair was rapidly expanding in every direction at the same time.

"Try this," Bolan suggested offering a black ski cap.

With no small amount of tugging, and a liberal use of inventive cursing, Montenegro finally got the woolen cap in place, her brilliant explosions of yellow hair properly under wraps. Almost instantly, she began sweating profusely.

"After a couple of hours of this, the alligators will come swarming after me," she muttered, tying a handkerchief across her forehead as a crude bandanna. "They like their meat ripe and reeking."

"So, no significant change to your general demeanor, then?" Kirkland said.

Spinning, Montenegro jabbed him in the ribs with an elbow. He grunted at the blow, but pretended it hadn't happened.

As midnight approached, Bolan finally throttled down the airboat, and the craft decelerated naturally until it was relatively motionless again. Drifting close to a mud island, Bolan stepped ashore and used his Gerber knife to hack down some saplings, then trim them into barge poles. Climbing back onto the airboat, he passed one to Kirkland and the two men started the long, slow process of stabbing the pole down into the water at the front of the craft, then walking the pole to the back, pushing with all of their might to make the craft slide a few scant inches forward.

Sitting on the dirty deck, Montenegro had her equipment bag open and was carefully monitoring for any live or passive sensors in the water or mud or hidden among the thick plants. So far, she had only found a few sonic fishing lures, the type that were sold on cable TV for a low-low introductory price, and were generally less useful than a flare gun for actually catching fish.

This deep in the swamp, the water was an oily deep black, impenetrable to their flashlights and thicker than porridge. How the countless underwater creatures lived in the muck was anybody's guess. But they constantly saw fish darting just below the surface, frogs hopping along the muddy banks and huge snapping turtles sitting like rocks among the reeds and aquatic plants. They seemed harmless enough, but everybody knew the jaws of the turtles were powerful enough to remove someone's hand in a single bite.

There was no indication of the countless alligators known to inhabit the swamp. They lived down deep in the mire, hidden and slow, lazy leather logs until violently exploding into deadly action.

Clusters of weeds and dense curtains of Spanish moss hung off every tree, sometimes making it difficult to know where the swamp ended and the land began.

"Why did I ever leave Miami?" Montenegro said, fine-tuning the controls on her scanners. Her shirt was thoroughly soaked, the fabric sticking to her figure.

"What, and miss this pleasant little tour of hell?"

Kirkland asked with a wide grin, yanking the sapling free from the sticky swamp bottom. A creature stirred.

With a mightly lunge, a hissing alligator tried to climb into the boat.

Guns were out of the question, the noise would travel for miles, so Bolan rammed the Gerber knife directly into the left eye of the swamp monster, trying for the brain, while Kirkland did the same thing to the tiny, almost hidden ear hole. Whipping out a military stun gun, Montenegro shoved the device into the creature's open mouth. A terrible light flashed as a half-million volts crackled into operation.

Going stiff, the alligator exhaled deeply as it slid backward into the swamp and sank from sight.

"Think we killed it?" Montenegro asked, squinting to try to see into the syrupy morass below.

"Absolutely," Kirkland replied, wiping his knife clean. "Go check, and we'll wait here."

"You first," she muttered, never taking her gaze off the oily surface of the swamp.

"It's dead. But more importantly, we can use the presence of the gator to our advantage," Bolan said, pushing an anchor over the side. The concrete block hit with a splash and settled to the bottom.

Outraged birds called out from the trees, a green snake slithered past the boat, and somewhere in the distance an alligator bawled.

Checking over the equipment, and especially their weapons, the three people slipped into the black liquid. The water rose only to their waists, but the bottom of the swamp was incredibly slippery. It was like trying to walk across marbles.

"Stay sharp for sink holes," Bolan said. "They sometimes go thirty feet deep."

"If you go down," Montenegro added, "just exhale a little and follow the bubbles. Those will lead you to safety."

All of the assorted creatures in the swamp became quiet at the approach of the humans, and several birds took flight as the team passed. That was a dead giveaway that outsiders were near, but since there was nothing they could do about it, Bolan and the others continued onward, staying alert for trouble under the black water and danger from above.

"Rumor has it there are land mines hidden in the mud, along with motion detectors and sonar sensors."

"There hasn't been anything detected so far," Montenegro said, constantly checking the EM scanner in her hand. "But then with all of the wildlife in this swamp, the guards would be out here every ten minutes thinking it was an invasion of Navy SEALs, or maybe a herd of elephants."

"So, we're safe?"

"Well, I didn't say that," Montenegro demurred as the meter on the scanner flickered, indicating a proximity sensor under the water.

Moving fast, she locked on to the pulse, duplicated it, and bounced it right back. For one long second, she thought the trick didn't work, then the needle on the meter dropped to the side, showing no presence of a live magnetic field. Whew!

Taking the lead, Montenegro wandered them all about the swamp, dodging land mines and sensors. If too many of the devices stopped working that would be as bad as one of them going off. There had to be no pattern to their approach. Chaos was the key to safety.

A long mile passed in silence before they gratefully walked out of the swamp and onto dry land.

Staying low in the bushes, Bolan and the others crept forward to peer out from between the prickly leaves. The interlacing tree branches blocked the moonlight, so they slipped on night-vision goggles and dialed for computer augmentation. Instantly, the darkness vanished, replaced by a clean green-and-white view of the Alabama wetlands.

"Target acquired," Bolan whispered, giving a brief smile.

Directly across a small inset of swamp was a smooth concrete wall that continued for hundreds of yards in both directions until eventually curving away out of sight. The base of the wall was studded with sharp spikes, several of them adorned with the rotting carcass of some small animal. Bare electric wires topped the wall, and the sides were festooned with coils of concertina wire.

Tall wooden guard towers rose on the other side, and they were equipped with searchlights and heavy machine guns. But the towers seemed to be empty, at the moment, anyway.

"What's over there?" Bolan asked, turning on his night-vision goggles.

"Sewer pipe," Montenegro stated, adjusting the controls on the handheld scanner. "But don't go near it! The interior is packed with Claymore mines rigged with sensors to blow if anything registering human temperature gets close."

"Can you jam them?" Kirkland asked.

She snorted. "Not all at the same time."

"And the front gate would be suicide," Kirkland said, then he turned. "Which means it's up to you, Tarzan."

Nodding, Bolan dug about in the equipment bags

until finding what he wanted. Climbing into the top branches of a banyan tree, he prepared a crossbow, aimed and fired. Whizzing through the night, the arrow slammed into another tree inside the compound, a black line trailing loosely behind. When nobody responded to the presence of the line, Bolan quickly hooked the crossbow onto the tree and cinched the line tight. Then he slipped on a pair of leather gloves and stepped off the branch. Silently, he slid down the zipline, passing over the wall and going past the guard tower. When he was near the end, Bolan let go and hit the ground in a roll, coming to a stop on his feet, a gun in his hand.

"Holy shit, who the fuck are you?" a man demanded, casting away a lit cigarette. He was wearing the uniform of Swampfox Security, and was carrying a holstered automatic, radio, tear-gas canister and a taser.

Kicking the man in the throat, Bolan took the stun gun away from the choking guard and zapped him twice in the chest before dragging the unconscious body into the bushes. A few minutes later Kirkland arrived, closely followed by Montenegro.

Bolan and the others studied the rows of buildings edging a central courtyard. All of them were dark and silent, but when they switched their goggles to infrared, the buildings glowed with hot spots. One large rectangular building showed numerous people lying down in neat rows. Clearly, that was the barracks.

The next building was the armory, the body heat of a large pack of guard dogs dimly illuminating the racks of assault rifles, rocket launchers and just about everything else imaginable.

Then they found a small brick building, centrally located, with a pole flying the American flag, as well as the flag of Swampfox Security. There were iron bars on every window, the front door was sheathed in steel, and the entire building was tightly enclosed in a web of UV beams, trip wires and proximity sensors.

"Could be the officer's club?" Kirkland asked, loosening both of his pistols. The big-bore Webley had joined with a Tokarev trauma pistol, a nasty weapon that fired rubber bullets using a half charge of powder. They hit with the force of a baseball bat and broke bones almost every time.

"Only one way to find out," Bolan replied, easing forward.

The security was good, but not perfect, and in only a few minutes, they were inside the building and moving through the stygian darkness. The lower levels were office space, with lots of desks and manual typewriters, but no file cabinets, wall safes or computers.

"Collar or cuffs?" Montenegro asked, deactivating an ultraviolet laser beam zigzag across a flight of stairs.

In the movies, spies and thieves would use a mirror to redirect the beams. But that didn't work in the real world. Well, not anymore. It worked for years, then computers got better, the sensors more sensitive, and if fifty percent of a beam failed to reach the target receptor, the alarms sounded, and the antipersonnel mines automatically detonated.

"Cuffs," Bolan decided. "The way I read Barrington is that he would always want to look down upon his kingdom."

"Zeus on high, eh?" Kirkland said softly. "Then show us the way, fearless leader."

Proceeding up the wooden stairs, Bolan kept his weight on the extreme ends where the wood would be the strongest and the least likely to creak. The second floor proved to only be a dining hall, the third was an indoor shooting range, and the door to the fourth floor opened onto a living room, complete with entertainment center, fish tank and fireplace. The walls were covered with gilded certificates of achievement for Edgar Barrington, sports trophies for the man, and a lot of framed pictures with him shaking hands with movie stars and famous politicians.

"I think my nose is going to start bleeding the air is so thin in here," Kirkland muttered.

Suddenly, Bolan held up a closed fist. Instantly, Kirkland and Montenegro went silent. Across the living room, an open doorway showed a kitchen, and a thin beam of light was coming from underneath a closed door.

Easing their way closer, Bolan and Kirkland stood guard while Montenegro checked for traps, explosives, pressure plates and everything else she could.

"Clear," she said, stepping back.

Pulling out the keywire gun, Bolan filled the lock with stiff wire, then twisted it hard. The lock disengaged with a soft click, and the door swung aside on oiled hinges.

The bedroom was large, with a lot of mirrors on the walls and deep shag-pile carpeting from another decade. There was an empty gun cabinet on the wall, as well as a lot of deer antlers used as decorations, and a stuffed grizzly bear stood in the corner.

Lying on a circular bed was a young woman wearing a pink slip and reading a hardback book. She was beautiful with long blond hair and a lush figure that the slip did nothing to hide.

Above the bed was a framed photograph of her in

a white dress and Edgar Barrington in a black tuxedo. They were standing at the altar of a church, and people were throwing rice. That was when Bolan noticed the chain shackled to the woman's ankle, the other end set into a steel bar bolted to the floor.

"If you've come to kill Edgar, you missed him," she said casually, turning a page. "If you plan to rape me as revenge for something he did, feel free. My so-called husband won't give a damn, and I haven't been touched by a real man in years."

"What if this is a rescue, Mrs. Barrington?" Bolan asked, sliding back his goggles so that she could see his face.

Slowly, she lowered the book, a dozen different expressions crossing her face in rapid succession.

"Emily," she said softly, then added, "Do I know you?"

"No, but we're not friends of your husband," Kirkland stated, removing his own goggles. "May I assume that taking you away would piss him off no end?"

Her face flickered into something that was almost a smile. "He would go ballistic!"

"Well, that's a good enough reason all by itself," Montenegro said, kneeling on the floor to start working on the lock.

"However," Bolan continued, "we would like something in return."

"Anything! Name it!" Emily cried, her cheeks flushing with excitement. "I'll do whatever you wish if you promise to get me out of here! There's millions in the safe behind the fish tank, and—"

"We want Edgar's files," Bolan interrupted.

Sighing deeply, Emily slumped her shoulders and opened the book once more. "Be sure to close the door on your way out," she mumbled, the sound turning into a sob. "Nobody can see the company files b-but Edgar. They're stored in a biometric vault that is located inside the armory, surrounded by guard dogs twenty-four hours a day, and covered with explosive charges."

Just then, Montenegro grunted in victory as the lock broke apart, and she moved to the shackle clamped on the woman's slim ankle.

"We can find a way in," Kirkland said confidently.

"What are you looking for that's so important?" Emily asked listlessly, "His tax records? Black-market arms sales? Illegal drug shipments? Trophies from the people he's tortured to death?"

Bolan arched an eyebrow. Obviously, Edgar was a lot worse than he had ever imagined. When this was over, he would have to return and have a short, loud, one-sided conversation with the Swampfox billionaire.

"If all of that is in the main vault, then what is in that wall safe?" Kirkland asked, pointing at the wedding picture.

"A rigged shotgun, and nothing else," Emily said. "Just another trap."

Kirkland gave a half smile. "I'm almost starting to admire the lunatic."

"Don't be deceived. Edgar would take you apart like a watch if he captures you alive." Lowering her slip, she partially exposed her breast. The company logo of Swampfox had been burned into the flesh. Branded like cattle.

Bolan was repulsed. Farm animals weren't treated this badly, and Barrington did this to his own wife? The man was clearly insane. If Edgar teamed up with the snake charmers, the world would be in for a new kind of hell on Earth.

"Oh, he has got to die," Montenegro growled, both hands busy.

"First, we need those files," Kirkland corrected, going to the window to keep watch on the compound below.

"After which, we blow his head off?"

"I have no problem with that."

With a click, the second lock came free and the chain rattled loosely to the floor.

"What are you searching for exactly?" Emily asked, massaging her scarred ankle. "I can tell you everything needed to put my dear husband in jail for life!"

Looking steadily at the woman, Bolan decided to take a gamble. "We looking for anything there is on a former member of Swampfox who went by the name Amir Bull."

"Zafar?" Emily gasped, smiling for the first time. "Are…are you from the major? Did he send you?"

Turning fast, Bolan stared at the woman. *The major?* But before he could ask the obvious questions, a siren started to howl outside, building rapidly in volume and power until the windows were shaking.

"God help us," Emily gasped in horror. "He's back! Edgar is back early!"

CHAPTER SEVENTEEN

Tavira, Portugal

As dawn crested the ocean horizon, the streetlights of the little fishing village went dark, and smoke began to rise from a hundred stone chimneys as the workday began.

Situated on a low cliff, Tavira overlooked a small peninsula that extended into the Atlantic Ocean. The shore was lined with tidal pools and irregular boulders that had broken off the face of the cliff over the millenium. Flapping furiously, a flock of seagulls hovered above a peninsula, their forward speed perfectly matching the push of the morning wind. Gentle waves crested on the golden sands of the irregular beach while countless tiny crabs scuttled along the rocks and tide pools in search of food.

Situated in the middle of the peninsula was a nameless steamship, the rusty hull ever so slightly tilted to one side. Roughly seventy years earlier, a terrible storm had deposited the vessel at that location, the crew long gone, along with any documentation of ownership. Even the name had been burned off the hull by fire. The cargo hold had been empty, and the hull badly breached, the jagged ends of the opening bent inward, which made many of the locals believe the vessel had been the victim of an attack by a Nazi submarine.

But that was ancient history. Nowadays, the rusting hulk was merely an eyesore, rubbish on the beach that was too big to haul away for junk, and too old for anybody to want to salvage. Bird nests festooned the sagging metal decks and corroded smoke stacks, the salty spray from the sea steadily washing away the streaks of filth dribbling down the sides of the hull and slowly finishing the destruction begun during a dark and stormy night so very long ago.

Moving in low and fast, two helicopters appeared in the sunny sky, both of them heading for the nameless wreck. Coming out of the dawn was a sleek Black Hawk and a Chinese-made Z-10 attack helicopter, bearing the name and logo of a commercial shipping company. Neither of the helicopters was armed in any way, and the identification numbers along their fuselages glistening with fresh paint.

Approaching the wreck, the Black Hawk and the Z-10 hovered in the air for a few minutes, the turbulence of the multiple spinning blades sending the squawking seagulls flying away, and even disturbing the golden sands just enough to make the tiny crabs turn rapidly in circles until disappearing underground.

With exaggerated grace, the helicopters landed on opposite ends of the peninsula, their blades continuing to spin at full speed, instantly ready to leave in case of trouble.

Maintaining strict radio silence, the two pilots did nothing until the swirling sands settled, then binoculars were used to visually scan the ocean, wreck, cliff and village. A few minutes later, the side hatches were pushed open and two people got out of each helicopter. A pair of men in business suits exited the Z-10, and Major Armanjani and Dr. Khandis left the Black

Hawk. Nobody was openly wearing weapons, and everybody was carrying a briefcase.

Walking slowly across the warm sand, Armanjani studied the people coming toward him. One was older, while the other was bald. They looked like ordinary civilians, which meant they were actually Red Star agents. That wasn't good. A wise negotiator would have sent one scientist and one guard.

The two groups stopped in the middle of the sandy beach, then had to wait a minute for the gulls to quiet down before they could talk.

"It rains in Russia today," Armanjani said in a French accent.

"But it never rains in America," the older Red Star agent replied in a thick German accent.

"Except on Thursday."

"Which is a holiday."

"Enough! Your masters were satisfied with what we did to the mountain?"

The first Red Star agent smiled, while his bald counterpart didn't. "Yes, it was most impressive."

"Thank you. Do you have the money?" Khandis asked, trying to keep the eagerness out of his voice.

"Right here, exactly as requested," the bald Red Star agent said, extending the briefcase. "As you requested—one hundred million in German bearer bonds, one hundred million in cut diamonds and an electronic deposit card for three hundred million in United States dollars."

"Check the card, Professor," Armanjani said.

"Yes, General," Khandis replied, handing his briefcase to the major. He felt silly using the fake rank and name, but then science was based on knowing the truth, while most business transactions were precisely the opposite.

Opening his own briefcase, the bald Chinese agent extracted a black card and passed it over. Pulling a compact scanner from his pocket, Khandis took the card and ran it through the slot. The indicator lights blinked twice, then a chime sounded.

"It's real, General," Khandis said.

Armanjani smiled slightly. "Give him the rest, please."

"No, we want your briefcase first."

Nervously, Khandis looked at the major.

"Do it," he said in an even tone.

"Here are the mechanical blueprints, mathematical formulas and electrical schematics," Khandis said, offering the briefcase.

The bald Red Star agent frowned. "The plans?" he demanded in a low voice. "We expected the command codes for the actual weapon!"

"That was not part of the deal," Armanjani growled, hooking both thumbs into his belt.

The mature agent smiled. "But it is now."

"We negotiated for the plans only."

"Things change, Arab."

"Unacceptable!"

"Ah, but we will pay twice what you asked for!"

"No!"

"Three times...four!"

Two billion U.S. dollars was a vast sum, but the major wasn't to be swayed by mere numbers. "Money is not the concern. You violated the contract," he growled. "Go home. We will now sell the Scimitar to somebody else."

"Idiot! You'll give everything to us right now!" the

bald Red Star agent shouted, thrusting out both hands. Instantly, a pair of slim Norinco .22 automatic pistols slapped into his palms from inside the sleeves.

"Now, do as you're told," he said with a sneer, cocking both hammers, "and maybe you'll live long enough to fuck another camel, eh?"

"As you command, you filthy...*yellow dog*," Armanjani whispered, folding his arms.

Instantly, they heard the report of a high-powered rifle, and the armed Red Star agent spun, his pistols firing wildly as red blood gushed from a hideous neck wound.

As the major and the doctor dove for cover behind a low dune, the dying Red Star agent tried to raise a pistol with a blood-streaked hand, and the distant sniper rifle sounded again. This time, his head erupted into chunks, teeth sailing away to patter into a shallow tidal pool.

Grinning widely, Khandis scrambled for the Chinese man's briefcase, but Armanjani tackled him and rolled away fast into the cresting waves. A split second later, the briefcase detonated, the assorted contents hurtling skyward on a searing column of burning thermite. Even yards away, the wave of heat forced the other man back.

"We must save the diamonds!" Khandis cried out, an arm covering his face.

While Khandis crawled for the ocean, Armanjani pushed aside a clump of seaweed to dig into the soft sand and extract a plastic food container containing a 9 mm Tariq pistol and spare magazines.

On the other side of the peninsula, a dozen heavily armed soldiers poured out of the Z-10 helicopter, their QBZ assault rifles firing steadily. They only got a

few yards before there was an answering barrage from
the ocean as ten Ophiuchus solders in scuba suits rose
from the waves, the M-16/M-203 assault rifle combos
in their hands now free of the sealed plastic bags that
kept out the saltwater.

As the Chinese soldiers dropped into defensive
positions, the Ophiuchus troops cut loose with a full
barrage of 40 mm shells. The combination of HE, thermite, white phosphorous and depleted uranium slugs
rocked the helicopter hard, punching soup-can-size
holes in the composite armor of the fuselage and shattering the windows. Riddled with lead, the dying pilot
instinctively tried to lift off. The Pratt & Whitney engines roared with power, which only made the ruptured
fuel lines ignite and catch fire.

Suddenly, two more Z-10 helicopters appeared in
the distance, their 30 mm nose cannons spitting flame.

In response, a dozen more Ophiuchus troops appeared along the sloping deck of the abandoned ship,
their arms cradling Stinger missile launchers. As the
incoming 30 mm rounds stitched a path across the
sandy shoreline, the Ophiuchus troops launched their
Stingers.

Accelerating to nearly mach 2, the deadly American antiaircraft missiles streaked across the sky to
converge on the hot engines of the armored Z-10
helicopters like avenging bloodhounds. The combined
detonations illuminated half the sky with smoky fire,
the burning wrecks tumbling into the warm Atlantic,
trailing fuel and oil.

In retaliation, a rain of grenades flew from the Chinese soldiers, the beach erupting in hammering explosions.

Without expression, Armanjani advanced on the

enemy troops, firing slowly and steadily. Faces disappeared in bloody explosions of brains and bone until the rest broke ranks and ran behind the burning Z-10 for cover.

"Blue dog, green dog," Armanjani whispered into the concealed throat mike.

Once more a full salvo of Stinger missiles lanced from the corroded ship, and the missiles slammed into the destroyed Z-10 with devastating force, the tattered bodies of the Chinese soldiers flying into the ocean or slamming against the rocky face of the low cliff.

"Check the bodies. Kill any survivors!" Armanjani commanded over his throat mike, the 9 mm Tariq firing into the broken corpses to make sure all of them were deceased.

"We should have known it was impossible to trust the Chinese," Khandis muttered, ripping open his shirt to inspect his body armor. "This was supposed to be a business deal, nothing more!" There were several gray lumps on the smooth black material, two of them directly above his heart, the rest in a ragged line across his stomach. He had abandoned the idea of trying to find the diamonds.

"Communists take everything personally," Armanjani replied, pausing in the executions to reload.

"Then they simply take everything!"

"That is their way, yes."

"So what now, sir? Must we deal with the Saudis?"

"No! They will not do business with us anymore," the major said with a pronounced note of annoyance. "They will assume that we have sold the weapon to the Chinese and now are trying to sell the Scimitar again." He paused, fumbling for the correct phrase.

"Double dip?" Khandis suggested.

The major smiled. "As you say, double dip."

"What should we do now?" Khandis asked.

Walking to a moaning Chinese soldier, Armanjani used his boot to push the wounded man over, then shot him in the face. "We go home," he said, holstering the pistol.

"I meant about the sale, sir," Khandis persisted. "Do we try the Russians again, or perhaps the Japanese?"

"After that earthquake they do not have the funds to purchase anything, much less a weapon system." Armanjani scowled, looking over the battleground. "No, we will have to try somebody else. Perhaps the United Nations."

"The United Nations?" Khandis gasped. "But sir, they do not negotiate with terrorists!"

"Perhaps this will be an exception." Armanjani laughed, starting back for the Black Hawk, his boots sinking deep into the soft golden sand.

Swampfox Firebase, Alabama

DRAWING BOTH OF HIS HANDGUNS, Kirkland took a position behind the living-room sofa, his weapons trained on the closed front door.

"Get dressed!" Bolan snapped, swinging around the XM-25 and going to the shaking window.

"Why?" Emily pleaded. "What can you possibly do that will—"

Interrupting the emotional torrent, Montenegro slapped the rattled woman across the face with the flat of her hand. With a cry, Emily hit the bed in a sprawl, her eyes wide.

"We are here to help you," Montenegro said firmly,

as if speaking to a child. "Now, do as we say, and you'll dance on his grave. Sound good?"

Rubbing her stinging cheek, Emily mutely nodded.

"Then please get dressed like the man said," Montenegro instructed her, pulling out a 9 mm Glock pistol. "But take this first!"

Looking as if she were being given the fabled Ark of the Covenant, the woman accepted the weapon, then surprised everybody by dropping the magazine to check the load.

Opening the window a couple of inches, Bolan aimed the grenade launcher at the building across the street. Stroking the trigger, the Executioner sent a 25 mm shell streaking down to detonate violently on the front door of the armory.

A maelstrom of wood chips and smoke blew across the green, and a moment later a snarling pitbull surged out of the building, closely followed by another, then six German shepherds, and finally a motley pack of assorted breeds.

"I would have preferred the 18," Emily said, a faint smile on her lips, sliding the magazine back into place and working the slide to chamber a round for immediate use.

"Ah, the woman of my dreams!" Kirkland chuckled, his full attention on the door. His first urge was to block the door with some furniture. There certainly was enough in the room to do a good job. But until they decided on a course of action, it was more important to maintain the ability to stay mobile than it was to dig in.

Casting the big man a furtive glance, Emily then scrambled out of the bed and rushed to a closet. With no concern for the others present, she stripped and quickly donned a mottled-green Swampfox uniform.

Charging out of the barracks, a large group of men carrying M-16 assault rifles stopped in their tracks at the sight of the slavering dogs. A few of the Swampfox guards drew weapons and started shooting, but the rest broke ranks and pelted madly back into the barracks. Choosing their targets, the pack of dogs separated and ruthlessly attacked, jumping on the armed men and driving them down to the street, then ripping out throats, and moving on to the next victim.

In the bright streetlights, Bolan could now see the scars on the backs of the animals where they'd been regularly whipped to make them more aggressive. Bad move, guys, he thought in cold irony.

Buckling a canvas gun belt around her waist, Emily tucked the Glock into place, then grabbed a pair of old sneakers.

"Better wear these," Montenegro suggested, tossing her a pair of U.S. Army combat boots that had been on the floor.

"Anything but those," Emily replied, lacing the sneakers on tightly. "The boots have an electronic tracking dot hidden inside the heel."

"Old Edgar doesn't miss a trick, does he?" Bolan said thoughtfully, firing another round into the second floor of the armory. As the glass windows exploded, more dogs came charging out of the front door, howling, yipping and snarling, looking eagerly for their unseen tormentors.

"Fifteen years ago Edgar was pumping gas at his uncle's service station. Now he's worth billions of dollars and guards kings," Emily said, buttoning her cuffs. "So you tell me...whatever your names are."

"It doesn't matter!" Bolan growled, this time firing a shell into the front door of the barracks.

The blast ripped the door off the hinges to sail away. Sensing a weak point, the circling pack of dogs charged into the barracks, howling for blood. Men cursed and dogs barked as assault rifles chattered away steadily, the bright muzzle-flashes illuminating the darkness in flickering strobes.

Unexpectedly, searchlights flashed into operation, the blindingly bright beams sweeping along the carnage-filled streets of the compound. Bolan used his last few shells to take them out, and the protective mantle of darkness returned.

"There are probably more 25 mm shells in the armory," Montenegro suggested with little interest. "If you want to give it a try."

"Rather stick my face in a lawnmower," Bolan said, casting away the exhausted weapon. He was down to the Desert Eagle and the Beretta now.

"Any weapons in here?" Kirkland asked hopefully, glancing over a shoulder.

"Where I might find them?" Emily laughed. "Good God, no! There aren't even any knives in the kitchen! This apartment is a prison cell, nothing more."

"Edgar Barrington slept in a prison cell?" Montenegro said slowly, testing the words. "No, that's bullshit."

"Where's the secret exit?" Bolan demanded, squeezing off a couple of rounds at the men on the green. As blood gushed from their wounds, the dogs went into a frenzy, and converged to tear the dying men apart. At the grisly sight, the rest of the Swampfox guards turned and ran.

"The what?" Emily scowled, her beautiful face distorted into a monstrous grimace. "Trust me, there isn't one!"

Holstering both of his guns, Kirkland shoved the

sofa firmly against the door to the apartment, then threw the dead bolt. "Let's see, shall we?"

Ignoring the closet where Emily had gotten her clothes, Montenegro went across the bedroom to a second door and stepped aside before pulling it open. As she'd expected, a shotgun roared, the blast hammering the opposite wall with deadly stainless-steel fléchettes. Cracked plaster fell off in chunks, exposing the splintered wood slats underneath.

"The man does like shotguns," Montenegro muttered, carefully removing the weapon from the clamp holding it in place.

"Edgar says that shotguns are manly," Emily said in a mocking tone.

"Just more proof that the man genuinely has shit for brains," Kirkland stated, glancing along the painfully neat rows of hanging shirts, pants and jackets. "The toughest guy I ever knew once took out an entire biker gang with a rolling pin."

"It was a baseball bat," Bolan corrected, staying alert by the window. Something was going on down there. Dogs were still barking, but the voices of the men seemed less frightened, and the random gunfire was taking on a measured quality. Almost as if they were trying to lure the intruders out of hiding by pretending the base was still in a panic.

"The shit is about to hit the fan," Bolan said. "We need that exit, Heather."

"Give me a minute," Montenegro replied slowly, concentrating on the details of the closet, looking for anything that seemed to be out of place. At first, there didn't seem to be anything odd or off-kilter, and that was when she noticed a bookshelf built into the wall. There were ten hardbacks, each of them a classic military tome: *The Art of War* by Sun Tzu, *Caesar's Gaelic Wars,* all six volumes of *The Gathering Storm* by Winston Churchill, and a single novel, *The Count of Monte Cristo* by Alexander Dumas.

"Now, what is an adventure story about a daring escape doing among all of these military volumes?" Montenegro muttered, pulling out the book.

The plaster wall behind it was blank, but on a hunch she gently pressed it with a fingertip. There was a subtle click, and a section of the closet floor swung away to reveal a dark opening.

"Houston, we have lift-off," Montenegro said hesitantly, shining a flashlight into the shadowy passage.

"Do…do you mean to tell me that's been here the whole time?" Emily asked incredulously, a hand going to her throat.

"Apparently so," Montenegro replied, studying the access ladder bolted to the side of the passage. She tried to see the bottom, but it was beyond the reach of her halogen beam. Then a subtle movement in the darkness below caught her attention, and Montenegro desperately threw herself backward to land outside the closet.

A split second later, a roaring column of fire rose from the darkness below to splash across the ceiling, and the entire apartment was filled with the telltale stink of jellied gasoline.

"Hello, my love!" a man shouted from the darkness. "Who are your new friends? FBI? NSA? You're certainly not smart enough to find the escape chute by yourself!"

"Eat shit and die, Edgar!" Emily screamed, rising shakily to her feet.

Grabbing her by the collar, Bolan dragged the enraged woman behind the aquarium tank. Kirkland and Montenegro were already there, stuffing sofa cushions under the raised platform.

Rising into view from the opening in the floor came the fluted barrel of a military M1A flamethrower, the tiny blue flame of the pre-burner hissing steadily. A pair of hands wearing thermal gloves were on the control levers. For a long moment, nothing happened, then the lights went out.

"Surrender, and I guarantee your lives!" Barrington called. "Release my wife, and you can live!"

"I'm not a prisoner," Emily screamed back, spittle flying from her mouth. "It's a rescue, not a kidnapping, you moron!" Her words hung in the air for long minutes, the silence almost deafening.

"Then it's time to die, bitch!" Barrington screamed, raising the wand higher.

Stepping quickly to the side, Bolan fired the Desert Eagle around the aquarium. The gun boomed, and Barrington shrieked in pain, a glove spurting blood as it jerked out of sight.

Screaming obscenities, Barrington angled the wand downward, and another column of fire gushed from the muzzle to reach across the bedroom, setting the sheets ablaze, then splashed across the front door to fill the living room with a chemical inferno.

As the flames washed over the aquarium, the glass cracked and water began to dribble onto the floor. Then the cushions burst into crazy green flames, and started giving off dense black smoke.Unconcerned, the tropical fish continued lazily swimming about, completely unaware of their impending doom.

Holding up a staying hand to the others, Kirkland took aim with the Tokarev trauma pistol, then emptied the entire magazine at the wall behind Barrington. The hail of rubber bullets cracked the plaster and bounced off to smack into the fuel tanks and hose of the flame-thrower.

"You missed, asshole!" Barrington said with a sneer, then stopped as he heard a soft hiss of escaping gas from the pressurized tank.

Quickly triggering the weapon again, Barrington got only a weak stream of fire that barely reached out into the smoky bedroom. Then the hissing stopped, and the burning fuel merely flowed out of the fluted end of the wand to puddle on the carpeting.

Snarling, Barrington quickly disappeared down the ladder, the dead flamethrower clanking and clattering along the way.

Rushing into the closet, Bolan and Montenegro both emptied their weapons down the passageway, the double barrage of 9 mm Parabellum rounds generating numerous death screams, along with an assortment of cries of pain. As they'd expected, Barrington hadn't been alone.

Then Kirkland pulled out a grenade. Tilting his head, Bolan looked at the man as if he was nuts, and Kirkland showed that the arming pin wasn't pulled, or safety tape removed.

Confused by that, Emily started to ask a question, and Montenegro put a hand over her mouth. "It wouldn't be very smart to blow up the only way out of here," she whispered softly into the other's woman's ear.

As Emily's face brightened in understanding, Kirkland dropped the grenade down the passageway, then tossed down another.

The military spheres disappeared into the shadows,

followed by the dull thumps of their landings. But there were no yells of surprise or scampering boots.

Tossing down a flashlight, Bolan got only a brief view of the bullet-riddled walls and ladder before it landed on something hard. The lenses noisily cracked, and the flashlight winked out.

Reloading the Beretta, Bolan took the lead. Pressing his boots to the outside of the ladder instead of using the rungs, he slid down the entire length in only a few seconds. As Bolan reached the bottom, he stepped aside and Kirkland arrived in the same manner, his Webley out and sweeping for targets.

The crumpled bodies of six men were piled before an open doorway, and lying on the other side was a short man with silver hair, a flamethrower still strapped to his back. Edgar Barrington. He was sprawled in a pool of his own blood, most of his head torn away by the barrage of 9 mm rounds.

"I think we won," Kirkland said, retrieving one of his grenades and polishing it like apple.

"Certainly seems so," Bolan replied, taking a camping flare from a dead man. Smacking it on a raised knee, he ignited the stick and tossed it through the doorway.

In the harsh red glow, Bolan saw a gunnite-lined tunnel extending into the distance, an iron gate nearby swung aside to allow the passage of an armored fighting vehicle, designation LAV-25. The amphibian armored vehicle was perfect for traversing the black waters of the Alabama swamp. Then he spotted the 25 mm chain gun mounted on the top cupola.

Instantly, Bolan and Kirkland separated to race along the opposite sides of the APC, yanking open the rear doors. Thankfully, the LAV-25 was empty, but the interior reeked of sour sweat, and the floor was littered with crushed cigarette butts, empty MRE food packs and beer cans.

"Must have been a hell of a party." Kirkland chuckled, the Webley never wavering. "Well, at least they died happy."

"The dead part is all that concerns me," Bolan stated, warily climbing inside the LAV-25 and starting to search for booby traps or other antipersonnel devices.

When Bolan made it alive to the driver's seat, Kirkland returned to the ladder and sweetly whistled like a whip-poor-will. In short order, Emily descended into view, closely followed by Montenegro. Both women had cut strips of bath towels tied around their faces as crude protection from the cloud of smoke billowing inside the closet.

"Where's Edgar?" Emily asked anxiously, her hands clasped together.

"Over here," Kirkland replied, using his boot to flip over the corpse with the flamethrower.

Staring at the dead man for a moment, Emily then hawked and spat in his face.

"Feel better?" Montenegro asked with a grin.

Emily nodded. "Much better."

Suddenly, the LAV-25's engine surged into operation, and the headlights came on, filling the dark tunnel with harsh illumination.

Herding Emily into the armored vehicle, Montenegro helped the woman strap down into a wall seat while Kirkland closed and bolted the rear doors.

"How's the fuel?" Montenegro asked, taking the seat alongside Emily.

"Just over half a tank, more than enough to get us

back to civilization," Bolan replied, awkwardly turning the vehicle around in the tight confines of the tunnel.

She smiled. "Good to know!"

Driving along the tunnel, Bolan turned off the headlights to keep from announcing their presence to any possible guards waiting in ambush, then he switched them back on, realizing the roar of the big Detroit engines was doing a fine job all by itself.

Climbing into the cupola, Kirkland inspected the 25 mm chain gun. Disgusted with what he found, the man shifted the belt of linked ammunition about until it fitted properly into the breech. Amateurs!

"Okay, Emily, we've kept our side of the deal," Montenegro said, rocking in the seat as the vehicle lurched over something. "You're free. Now tell us about Amir Bull."

Keeping a grip on her safety harness, Emily took a deep breath. "His real name is Zafar Armanjani, Major Armanjani. Edgar didn't like him very much because…well…"

"Because he wasn't white enough," Kirkland supplied from the cupola.

She nodded, then smiled. "But the men loved him! He was an excellent shot, and taught them knife-fighting and about swords, and…Zafar knew everything about military history. He was always telling the men stories about Rommel and Roarke's Drift and such."

"Which I'm sure made Edgar like him even less," Montenegro guessed.

"He was also my… That is…we…" Unsure how to proceed, Emily paused to chew a lip.

"You were lovers," Montenegro said gently. "After

meeting Edgar, I wouldn't blame you for making time with a gator."

Blinking back tears, Emily tried not to smile, but did anyway, then burst into racking sobs.

Coming out of the tunnel, Bolan banked hard at the sight of five men in Swampfox uniforms sitting around a campfire.

"Showtime!" he barked, revving the engine to maximum. Ramming directly through the group, the armored prow of the LAV-25 sent their broken bodies sailing away into the dirty swamp water.

Looking confused and frightened, the sole survivor turned to race into the bushes.

"Three o'clock!" Montenegro announced, drawing her Glock and trying for the guard. But the angle was wrong, and she could only hit the Spanish moss hanging from the trees.

Just then, the guard reappeared holding an LAW rocket launcher. He barely managed to extend the tube when Kirkland cut loose with the chain gun, the hammering stream of 25 mm rounds tearing the man apart as he went stumbling backward into the muddy weeds.

"You were telling us about Zafar," Bolan said, shifting gears.

"We… He talked a lot…afterward, you know," Emily said, blushing all over. "He had big plans for taking over his homeland and restoring order. In a way, he sort of reminded me of Edgar, only much nicer."

Couldn't be any worse unless he drowned you in the bathtub, Kirkland mused privately. "Did he ever mention a base of operations, a mansion, castle, hardsite, anything like that?"

"He had several, the main one was a cargo ship,"

Emily said. "I think it was called the *Red Rose,* or maybe just the *Rose,* something like that."

Dodging a sleeping alligator, Bolan frowned. A ship could be anywhere in the world. "Did he have someplace that wasn't mobile?" he asked hopefully. "A firebase, military installation or an island?"

"Fort Ithnaan," she said, stumbling over the foreign word. "He used to boast that if anything went wrong, we would be safe there because of the constant cloud cover." She gave a nervous laugh. "Whatever that meant!"

Driving around their abandoned airboat, Bolan scowled. *Ithnaan* was the Arabic word for *two.* That was probably the fallback position for Ophiuchus in case of trouble. The cloud cover would give them all the protection needed with unlimited lightning bolts. This was not what he had hoped for. However, Ithnaan base might just tell them where the *Red Rose* was located.

"Did he ever mention where the base was hidden?" Montenegro pressed gently. "Iraq, Kuwait or maybe Afghanistan?"

"Pakistan, Latveria?" Kirkland supplied. "Sheboygan, Kalamazoo, Outer Mongolia?"

Emily laughed, then abruptly stopped. "You're going to kill him?" she said as a question.

"Yes, we are," Bolan said honestly. "Major Armanjani is a terrorist and directly responsibly for killing thousands of innocent men and women."

Rocking to the motion of the speeding vehicle, Emily said nothing for a long time, lost in somber contemplation.

"It's true, we can prove it if necessary," Montenegro

said gently, sensing the other woman was on the cusp, but not yet ready to betray her former lover.

"Yes, I believe you," Emily whispered, massaging her temple. "Or else you wouldn't have wanted the files so much. I suppose."

"Yes?"

"Mousehole." Emily sighed, hanging her head. "It's located at the bottom of a tin mine at someplace called Mousehole. That's all I know."

Immediately, Montenegro typed the word into her smartphone to start an internet search.

"It's a small town in Cornwall," Kirkland supplied, climbing down from the cupola. "But England has dozens of abandoned tin mines, maybe hundreds, and even more stone quarries."

Montenegro scowled at the map displayed on the smartphone's screen. The whole peninsula was a warren of tunnels, cisterns, aqueducts, quarries, caves and mine shafts. "How can we find the right one before the major blows us off the face of the map?"

"We check the weather reports," Bolan said, shifting gears again.

"For rainstorms?"

"No," he said grimly. "Smog."

CHAPTER EIGHTEEN

Washington, D.C.

A warm rain fell across the city as Hal Brognola stood on the balcony just outside the Oval Office. Until Bolan called, there wasn't much he could do, so the big Fed decided to stay as close to the President as possible. If the snake charmers attacked, he might see something important that the Secret Service agents would miss. After all, their attention was focused on the President, while his was on the sky. Big difference.

His cell phone buzzed. Snapping it open with a flip of the wrist, Brognola grinned when he saw there was no caller ID. Thank God!

"Brognola," he said into the phone, knowing the signal would be scrambled. "Go ahead, Cooper."

"They're hidden somewhere in a tin mine in Cornwall," Bolan announced without preamble. "No precise location yet. We're checking the weather reports for unusual amounts of smog."

"The ozone from the equipment," Brognola said in slow comprehension. God, that was brilliant!

All electrical devices created trace amounts of ozone, an unbreathable version of oxygen. The bigger the equipment, the more it made. Logically, controlling lightning had to use a lot of power, and trapped inside the closed environment of a mine, the ozone would soon prove fatal to the terrorists. They would be forced to constantly vent outside, which would create localized smog.

"Okay, now what?" Brognola asked. "Do we send in the troops, or bomb them from orbit?"

Bolan's reply was lost in a burst of static. A split second later, lightning flashed to hit the decorative iron tables in the Rose Garden. Partially melted, the furniture tumbled away to hit a window and bounce off the bulletproof plastic.

"Red alert!" a hidden speaker blared inside the White House. "Repeat, this is a red alert!"

"Cooper?" Brognola asked, but there was no response. Damn! Snapping the phone shut, he quickly went back inside.

Surrounded by a living wall of Secret Service agents, the President of the United States was bent over his desk, both hands full of top secret documents.

"What's the situation?" he demanded in a rich, cultured voice.

"Storm clouds cresting the horizon," Brognola said, checking his laptop.

"Sir, we have to get you to the bunker right now," said the FBI liaison.

"No more delays!" added the head of the CIA with a stern expression.

Still rifling through the decoded papers on his desk, the President frowned. He hated the bunker; it sent a bad message to the people of America. Built under the West Wing as protection against a nuclear attack, the bunker should prove resistant even to lightning.

"Time to go, sir," Brognola added curtly.

"I'm sorry, Hal, but that's still impossible." The President sighed, then gasped in surprise as two of the larger Secret Service agents grabbed him under the arms.

"Sorry, sir, we make the decisions when it comes to your safety," the special agent in charge stated bluntly.

With that as their cue, the cadre of agents bodily hauled the duly elected leader of the nation out from behind the desk and across the room.

"Y-you can't do this!" the President said furiously, struggling to escape. "I order you to stop!"

"Sorry again, sir, but you have no direct authority over us," the chief agent replied curtly as the President went out the door.

"Hal, do something!" the President ordered as his entourage of Secret Service agents rushed through the maze of deserted secretarial desks.

"Absolutely, sir. Move faster, guys!" Brognola yelled as the agents took a corner and disappeared from sight.

In stony calm, an Air Force lieutenant with a steel briefcase handcuffed to his wrist calmly walked from the office. Several of the remaining Secret Service agents followed close behind, drawn pistols in their hands. Softly in the distance, they heard a low peal of thunder.

In Washington, D.C., slang, the lieutenant was the quarterback, and the briefcase was the football. It contained the launch codes for America's imposing arsenal of thermonuclear missiles. Day or night, it was never more than fifty feet away from the chief executive.

"How soon until Eagle is safe?" Brognola asked, closing his laptop.

"Already is," the SAC said, glancing at his watch.

Stuffing the computer into a briefcase, Brognola arched an eyebrow at that statement. "Really?"

"We've practiced this a hundred times before with

the chief of staff as a stand-in," the SAC explained as the clouds rolled over the building, casting it into dark shadows.

"Good to know." Brognola exhaled in relief. "What about the First Family?"

"They've been in the bunker since we heard from what remains of Cheyenne Mountain," the SAC replied, slapping a small discolored section of the executive desk.

As the disguised biometric reader identified the special agent in charge, every drawer slammed shut and triple locked, the telephone went dark as the internal memory chips melted, and everything inside the nearby waste basket flashed into carbonized ash.

"Okay, let's go," Brognola said, stuffing the laptop into a nylon carrying case.

Rising from chairs around the office, a dozen men and women briskly exited using different doors. Along with the head of the FBI, CIA, NSA, and several other members of the alphabet soup club, Brognola had been discussing contingency plans with the President in case Bolan failed in his mission.

Unfortunately, nobody had been able to come up with anything worth considering. There simply wasn't enough information about these impossible attacks. Maybe they were terrorist strikes, or perhaps just a long series of freak events. Such things had happened before in the history of the world, just not on this devastating a level. However, as the old saying went, there was always a first time for everything.

Without warning, a platoon of U.S. Marines in Class-A uniforms crashed into the Oval Office, their weapons at the ready.

"Has Eagle One left for the bunker?" a master sergeant growled, his white gloves tight on a spotless M-4 rifle.

Nobody moved or flinched as sheet lightning crackled across the sky. The stark white light flashed bright as a bomb in the Oval Office, reflecting off the assortment of highly polished surfaces of the assorted pistols and rifles.

"Yes, Eagle One is secure," the SAC confirmed. "What about the Veep?"

As thunder rumbled overhead, the Marines scowled in disapproval, but nobody spoke.

"Where is the vice-president?" Brognola translated diplomatically.

"Eagle Two is at the Ellipse, waiting for his wife to arrive in an armored limousine," the master sergeant replied crisply without any trace of emotion.

"He's...outside?" the SAC asked in a strained voice.

"Yes, sir. The military can only obey direct orders," the master sergeant growled, twisting his gloves on the assault rifle. "If the vice-president wants to wait at the Ellipse, we can't stop him."

He turned to face Brognola. "Nor can the Justice Department." Then the master sergeant smiled briefly. "But you Treasury boys sure can."

"Understood. Let's go!" the SAC shouted, charging forward at a full run and touching his throat mike. "Break pack! Repeat, break pack! Eagle Two has gone rogue at the Ellipse! Repeat, Eagle Two is at the Ellipse! Find and detain!"

"Screw that crap!" Brognola growled, slinging the nylon strap of the laptop case over a shoulder. "Get the fucking Veep inside the bunker right now!"

Sprinting past the empty Roosevelt Room, the SAC

scowled at the vulgarity, but relayed the suggestion anyway word for word.

"Nicely done," the master sergeant said out of the side of his mouth.

Moving at his best speed, Brognola merely snorted in reply, saving his breath to keep up with the Secret Service agents and Marines. There was too much procedure and protocol in Washington these days, and nowhere near enough plain common sense!

As the heavily armed group raced past a series of small offices, Brognola noted the dozens of clerks, aides, interns and secretaries still diligently working at their desks. Even with the nation under attack, the day-to-day work of government had to continue. The citizens of America expected no less. He knew the staff wasn't paid enough to risk their lives, it was simply their deeply rooted sense of duty that kept them here.

Racing around a corner, Brognola saw the vice-president standing under the portico of the Ellipse. He was talking on a cell phone, a pretty young aide protecting him with an umbrella. The rain was coming down hard by now, the droplets bouncing high off the pavement and, oddly, sounding exactly like frying bacon.

From the rooftop of the Old Executive Building across the street, an Army MRL started firing rockets into the clouds. Some of them were destroyed, but others weren't, and the multiple-rocket launcher went untouched.

Feeling the hairs rise on the back of his neck, Brognola frowned at that. The enemy was getting smarter. Not good news.

"Mr. Vice-President, get inside, now!" the SAC bellowed as the group raced past a set of marble pillars.

As the vice-president started to turn there was a blindling flash of light and the man's aide was struck as lightning flashed through the umbrella to course through her body. Arms and legs flailing, the horrified aide staggered backward, her tattered clothing in flames. The vice-president toppled to the ground.

"Eagle Two and his aide are down! Medical at the Ellipse, stat!" the SAC shouted into his throat mike.

"Down? She's dead, you idiot!" the master sergeant snarled furiously, staring hatefully at the rumbling sky. "Maybe him, too. What in the hell is going on here?"

As the searing after-glare faded, soldiers, sailors and Secret Service agents rushed to check the victims in the rain, the SAC running down the pavement to wave off the approaching limousine.

Suddenly, the lightning returned, a thick blue bar of blinding annihilation that struck the left hand of the dead aide then crawled along the pavement, chewing a path of crackling destruction directly to the limousine.

Instantly, the military tires exploded off the rims, the bulletproof windows shattered, people screamed and the fuel tank detonated. The combined blast flipped over the armored vehicle and it came crashing back down onto top of the SAC with grisly results.

As the stunned survivors staggered about trying to get their bearings again, everything seemed strangely silent, almost surreal, and Brognola realized that he couldn't hear anything. Goddamnit, he had to be temporarily deaf from the concussion! More importantly, he had seen the lightning hit the cell phone of the dead aide when there were dozens, no, hundreds of better targets. Could the terrorists be using cellular transmissions to aim the attacks?

Starting to go for his cell phone, Brognola abruptly

stopped, then swung around the nylon case and hauled out the laptop. That was when lightning flashed again, striking the group of Marines and then the Secret Service agents. Burning bodies scattered wide and far, their weapons discharging randomly.

The teams were hit separately. That sent a cold sword of comprehension through Brognola as he retreated under the safety of the portico. It now seemed a safe bet that these were controlled attacks! The lightning had gone from a Marine talking on the radio to a Secret Service agent opening a cell phone. He had to tell Bolan this! It could mean all the difference when he faced them in Cornwall!

Kneeling on the sidewalk, Brognola started hurriedly typing, his fingers flashing across the miniature keyboard when the terrible white light returned. There was a bone-breaking surge of incredible pain through his entire body and Brognola felt himself flying. He landed on something hard with a jarring impact, and lost consciousness, still struggling to reach the blasted ruin of the scorched laptop....

Cornwall, United Kingdom

HORN BLARING, HEADLIGHTS flashing, a huge tanker truck rumbled along the mountainous road at breakneck speed. It appeared to be driverless.

"We don't know for certain that your contact is dead," Kirkland said into his throat mike while running across the irregular countryside. "The transmission was terminated early, that's all."

"Have there been many survivors before?" Bolan asked, adjusting his parachute while keeping pace.

"Very few," Kirkland grudgingly admitted.

Tilting dangerously, nine of the eighteen wheels of the Bug-B-Gone vehicle squealed loudly as the colossal truck took a tight curve, then came crashing back down to continue faster than ever.

"Razor up, boys," Montenegro said, delicately turning the miniature steering wheel on the remote control. "We're almost there!"

Quickly, everybody banished all considerations for absent friends, and concentrated on crossing the rough hills of Cornwall. This next part was going to be extremely difficult.

While flying from Alabama to England, Bolan and Montenegro had been able to ascertain that the most likely location for the hidden base was the Hercules Granite Mine and Quarry, just outside Mousehole. Aside from a staggering surge of ozone in the atmosphere of such a nonindustrial area, the local UFO clubs had also reported a startling increase in recent sightings. It had always been Kirkland's experience that what many UFO buffs thought to be alien visitors were in fact covert military helicopters not using their running lights while flying under the national radar grid.

"Sorry that we had to leave Emily in your jet at Heathrow Airport," Bolan said, checking his body armor. "But we're racing against the clock."

"I'm sure she understands these things. The mission always comes first," Kirkland said.

"Has the RAF been told this is a no-fly zone?" Montenegro asked, checking the GPS on her watch, while braking the tanker truck into another curve. "A helicopter skimming the trees might be us running for our lives."

"I don't know if they'll listen, but they have been

told," Bolan stated, checking his pockets for any loose items. Extracting a couple of quarters and a dime, he tossed them into the tall grass. Going into battle with loose coins in a pocket was an excellent way to inform an enemy you were nearby and please-come-kill-me.

"SAS, too?" Kirkland asked.

"Everybody in British law enforcement, except for Sherlock Holmes."

"Good enough!" Montenegro said, accelerating. "Because, here we go!"

Horn still blaring, the rattling Bug-B-Gone truck charged past the chained access road to the quarry and drove over the edge of the cliff. Soaring gracefully into the quarry, the tanker truck rotated slightly as if doing a swan dive before thunderously crashing onto the rocky bottom. Broken bits of metal and glass sprayed out in every direction as the truck compacted like an accordion, but, almost out of gas, there was no fiery blast from the engine or fuel tanks. However, a thick greenish fluid squirted out from a hundred rents in the pressurized tanker, the viscous fluid splashing like mutant gore across the smoothly cut walls.

Even as it trickled along the rock face, the ten thousand gallons quickly evaporated into a heavy swirling mist that flowed across the quarry to the lowest point—the mouth of the abandoned tin mine.

The problem of how to invade the terrorist hardsite without getting killed in the attempt had been solved by the simple procedure of using poison gas. There were a lot of military gases much heavier than air that would flood the underground mine, killing everybody down there.

The trouble was that those sorts of chemical weapons were obviously unavailable to the team. Also, there might be civilians present—either prisoners of the terrorists down in the mine, or just walking past the quarry. Bolan and his people needed some sort of a gas that was heavier than air, and extremely painful, but not overly toxic. The answer had been simple: a chemical compound used by exterminators to kill termites.

Moving faster than water flowing down a drain, the green mist entered the mine, rushing to find any and all crevices, vents, cracks and doorways.

Reaching the edge of the pit, Bolan, Kirkland and Montenegro dove into the quarry, immediately pulling the ripcords on their parachutes. As the chutes opened, their descent rapidly slowed but they still hit the pool of drainage water hard, going deep, their boots actually brushing the bottom before they were able to start swimming to the surface.

Scrambling out of the stagnant water, they slapped the releases on their chest harnesses and dropped the parachutes behind, sprinting toward the tin mine.

"Now, that was close!" Kirkland panted, flashing a crazy grin. "If that water had been just a little more shallow, we would have broken both legs on the bottom!"

"It was either jump or chance the access road," Bolan countered, swinging up the XM-25 grenade launcher.

"No, thanks!" Montenegro chuckled, clicking off the safety on the Neostead. "Land mines are bad for my figure!"

Reaching the entrance of the mine, they dove over the threshold, fully expecting there to be trip wires, explosive charges or deathtraps of some kind. But their arrival only invoked a cloud of dust as they landed on the wood floor.

"We're going to look pretty stupid if this is not the right place," Kirkland said.

Suddenly, there came a rumble of thunder from outside the mine, followed by a bright flash as a lightning bolt slammed into the crashed truck.

"Nope, this is it," Bolan growled, staying alert for any possible deathtraps.

So far, all they had encountered was some artificial trash and a lot of dead rats. That was just camouflage to distract any curious tourists or wandering constables. The real defenses would be located much farther in the mine, where the explosions and screaming couldn't be heard by outsiders.

Following the flow of green fog, Bolan and the others zigzagged their way deeper into the mine, bypassing many side tunnels, until they reached a dead end.

"Now what?" Montenegro demanded into her throat mike.

Before anybody could answer, the rock wall ahead of them broke apart and out rolled a British army Warrior armored vehicle, its 7.62 mm machine gun blazing away as the 30 mm cannon fired.

The shell missed the Americans by inches, and disappeared down the tunnel to explode in the far distance. The concussion of the muzzle-blast slammed Bolan and Kirkland into the rock walls, while Montenegro was thrown flat on her back and rolled directly into the stream of copper-jacketed death pouring from the chattering machine gun.

CHAPTER NINETEEN

Firebase, Ithnaan

Slamming the door aside, Major Armanjani burst into the control room, coughing and hacking. The air in there was also misty with the emerald-colored gas, and every inch of his exposed skin was beginning to itch fiercely.

Rudely pushing a path through a crowd of coughing people, the major reached the pressurized air tanks in the corner. Twisting the release handle, he let the stream of pure air fill his aching lungs and wash the stinging fumes from his tearing eyes.

In spite of his many years of using chemical weapons on insurgents, the major had absolutely no idea what was being pumped into the base, yet the reeking fumes had spread through the entire underground base like wildfire. Listening to the chatter coming over the intercom and radio links, Armanjani was seriously displeased. Frightened by the gas, and unable to see clearly, soldiers were allegedly shooting one another by mistake in the swirling clouds.

What was this shit? The major frowned. It wasn't toxic enough to activate the bio-sensors, but it was more than caustic enough to incapacitate most of his staff. It almost seemed like some odd kind of tear gas....

That was when it hit him. Bug spray! This was exactly the sort of chemical gas the American Army used to fumigate a house infested with insects: fire ants, termites and such.

The realization sent a surge of cold fury through the major. They're trying to kill us like vermin? he thought. Somebody would pay dearly for this mortal insult. Pay for it with their lives.

Grabbing a gas mask from a shelf above the air tanks, Armanjani had the stream of air to wash it clean first, then hurriedly pulled it over his head, and headed to the main console.

"Red alert, gas attack!" Armanjani coughed into a microphone. "Don masks immediately! Get to your gas masks before anything else! Then seal every d-d-d…" He stopped to draw in some deep breaths of filtered air until he was able to speak clearly once more.

Nearby, Nasser and Hassan were working in unison, cutting towels into strips and soaking them in the washroom sink before tossing them to Khandis. Kneeling on the floor, he was packing the material along the bottom of the door to try to block the advance of the disgusting vapors. The tactic seemed to be working, and soon the humming air purifier had the atmosphere clear of the vile green tinge.

"Gas attack!" Armanjani repeated. "Use wet clothing to block the doors, and execute emergency protocol five! Repeat, emergency protocol five!"

"Orders, sir?" Nasser demanded, drying her hands on a cloth. A Russian gas mask was in place, but her eyes were terribly bloodshot from just a brief exposure.

"Lieutenant, find the intruders and kill them!" he barked, working the slide on the Tariq pistol to chamber a round. "Those orders are to stand until revoked by me personally. Personally, not by radio! Understood?"

"Yes, sir! The invaders may try to issue false commands!" Nasser replied with a salute. "Sergeant, with me!"

Hesitantly, Hassan glanced at the major first, then nodded and retrieved his Atchisson autoshotgun before he followed the departing lieutenant.

"Dr. Khandis, I want you to contact the British government," Major Armanjani said with a gesture, stepping away from the console. "Tell them to immediately stop this attack, or else we will level London!"

"At once, sir!" Khandis replied, tightening the strap on his gas mask. "And if they don't think that we are serious, what then?"

"Convince them otherwise," Armanjani growled, striding from the room with a gun in each hand.

THE MACHINE GUNS ON THE armored vehicle fired again.

Grunting loudly as the 7.62 mm rounds painfully bounced off her body armor, Montenegro rolled out of the way of the bullets and came up in a kneeling position with the Neostead shotgun roaring. The stainless-steel fléchettes mercifully hammered the machine gun, tearing off tiny flecks, and it instantly jammed. She fired again, and a man inside the armored vehicle screamed, blood splattering onto the ceiling.

However, even as the machine gun went silent, the 30 mm cannon noisily swung to a new position. Moving fast, Bolan and Kirkland dove headfirst at the vehicle, and rolled underneath just as the cannon cut loose again. Angled downward, the 30 mm shell punched a big hole in the wooden floor, but the distance had been too short for the warhead to arm, and there was no explosion.

Still reeling from the concussion, Montenegro swept the Neostead across the front of the Warrior, the fléchettes wildly ricocheting off the armored prow, but smashing both of the headlights. As they winked out, darkness filled the mining tunnel once more.

Appearing behind the armored vehicle, Bolan killed a guard while Kirkland whipped out a thermite grenade and gently lobbed it onto the top of the tanks. "Move it or lose it!" he snarled. But Bolan was already in motion, firing the XM-250.

Lurching into action, Montenegro sprinted past the men, and they turned to join her escape only seconds before there came a powerful exhalation followed by a searing wave of heat that forced away the swirling green mist.

The 30 mm cannon fired again at nothing in particular as the surging thermite grenade reached operational levels, and rivulets of glowing red steel began to trickle down the armored sides of the vehicle.

Muttering curses, the men inside tried to open the softening rear doors, but they were already misshapen and refused to budge. As the roof turned white-hot, it began to sag, then the gunner's hatch buckled, and the ammunition belt for the machine gun ignited. The linked 7.62 mm rounds cooked off like a string of fire-crackers inside the armored cupola. The cursing turned to screams as the exploding ammunition and internal ricochets escalated into a nightmarish rattle.

With a hard clatter, the diesel engine stopped, then so did the screaming.

Moving away from the conflagration, Bolan and the others were headed directly to the opening in the tunnel wall, when the fuel tank erupted and the Desert Eagle vanished inside a writhing fireball of its own creation.

Assuming the lead, Bolan charged into the next tunnel, with Kirkland and Montenegro tight on his flanks. On either side of the entrance was a pair of Remington .50-caliber heavy machine guns situated behind sandbag walls. However, the gunners were staggering out in the green mist, hacking and coughing. Clutching his stomach, one of them doubled over to be sick while another popped the tab on a can of soda and poured the contents onto his head in an effort to wash away the debilitating chemicals.

Kirkland smacked the first terrorist in the head with the stock of the Black Arrow, while Montenegro slapped the next man with the barrel of the Neostead. Both men dropped to the floor, feebly twitching.

Snarling something in Arabic, the last terrorist drew a 9 mm Tariq pistol and began shooting blindly. He hit the floor, the roof, several sandbags, and killed one of his unconscious comrades before Bolan managed to take him out with a blow to the back of the head with the XM-25 grenade launcher.

If at all possible, the Executioner wanted some of these people alive for debriefing, just in case their commander escaped, and he had to continue the hunt for Major Armanjani somewhere else in the world.

"You okay, Heather?" Kirkland asked, turning the woman around to inspect her clothing. There were a lot of holes in the ballistic cloth, but no sign of blood.

"Doing better than these poor bastards," Montenegro replied, twitching a little while reloading her shotgun.

Just then, somebody wearing a gas-proof hazard suit stepped around a corner firing an AK-47 assault rifle.

Shooting from the hip, Bolan and Kirkland blew the terrorist into screaming hamburger, the grisly residue smacking into the brick walls to dribble onto the smooth floor.

"Bill, check for a radio!" Bolan commanded, the XM-25 poised and ready while he watched the clouds of bug spray for any suspicious movements.

"Roger that, Matt!" Using a knife to pull apart the tattered sections of the destroyed suit, Kirkland briefly inspected the corpse.

"Clean!" he reported, standing. "No radio."

"Then keep moving," Bolan directed, using the butt of the grenade launcher to disable first one, then the other machine gun.

Staying close to the walls where their presence would be less noticeable, the three people heard strange noises echoing in the emerald fog: mechanical clanks, muffled voices and doors slamming. Major Armanjani and his people were regrouping faster than expected.

Turning a corner, Bolan almost fired at the sight of a man in a hazard suit, but stopped at the last moment when he saw both arms were raised in surrender.

"Don't move, and drop your weapons," Bolan called in a graveyard voice.

"I am Agamemnon, seeking enlightenment," the stranger said.

Even though he recognized the Interpol code for an undercover agent, Bolan didn't relax his stance. "Shall we divide and conquer?"

"Not in the light of knowledge."

"Good enough for me," Kirkland said, lowering his sniper rifle. "We're CIA."

"Rock," the stranger replied, lowering his arms.

Impressed, Bolan shouldered the grenade launcher and stepped forward to shake the other man's hand. In spite of his detailed knowledge of the underworld, there hadn't been the slightest hint that the Sons of the Rock had an agent inside Ophiuchus.

As with most of the major religions, the vast majority of Muslims were peaceful people, just ordinary folks trying to make a living and raise a family, nothing more. But with the advent of international terrorism, much of it done under the dubious cloaks of religious zealots. Muslims were coming under harsh scrutiny, and their beloved religion was being cast as a harbinger of evil. In order to clean their name, the Sons of the Rock had been created, the name being a poetic allusion to the prophet Mohammed.

Composed of soldiers from a dozen different nations in the Middle East, including Israel, the Sons of the Rock was an antiterrorist organization created by and wholly staffed by Muslims. They were devout believers in the peaceful teachings of the Koran, and were sworn to stop terrorism at any cost, even of their own lives.

"Where's Armanjani?" Bolan demanded.

"Control room, one level down, two over," the Rock agent said swiftly. "But be warned! Our people almost got him a few days ago on a cargo ship at sea, but apparently he—"

Oddly jerking forward, the Rock agent threw his arms wide as if trying to embrace the world, then silently crumpled to the misty floor with a huge gaping hole in the middle of his back.

"Traitor!" another man screamed from the murky shadows.

Instinctively, Bolan and the others dropped.

A split second later, the tunnel strobed to the muzzle-flashes of a dozen AK-47 assault rifles firing in an orchestrated attack pattern.

CHAPTER TWENTY

Ruthlessly gunning down a coughing group of Ophi-uchus terrorists fighting over a hazard suit, Bolan assumed the lead once more, with Kirkland and Montenegro flanking him. After a couple of hundred yards, they reached a T-intersection and went to the right. But that soon reached a dead end, and they had to race back.

Unfortunately, the left branch soon formed a Y-intersection, followed by countless side tunnels. Most of those didn't have brick walls for additional support, so Bolan made a battlefield decision to ignore those unless absolutely necessary.

"This place is a freaking maze," Kirkland said into his throat mike, as they stopped to change the filters in their gas masks. "How deep could these old mines go, anyway?"

"A mine from last century?" Montenegro asked, shooting out a video camera attached to the ceiling. "Probably no more than a mile."

"How deep?" Kirkland asked.

"Maybe two miles, but certainly no more than three tops," Bolan added. "How much liquid bug spray was in the tanker?"

"Nine thousand gallons."

Taking a fast sip of water from a hip flask, Bolan did some math in his head. Assuming a standard dispersal ratio of one part to a thousand, plus the internal volume of the tunnels, minus leakage, plus men and machinery yielded, there weren't enough fumes to effectively cover two miles of the underground complex, much less three.

"We're short," Kirkland stated, firing the Black Arrow from the hip. A dagger of flame extended almost a foot from the barrel of the sniper rifle, and a hundred yards down the tunnel, a man in a Russian gas mask cried out and flipped sideways, his AK-47 chattering briefly toward the ceiling.

"We have to move faster, guys," Montenegro growled, hefting the Neostead. "Double-time, march!"

The short rest over, the team broke into a full sprint, ruthlessly blowing away anybody encountered who was armed. Which was everybody so far. Terrorists were everywhere, some of them trying to get out of the foggy base. Each was met with swift and absolute justice.

A ramp took the three down a level, and the fumes were thicker here. Checking a side tunnel, Bolan saw a section of the brick wall swing aside on disguised hinges, and out walked a large, dark-skinned man wearing military fatigues and armed with an oversize Tariq pistol.

"Major Armanjani!" Bolan yelled, triggering the XM-25 grenade launcher.

Instantly dodging out of the way, the major returned fire with the Tariq as the 25 mm shell streaked past to explode farther down the tunnel.

Shooting again, Bolan heard the round hum by dangerously close as a boiling wall of green fog came rushing back up the tunnel. Temporarily blinded in the chemical wind, Bolan lost track of the major and, as the air cleared, there was no sign of Armanjani.

Starting into the tunnel, Bolan felt the floorboards shift and threw himself backward just in time to avoid being crushed as the brick walls moved inward, crushing the boards into kindling until forcefully ramming together in a stentorian crash.

Getting back to his feet, Bolan scowled at the shifting pile of broken debris completely blocking the tunnel. This mine was more than just a firebase, it was a deathtrap. One wrong move and they would never see the outside world again.

"Surrender, Major!" Bolan shouted, reloading. "The SAS is on the way, and they'll hang you from a tree like a chicken thief! That's no way for a soldier to die!"

The Executioner heard a muffled laugh. "You lie, Yankee!" Armanjani said, his words fading into the distance. "If they were coming, you would be stalling for time, not attempting to blow off my head."

Unfortunately, the man was right.

Charging into the tunnel, Kirkland and Montenegro scowled at the destruction.

"What happened?" Kirkland demanded.

"Secret passage," Bolan replied.

"The major?"

"He escaped," Bolan admitted, then added resolutely. "But not for long!"

Expecting prompt retaliation, the three Americans weren't overly surprised when at the next branch, several soldiers in hazard suits were waiting for them, and opened fire with a 7.62 mm RPK machine guns. Most of the incoming lead missed completely or bounced off their body armor. Then Bolan and the others returned fire, the high-explosive 25 mm shells, .50-caliber rounds and swarms of stainless-steel fléchettes taking the terrorists out of play.

"Kind of hard to aim when you can't see the target," Kirkland said to a corpse as reloaded the Black Arrow.

"That was the idea," Bolan commented wryly, advancing into the billowing mists.

As he did, a bloody hand clawed for a holstered weapon. Instantly, Bolan turned and fired the Beretta just as the soldier on the floor cut loose with his 9 mm Tariq. The two weapons roared in unison. Then Bolan moved on, and the terrorist didn't, groaning into death.

Encountering a wide set of double doors set into a brick wall, Bolan took left, Montenegro right and Kirkland took the slot, charging up the middle at a full run.

Bursting through the doors, Kirkland dove to the side and came up with the Black Arrow ready, but he proved to be alone in the spacious garage. There were several more Atkinson trucks parked against the far wall, along with numerous motorcycles and several forklifts. At the far end was a machine shop, in one corner was a stash of pressurized oxygen tanks and in the exact middle of the garage was an industrial air cleaner, all of the indicator lights flashing a silent warning.

"Clear," Kirkland announced, inspecting the shadowy recesses of a grease pit.

"Same here," Montenegro reported, checking for lurkers behind the lathe and drill press.

"Then let's call for room service," Bolan said, walking to a wall phone.

First checking for traps, he removed the receiver and pawed at the buttons. Just for a moment, he thought nothing would happen, then there came a fast series of clicks, and a woman barked a question in Arabic.

Moaning in pain, Bolan dropped the receiver and let it dangle, twisting and turning on the end of the cord. Almost immediately, the voice stopped talking.

"Okay, they're on the way," Bolan said, going into the grease pit and resting the XM-25 on the floor.

"Think the major will fall for that obvious trick?" Kirkland asked, replacing the nearly empty magazine in the Black Arrow with a full one. He was almost out of spares.

"Not a chance," Montenegro stated with conviction. "So, what's the plan, Matt?"

"Kill the bastards," Bolan said, heading for the fuel pumps.

"Good plan!"

Moments later, the three Americans raced out of the garage riding motorcycles. As they drove into the cloud of bug spray the grenades rigged to the fuel pumps detonated. An inferno of burning gasoline flooded the garage, quickly setting the other vehicles ablaze, rupturing the tanks of pressurized air and finally setting off the stores of ammunition.

Explosion after explosion shook the tunnels, dust raining down from the dimly seen ceiling, and wild bullets zinged everywhere, endlessly ricocheting off the walls, ceiling and floors until making it out of the garage and into the misty tunnel.

"Sounds like World War III back there," Kirkland said with a snort, revving the motorcycle engine. The Twin-V 88 answered with a classic burst of power, and the bike surged forward to pop a wheelie before he could get it back under control again.

"The louder, the better," Bolan said, hunching over the handlebars. Trick, trap or diversion, the major would have no choice but to send people to check the garage and determine if the invaders were dead. That would divide his attention and weaken his defenses. It wasn't much, but every point in their favor would help now. Secret passages hadn't been considered in the original invasion plans, and this was the only way Bolan had of canceling out their effect.

Almost immediately, the bikes' windshields began to speckle with droplets of condensed mist, and the headlights dimmed. Next, the engines began to cough, sputter, then promptly died.

Coasting to a stop, Bolan kicked down the stand and climbed off. "We got a lot farther than I expected," he said, priming a grenade and tucking it under the seat.

Stashing the bikes in an empty side tunnel, the three waited as a group of terrorists marched by, obviously heading for the garage. Once they were past, Bolan and the others stepped out of hiding and mowed them down from behind. Grenades and spare ammunition were taken, then they continued on, killing everybody they encountered until they found the next downward ramp.

The fumes billowed like winter fog along the tunnels, coating the overhead lights until they glowed faintly green, as if the entire complex was radioactive. Twitching bodies of armed soldiers lay everywhere. None of them were wearing hazard suits, only gas masks, and many were sprawled in puddles of their own stomach contents.

"Must be cheap gas masks," Kirkland said, sneering just as two of the supposed corpses rolled over firing AK-47 assault rifles.

Hammered backward from the stream of 7.62 mm rounds, Kirkland hit the wall hard and fired the Black Arrow, but missed. Then Bolan and Montenegro opened fire with their weapons, ending the matter forever.

Nasser and Hassan appeared out of the thick cloud. Caught in the act of reloading, Bolan and Montenegro dove to the sides as the terrorists cut loose and thundering hell filled the tunnel. Bolan was hit a dozen times by fléchettes from the roaring Atchisson, and the rock wall behind Montenegro exploded, rock shards tearing gouges in both of her arms and ripping off her gas mask.

Clamping her mouth shut, the woman rolled over, trying to find the mask, when Kirkland kicked it closer, then triggered the Black Arrow.

Nasser grabbed her throat in both hands, trying to staunch the blood flow.

As Kirkland swung the weapon toward the sergeant, Hassan raised the Atchisson—and Bolan fired from the floor. The triburst of 9 mm rounds from the Beretta drilled into Hassan, the Atchisson flying away from his spasming fingers.

Gurgling horribly, Nasser attempted to pull a grenade from her pocket, and Kirkland put a .50-caliber round directly into her temple. With half of her head gone, the lieutenant dropped to the floor, twitching once before going motionless forever.

Montenegro stood weakly just as another section of the brick wall swung open. With no time to grab the Atchisson on the floor, Montenegro drew both of her Glocks as three more terrorists rushed out with RPK machine guns blazing.

Firing both weapons, Montenegro almost lost control of the Glock 18 as it emptied the entire clip in two seconds flat, the hellish barrage killing two of the terrorists outright, but only wounding the third.

As the third man shot Montenegro in the face, Kirkland and Bolan unleashed their weapons, and the terrorist ceased to exist.

"Heather!" Kirkland called out, rushing to her side and ripping off the gas mask.

"Fine...mask!" she wheezed, a hole in the mask perfectly matching a bloody gouge along the side of her temple.

Kirkland inspected the wound, as Bolan did a fast recon into the secret passage. It ended at a plain wooden door.

Blowing off the lock, the Executioner discovered a large room full of control boards and flat-screen monitors. The control room!

Sitting before a complex console, a handsome man with a mustache spun in a chair and started shooting with a 9 mm Tariq pistol. The XM-25 was torn from Bolan's grip, so he drew the Beretta and pulled the trigger. The machine pistol chattered, and Dr. Khandis fell backward, his life splashing across a samovar and bathroom door.

Turning toward the control board, Bolan saw that all of the labels were in code. With no time even to attempt an educated guess, Bolan reached for the XM-25 and saw that the grenade launcher had been seriously damaged. With no other choice, the Executioner emptied both of his pistols into the console, exploding the dials, punching holes in the casing, blowing apart the monitors and shattering the keyboards. Even as he reloaded, short circuits began to crackle among the ruined electronics, and a sharp metallic stink cut through the filters of his gas mask.

Turning fast, Bolan rushed toward the open door and barely got there before a powerful explosion filled the room. The concussion shoved him out the doorway, and he hit the floor rolling to land on his feet. He kept running until he found Kirkland patching a pale, sweaty Montenegro.

"You okay?" Bolan asked in concern.

"Flesh wound," Montenegro grunted.

"What was in there?" Kirkland asked, tying off the bandage.

"Control room."

Montenegro almost smiled. "Then we won?"

"Not till the major is dead," Bolan replied bluntly, when there came the sound of rocks grinding against each other.

Bizarrely, sunlight flooded the tunnel and the swirling bug spray began to uniformly flow toward the light. Grabbing weapons, Bolan and the others charged in that direction, cursing at the sight of another section of the brick wall swinging aside. But this time they saw that it opened onto a rock-stewn hillside.

A swarm of motorcycles came into view from behind a rocky escarpment. Bolan fired first, but the others were right behind, and they blew the escaping terrorists off the machines, the tattered corpses rolling along the smooth grassland of the sloping hillside.

Unexpectedly, they heard a powerful engine, and a man who fitted Major Armanjani's description appeared riding a Harley-Davidson. Heading for the coastal highway, the major was flying across the hillside, both tires often off the ground at the same time.

Bolan snapped off a couple of rounds. He hit the major twice, but only succeeded in ripping away large swatches of his fatigues to reveal molded body armor.

"We can't let him get away!" Montenegro snarled, unleashing the Neostead. "He'll only start again someplace new!" However, the major was already out of range, and the barrage of rounds fell short of the Harley.

"Not going to happen!" Kirkland stated, raising the Black Arrow and squeezing off a round. The massive rifle boomed, and the bike's sideview mirror exploded directly alongside the fleeing major.

Even though the terrorist was just about out of range, Bolan continued to fire the Beretta and the Desert Eagle at the zigzagging terrorist, Kirkland levered in another cigar-size bullet and tried again. This time it was a clean miss, and Armanjani raced over the crest of the hill and out of sight.

"Son of a bitch escaped!" Montenegro cursed, shaking the Neostead in rage.

"Not yet, he hasn't," Kirkland retorted, offering Bolan the rifle.

Dropping the handguns, Bolan accepted the Black Arrow and lay on the soft grass. Carefully sighting through the telescopic sight, he put the crosshair on a patch of empty air. He could still hear the Harley, but the sound was getting farther and farther away with every passing tick of the clock.

However, the way Bolan read the man, Armanjani had once been the head of the infamous Republican Guard, and the he wouldn't be the sort of man to cut and run from a battle unless being actively chased. If Bolan was right, the major would take a fast look over the hill to assess the situation. There was a blur of movement near the side of the hill overlooking the coastline. Instantly, Bolan fired.

A split second later, the major tumbled into view, both hands holding a gushing, bleeding wound on the top of his head. As Bolan fired again, the major flipped off the Harley, tumbled over the cliff and plummetted onto the jagged rocks below. He bounced the first time, but splattered crimson on the next. There was no question that he was dead.

Not yet finished with their mission, Bolan and the others went back into the tin mine to complete their blitz. But there was nobody left alive, and, as they stumbled onto the grassy hillside once more, a gentle rain began to fall.

However, this time there was no sound of thunder.

"YOU OKAY?" MACK BOLAN ASKED.

"Been better," Brognola replied, pushing his wheelchair a little closer to the table. He was covered with bandages, and had spent an entire week at the Army hospital recovering from the near-miss of the lightning strike.

At the moment, though, every inch of him ached so badly—especially his kidneys—that he almost wished the lightning had finished the job the first time.

"By the way, are you interfering with TV reception yet?" Bolan asked in a deceptively pleasant tone.

Brognola snorted. "No, and magnets don't stick to my ass, either. These hit-by-lightning jokes are getting old fast."

"Fair enough." Bolan laughed, leaning back in his chair. "By the way, did you hear that Edgar Barrington left everything to his wife? She's a rich woman now."

"That's hardly compensation for being chained like a dog, but I suppose it's better than starting over without a dime to your name."

"Damn near. She's hired Bill and Heather to help her dismantle Swampfox. By force, if necessary."

"Delighted to hear it!" Brognola said, then added,

"She's a fine-looking woman. Do you think Bill will settle down, start raising a family?"

"Wild Bill Kirkland, the playboy of Brazil? Unlikely. But stranger things have happened."

"If he does get married, that would leave Heather available…" Brognola didn't finish the sentence.

Finishing the mug, Bolan made a face. "Better lighten up on those pain medicines, Hal, they're making you hallucinate."

"No, they're not! And why are you dressed as Godzilla?"

"Hey, don't ask, don't tell."

"My apologies, soldier. Enjoy your fins."

"Thank you, Hal!"

Pouring himself a fresh cup from the small carafe on the table, Brognola smiled. "By the way, we found a third Ophiuchus base down in Australia on the Nullabar Plains."

Bolan frowned. "Was the equipment recovered intact?"

"No. Killing the major seemed to forced the terrorists to trigger a self-destruct sequence. The whole base is just rubble now, so we may never know how it was done."

"That's probably for the best," Bolan said with a shrug. "Every time humanity tries to outwit Mother Nature, she consistently bites us in the ass."

"Yet somebody will keep trying."

"That's why we're here, Hal, to stop them," Bolan said gravely.

"Till the day we die," Brognola stated.

* * * * *

TAKE 'EM FREE
2 action-packed novels plus a mystery bonus

NO RISK
NO OBLIGATION TO BUY

JAMES AXLER

DEATH LANDS

Crimson Waters

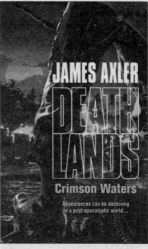

Appearances are almost always deceptive in the postapocalyptic new world of Deathlands.

When a mat-trans malfunction strands Ryan Cawdor and his friends in a gutted redoubt in the West Indies, the crystal waters offer them a tantalizing glimpse of untouched splendor. But the oasis is abruptly shattered by violent and ruthless pirates…and the group rushes to escape paradise before it destroys them.

Available September wherever books are sold.

strategically planted around the world. Nations race
to contain massive spills occurring worldwide, and
simultaneously Stony Man faces the mother
of all do-or-die missions.

STONY MAN®

*Available in August
wherever books are sold.*

Or order your copy now by sending your name, address, zip or postal code, along with a check or
money order (please do not send cash) for $6.99 for each book ordered ($7.99 in Canada), plus
75¢ postage and handling ($1.00 in Canada), payable to Gold Eagle Books, to:

In the U.S.
Gold Eagle Books
3010 Walden Avenue
P.O. Box 9077
Buffalo, NY 14269-9077

In Canada
Gold Eagle Books
P.O. Box 636
Fort Erie, Ontario
L2A 5X3

Please specify book title with your order.
Canadian residents add applicable federal and provincial taxes.

GOLD EAGLE®

www.readgoldeagle.blogspot.com

GSM120